Snug Harbor Stories

a WALLACE the BRAVE collection!

Will Henry

Andrews McMeel
PUBLISHING®

to my wife

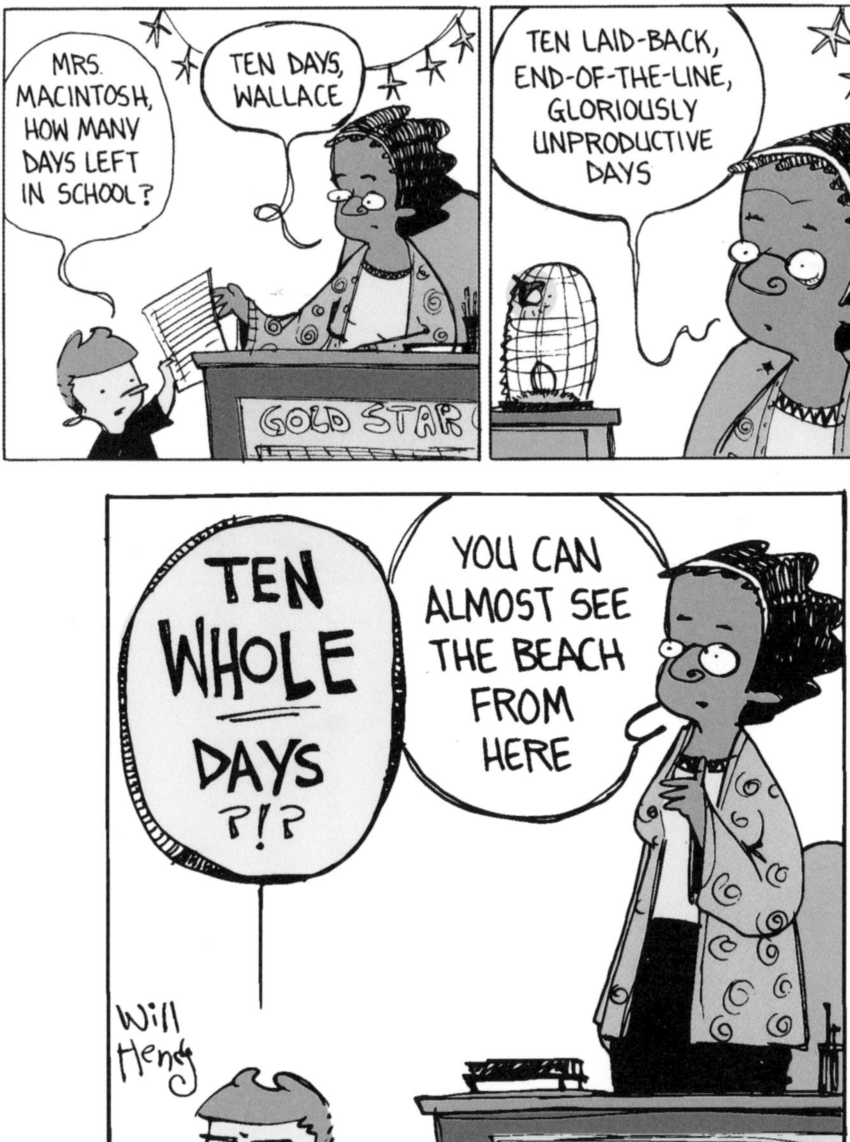
MRS. MACINTOSH, HOW MANY DAYS LEFT IN SCHOOL?
TEN DAYS, WALLACE
GOLD STAR
TEN LAID-BACK, END-OF-THE-LINE, GLORIOUSLY UNPRODUCTIVE DAYS
TEN WHOLE DAYS ?!?
YOU CAN ALMOST SEE THE BEACH FROM HERE
Will Henry

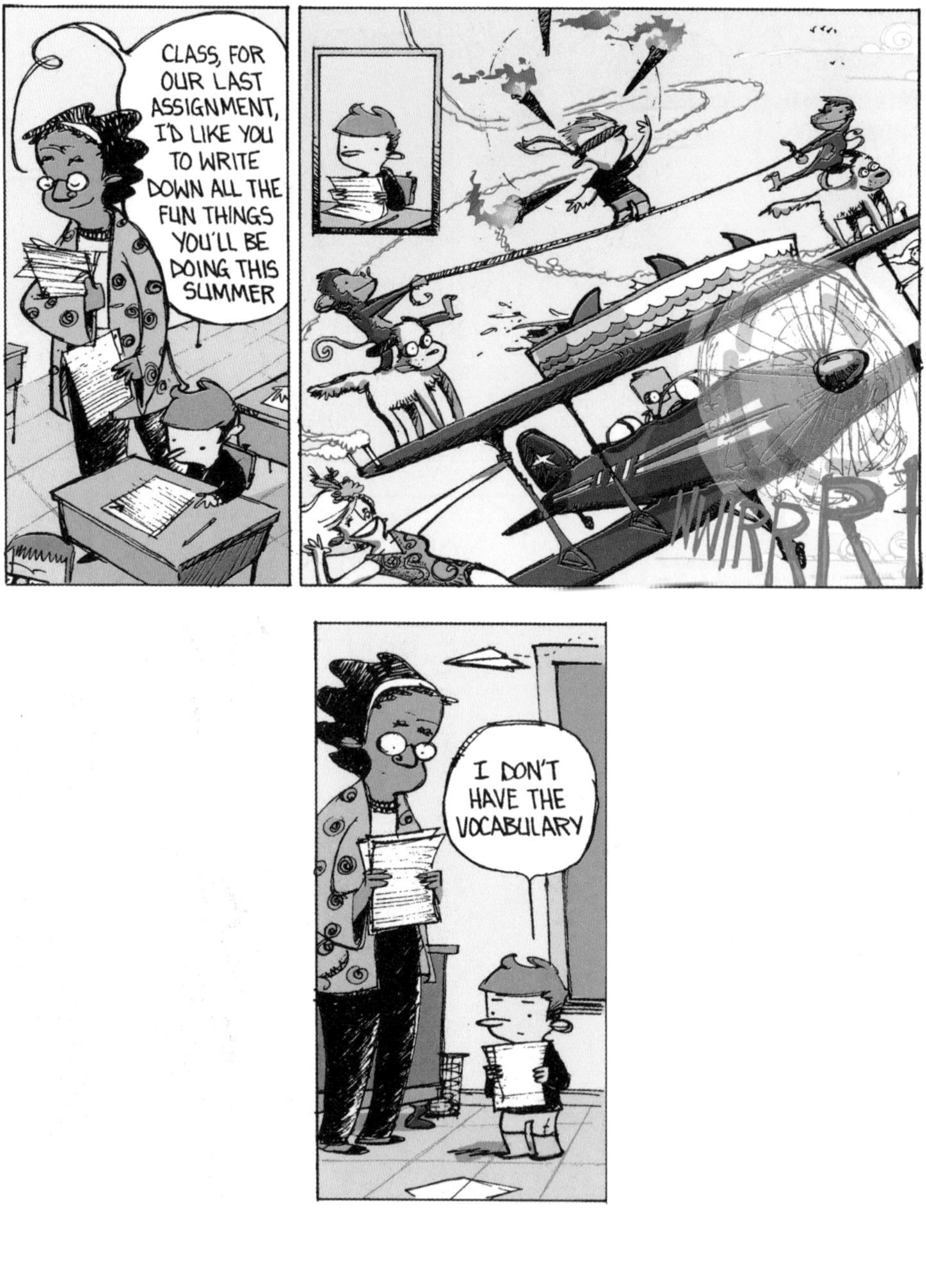
CLASS, FOR OUR LAST ASSIGNMENT, I'D LIKE YOU TO WRITE DOWN ALL THE FUN THINGS YOU'LL BE DOING THIS SUMMER
WWIRRR
I DON'T HAVE THE VOCABULARY

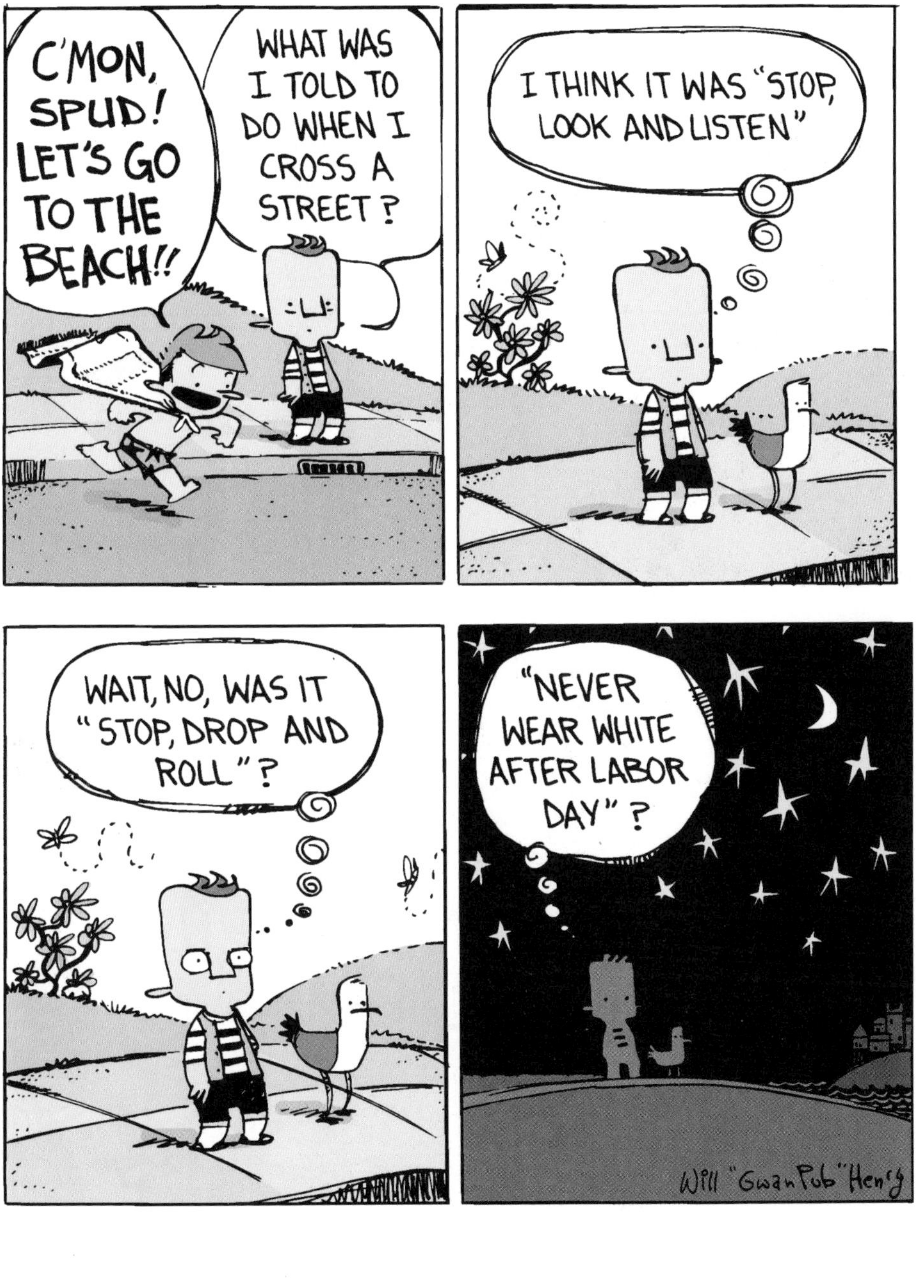
C'MON, SPUD! LET'S GO TO THE BEACH!!
WHAT WAS I TOLD TO DO WHEN I CROSS A STREET?
I THINK IT WAS "STOP, LOOK AND LISTEN"
WAIT, NO, WAS IT "STOP, DROP AND ROLL"?
"NEVER WEAR WHITE AFTER LABOR DAY"?
Will "GwanPub" Henry

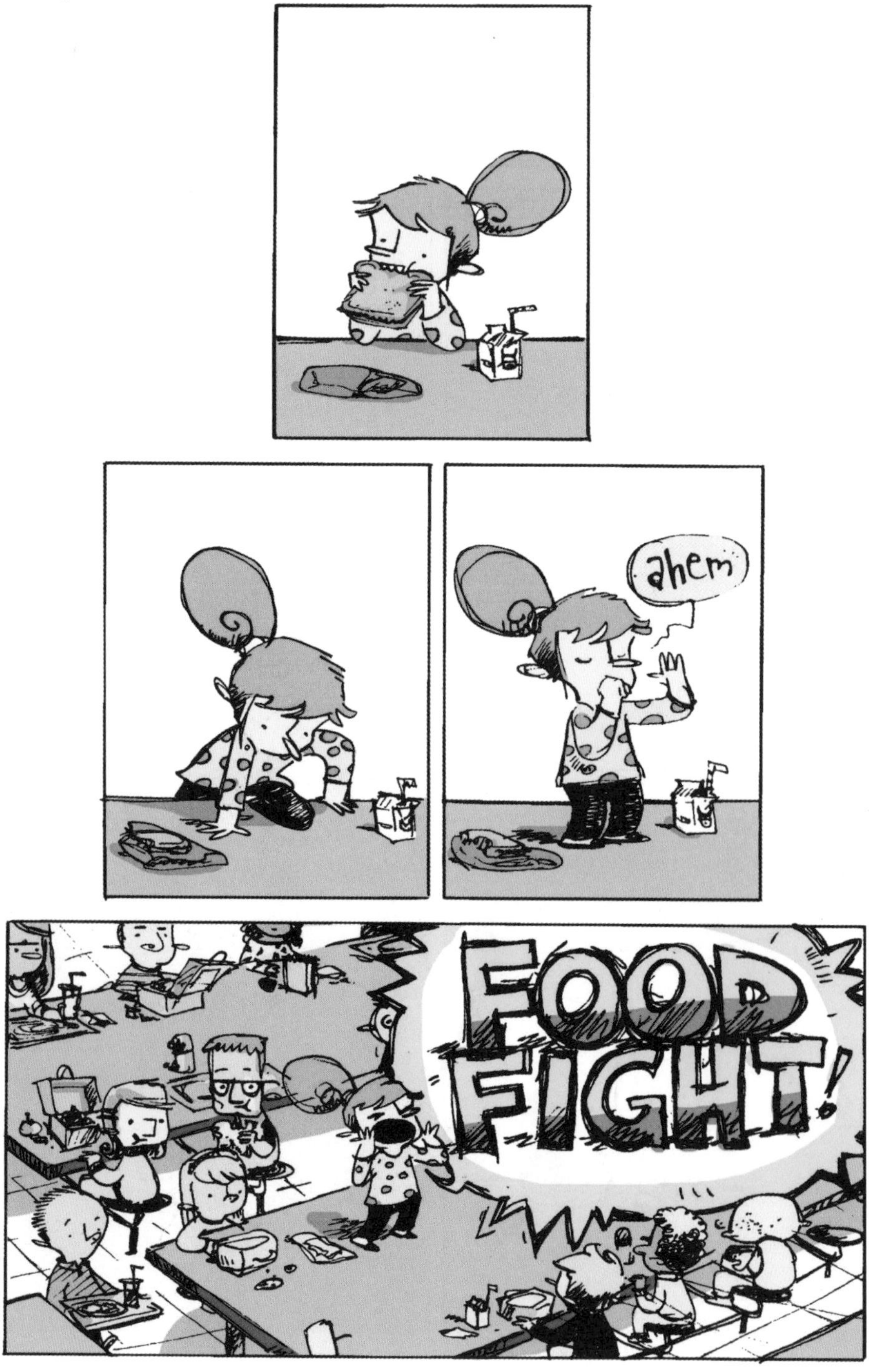
ahem
FOOD FIGHT!

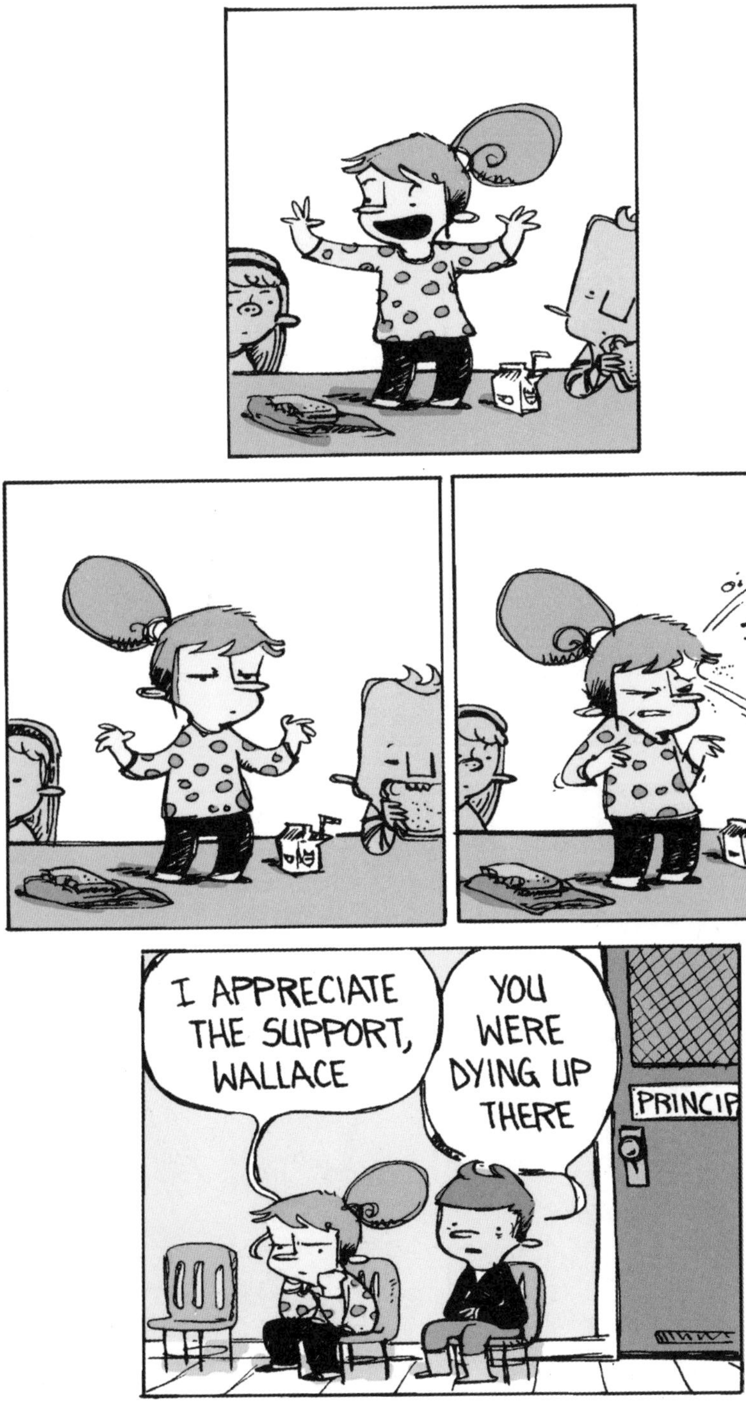
PLIP
I APPRECIATE THE SUPPORT, WALLACE
YOU WERE DYING UP THERE
PRINCIP

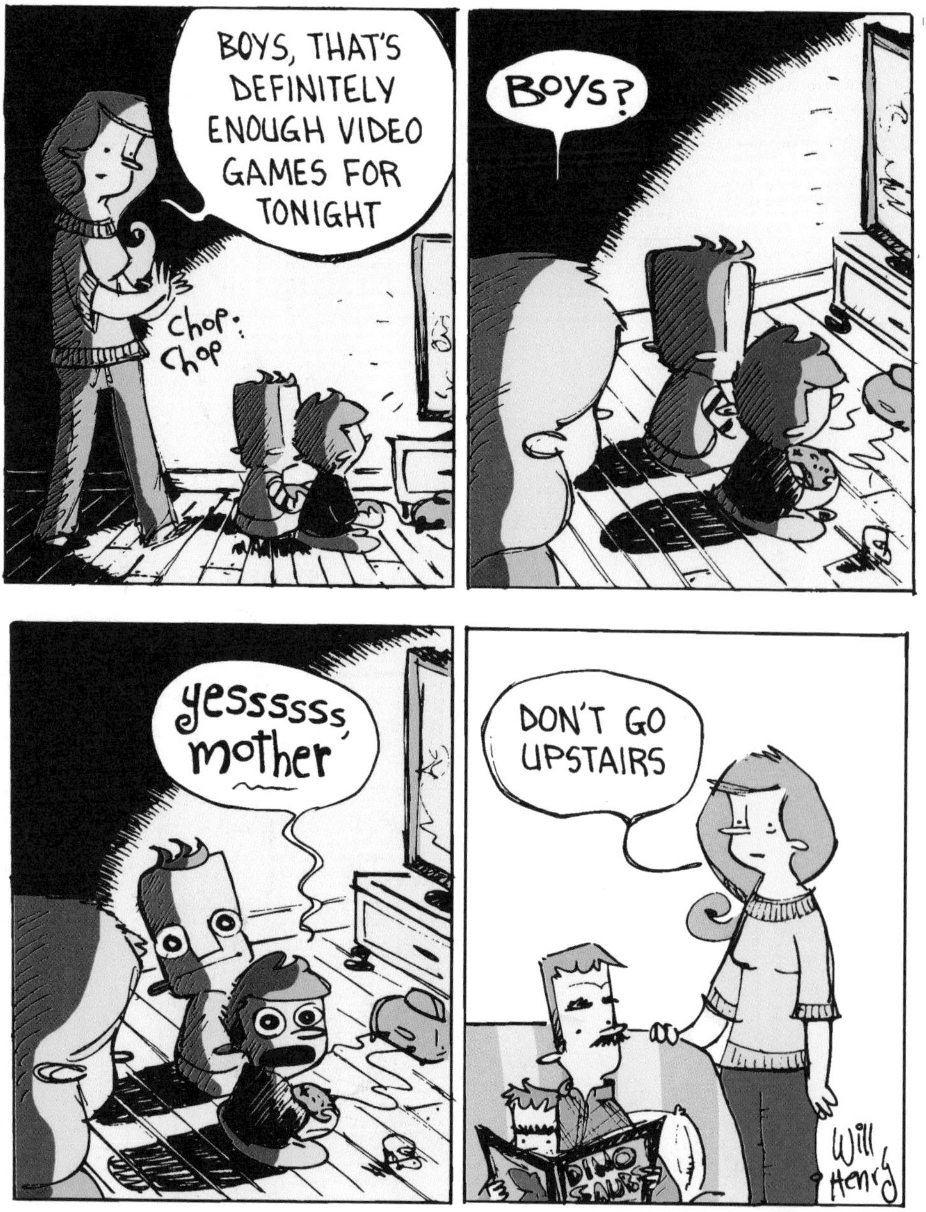
BOYS, THAT'S DEFINITELY ENOUGH VIDEO GAMES FOR TONIGHT
Chop. Chop
BOYS?
yessssss, mother
DON'T GO UPSTAIRS
DINO SAURS
Will Henry

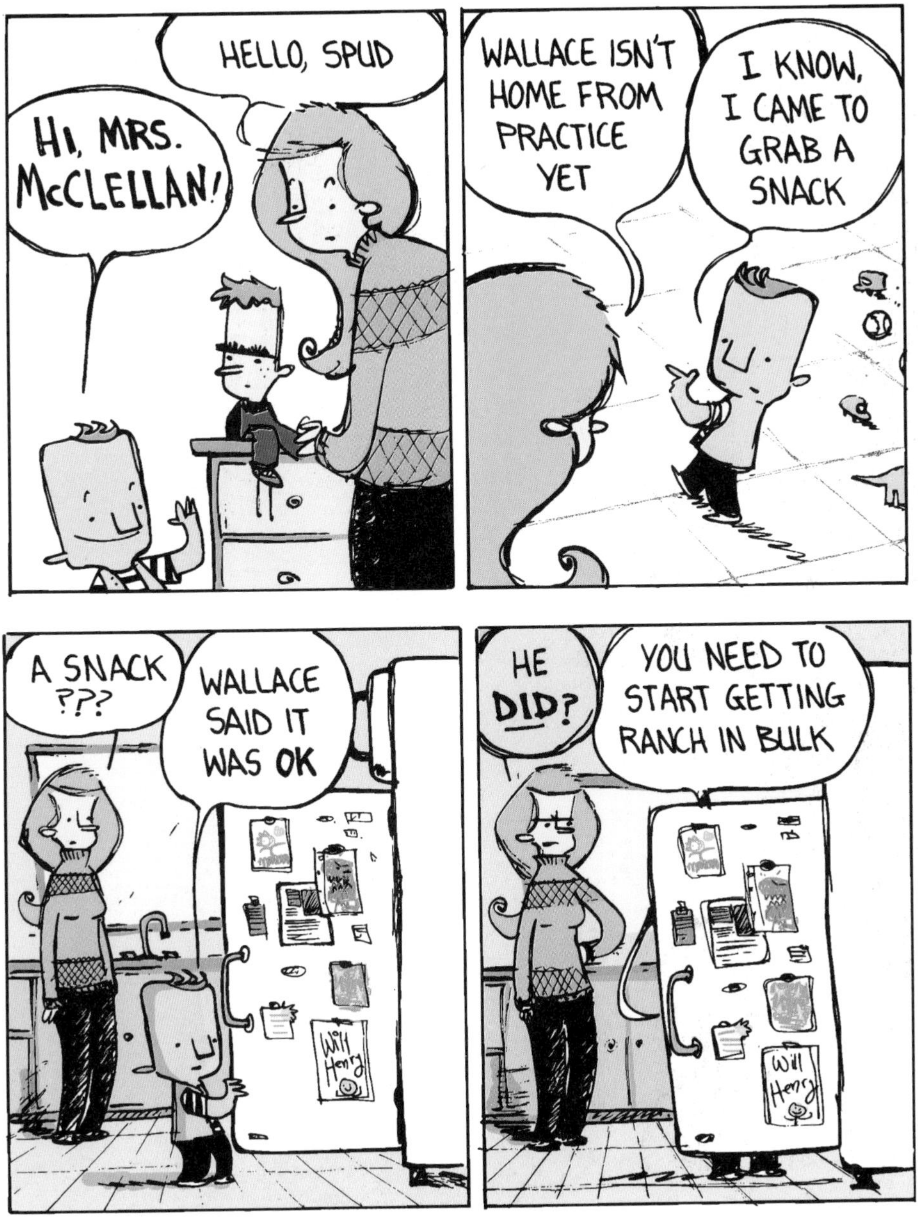
HI, MRS. McCLELLAN!
HELLO, SPUD
WALLACE ISN'T HOME FROM PRACTICE YET
I KNOW, I CAME TO GRAB A SNACK
A SNACK ???
WALLACE SAID IT WAS OK
Will Henry
HE DID?
YOU NEED TO START GETTING RANCH IN BULK
Will Henry

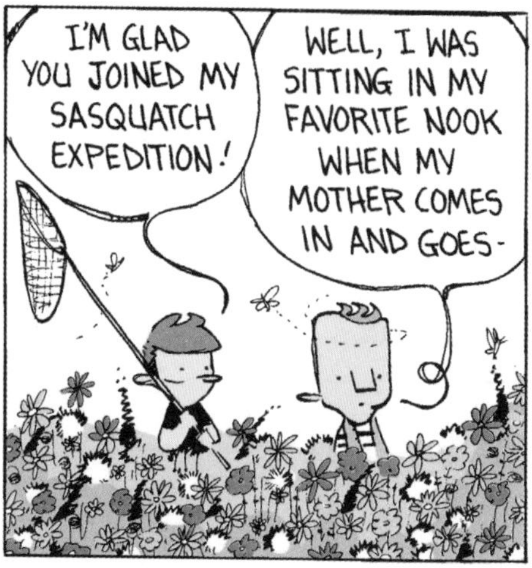
I'M GLAD YOU JOINED MY SASQUATCH EXPEDITION!
WELL, I WAS SITTING IN MY FAVORITE NOOK WHEN MY MOTHER COMES IN AND GOES-

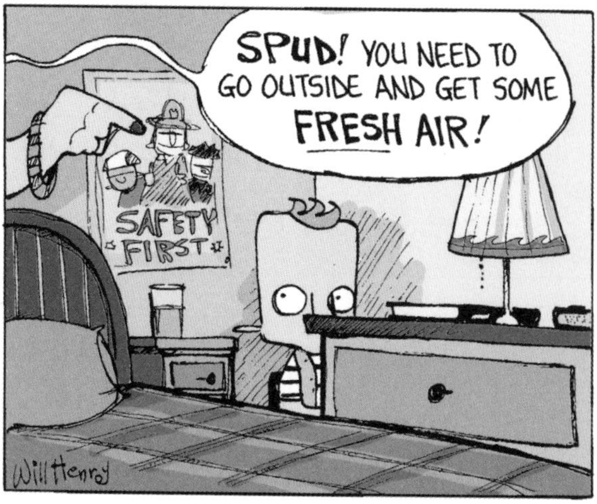
SPUD! YOU NEED TO GO OUTSIDE AND GET SOME FRESH AIR!
SAFETY FIRST
Will Henry

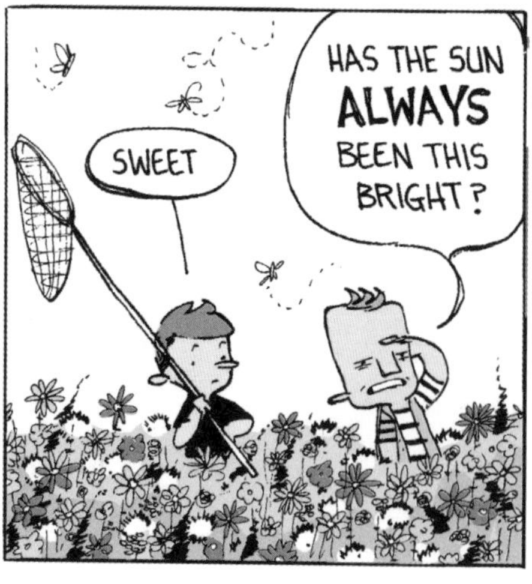
SWEET
HAS THE SUN ALWAYS BEEN THIS BRIGHT?

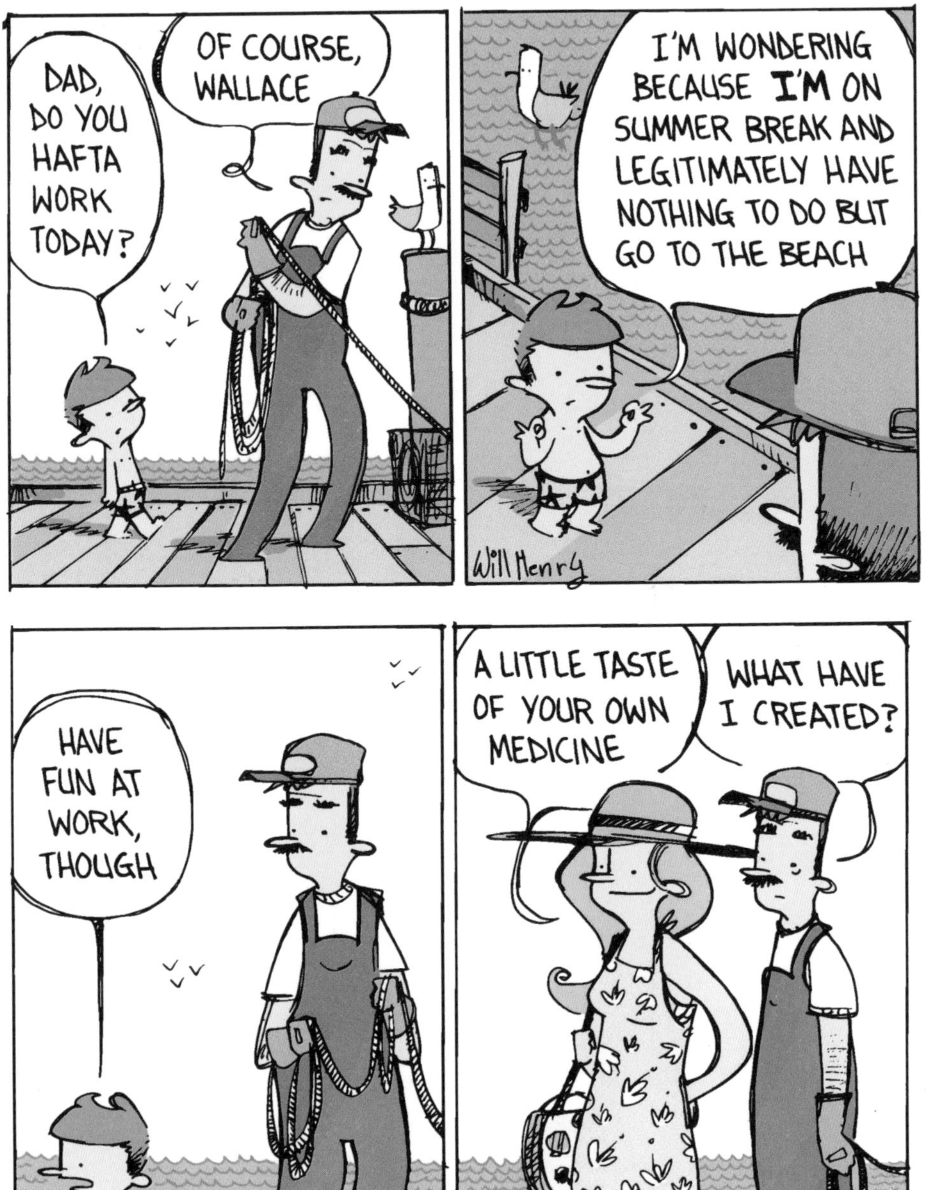
DAD, DO YOU HAFTA WORK TODAY?
OF COURSE, WALLACE
I'M WONDERING BECAUSE I'M ON SUMMER BREAK AND LEGITIMATELY HAVE NOTHING TO DO BUT GO TO THE BEACH
Will Henry
HAVE FUN AT WORK, THOUGH
A LITTLE TASTE OF YOUR OWN MEDICINE
WHAT HAVE I CREATED?

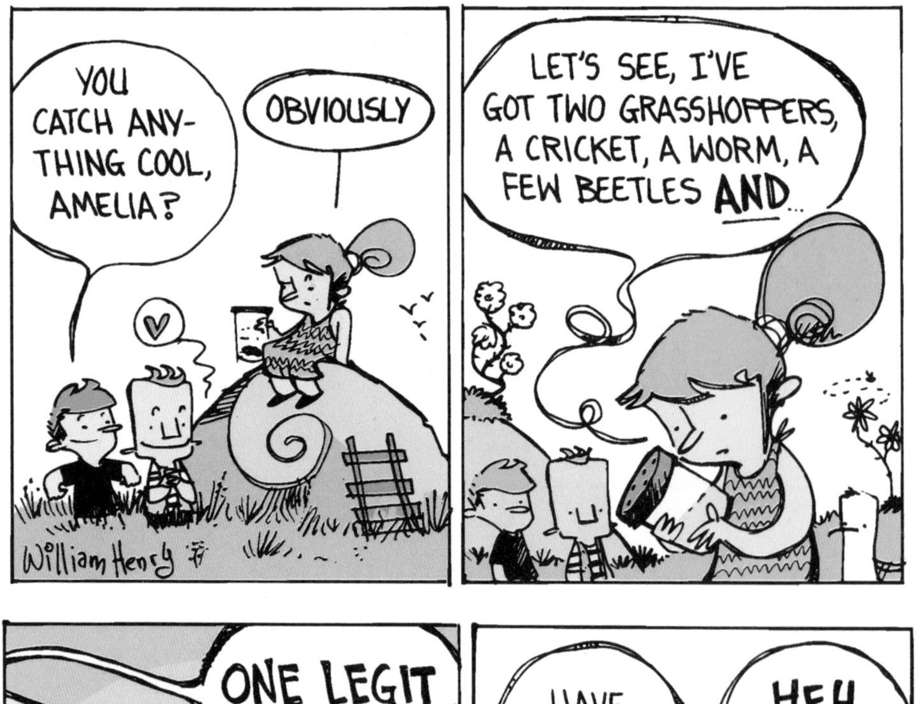
YOU CATCH ANYTHING COOL, AMELIA?
OBVIOUSLY
William Henry
LET'S SEE, I'VE GOT TWO GRASSHOPPERS, A CRICKET, A WORM, A FEW BEETLES AND...
ONE LEGIT TOAD!
WOW
EW
HAVE YOU TRIED TO KISS IT YET?
HEH, LIKE I NEED A PRINCE

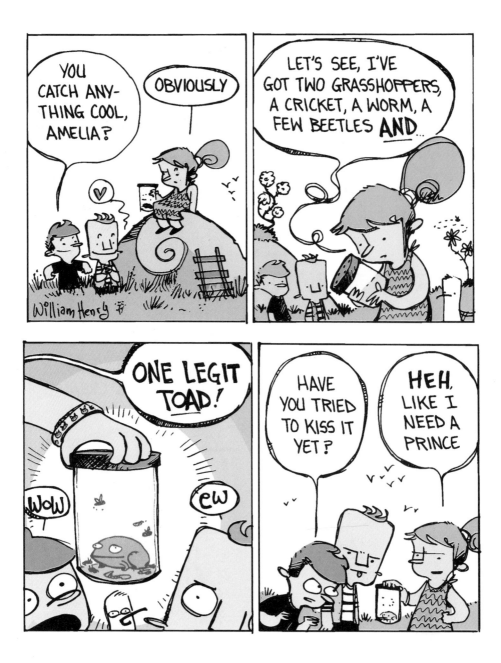

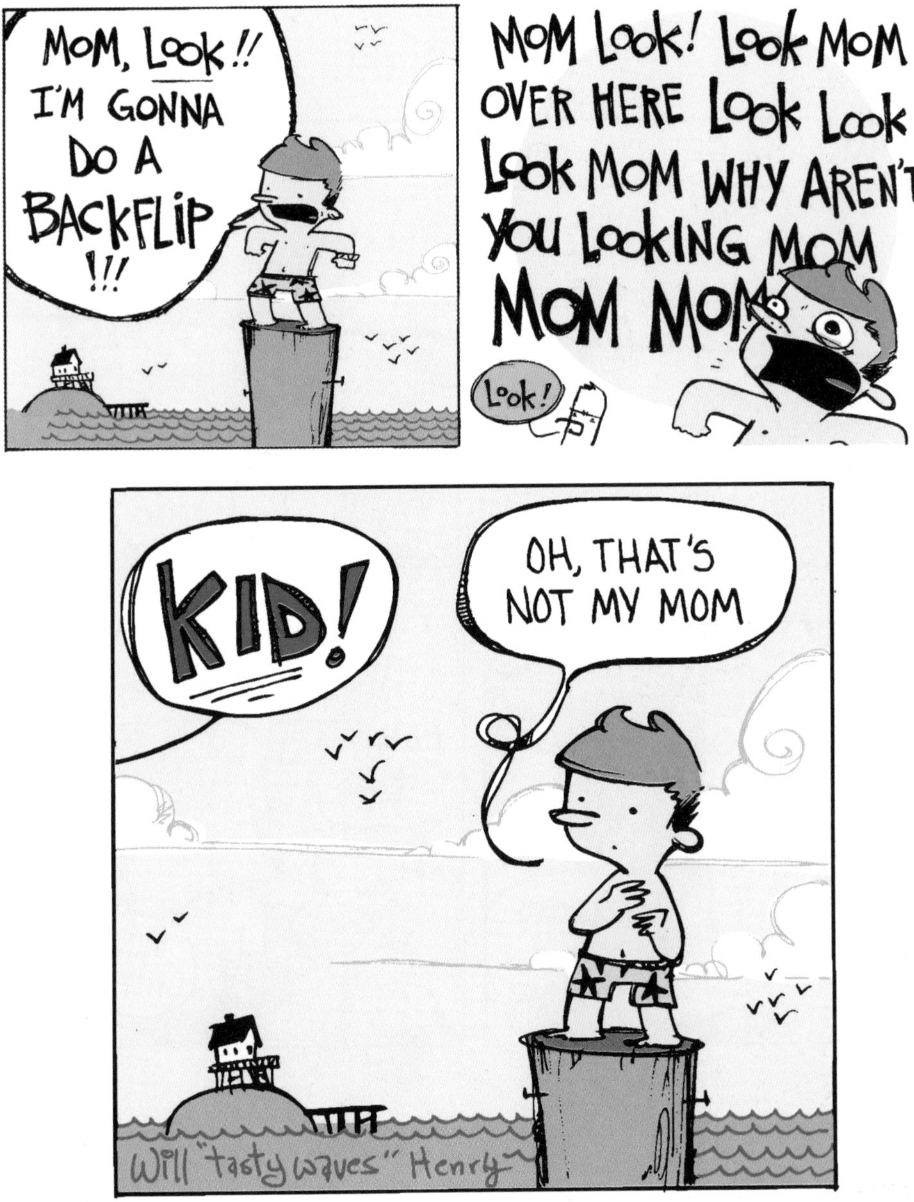
MOM, LOOK!! I'M GONNA DO A BACKFLIP !!!
MOM LOOK! LOOK MOM OVER HERE LOOK LOOK LOOK MOM WHY AREN'T YOU LOOKING MOM MOM MOM
LOOK!
KID!
OH, THAT'S NOT MY MOM
Will "tasty waves" Henry

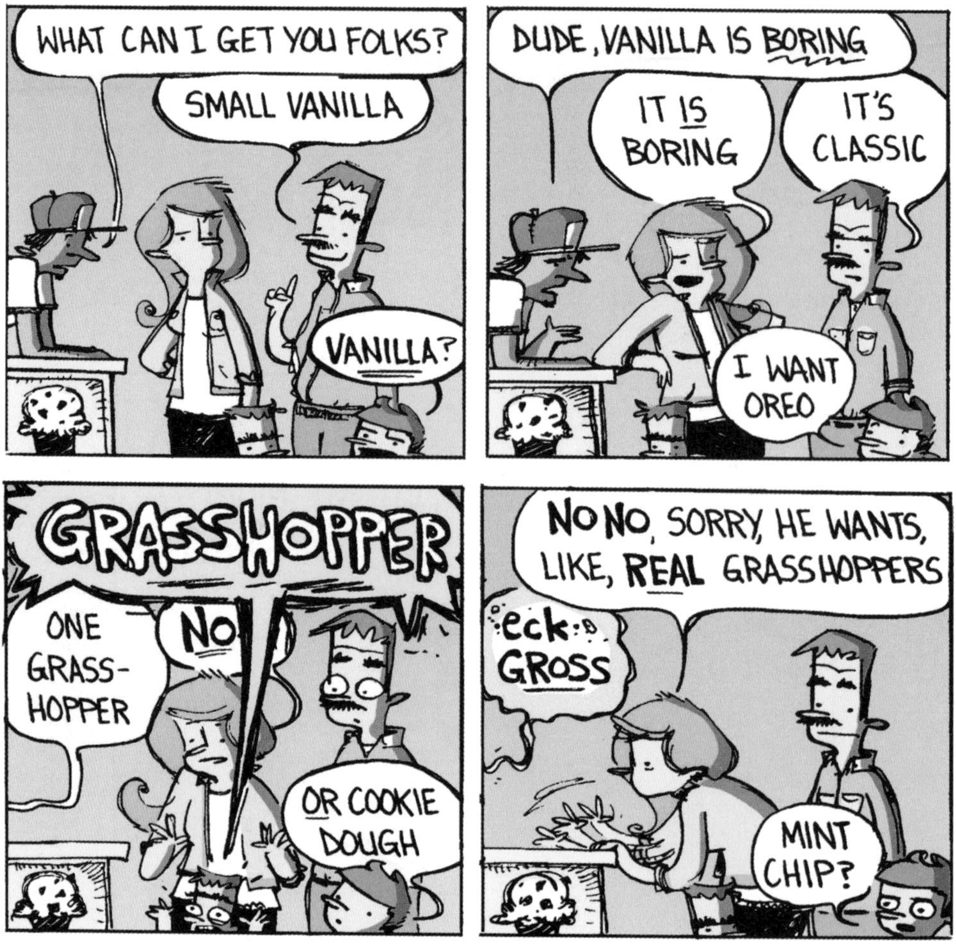
WHAT CAN I GET YOU FOLKS?
SMALL VANILLA
VANILLA?
DUDE, VANILLA IS BORING
IT IS BORING
IT'S CLASSIC
I WANT OREO
GRASSHOPPER
ONE GRASS-HOPPER
NO
OR COOKIE DOUGH
NO NO, SORRY, HE WANTS, LIKE, REAL GRASSHOPPERS
eck GROSS
MINT CHIP?

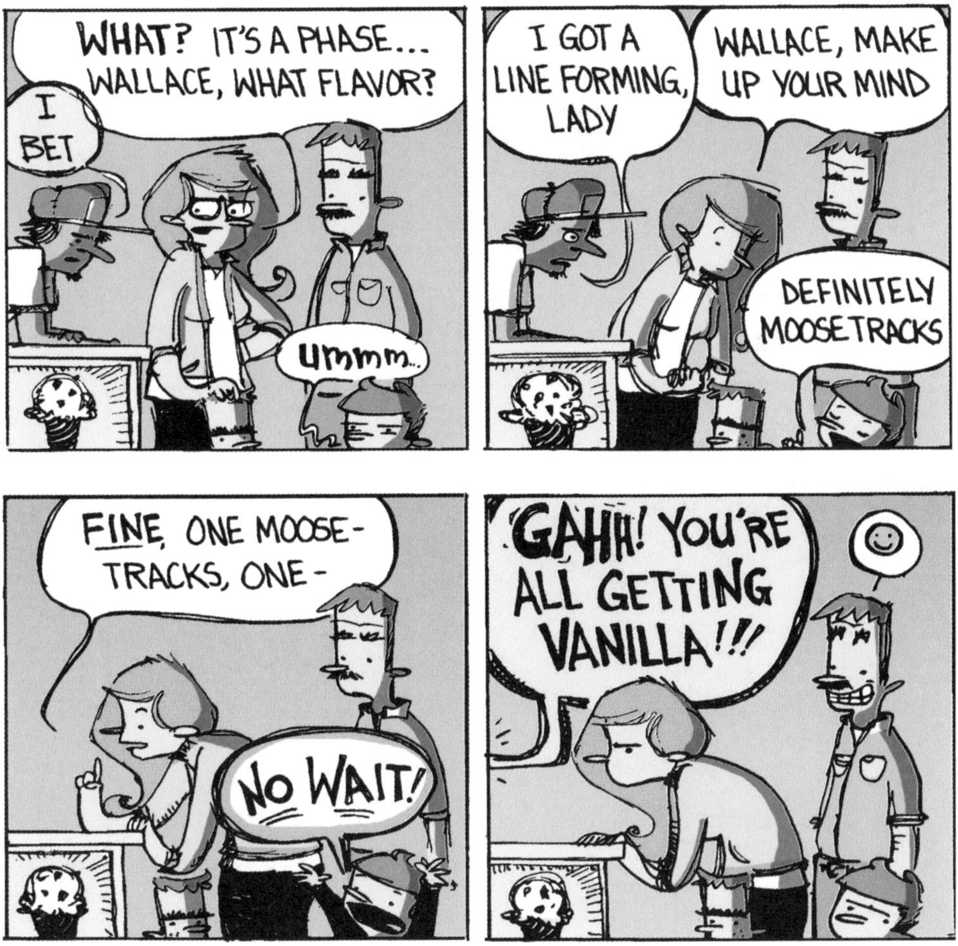
WHAT? IT'S A PHASE... WALLACE, WHAT FLAVOR?
I BET
ummm...
I GOT A LINE FORMING, LADY
WALLACE, MAKE UP YOUR MIND
DEFINITELY MOOSETRACKS
FINE, ONE MOOSE-TRACKS, ONE -
NO WAIT!
GAHH! YOU'RE ALL GETTING VANILLA!!!

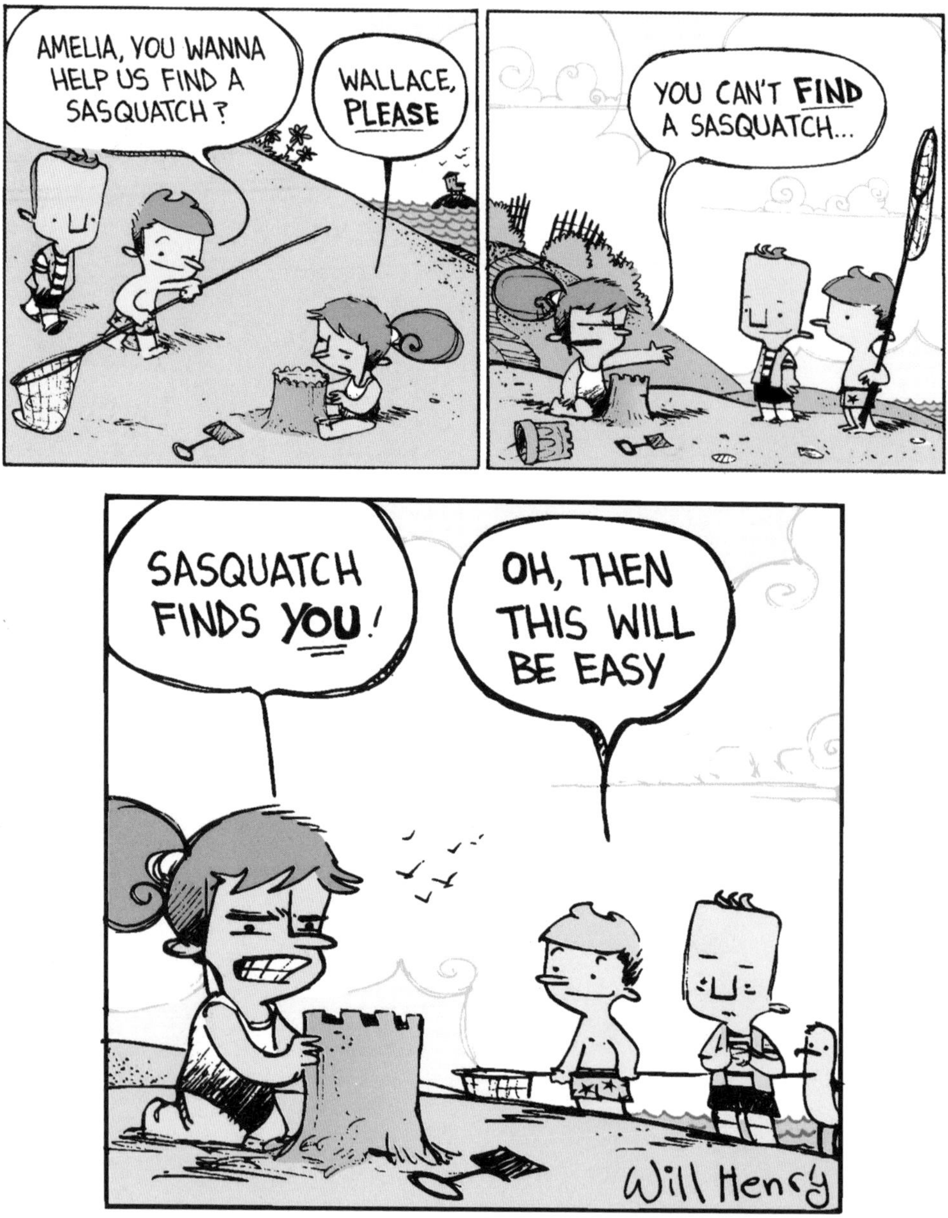
AMELIA, YOU WANNA HELP US FIND A SASQUATCH?
WALLACE, PLEASE
YOU CAN'T FIND A SASQUATCH...
SASQUATCH FINDS YOU!
OH, THEN THIS WILL BE EASY
Will Henry

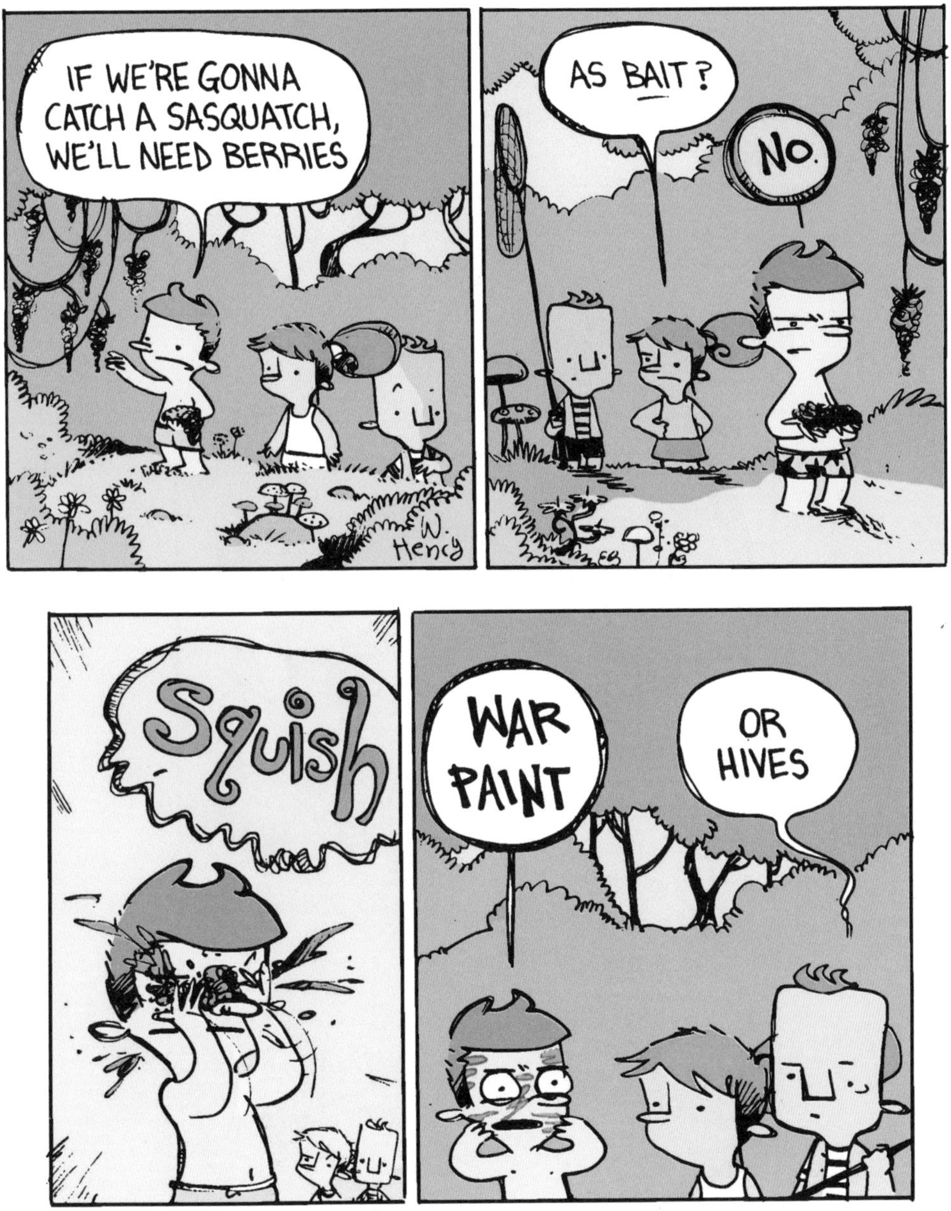
IF WE'RE GONNA CATCH A SASQUATCH, WE'LL NEED BERRIES
W. Hency
AS BAIT?
NO.
Squish
WAR PAINT
OR HIVES

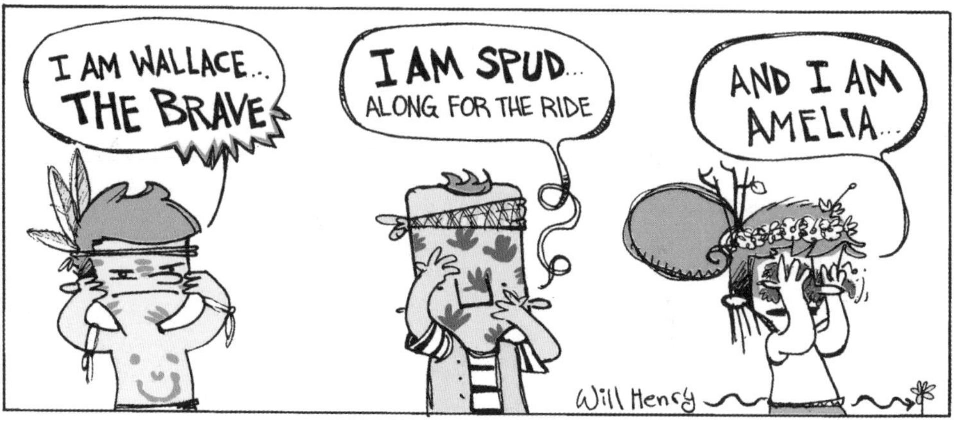
I AM WALLACE... THE BRAVE
I AM SPUD... ALONG FOR THE RIDE
AND I AM AMELIA...
Will Henry

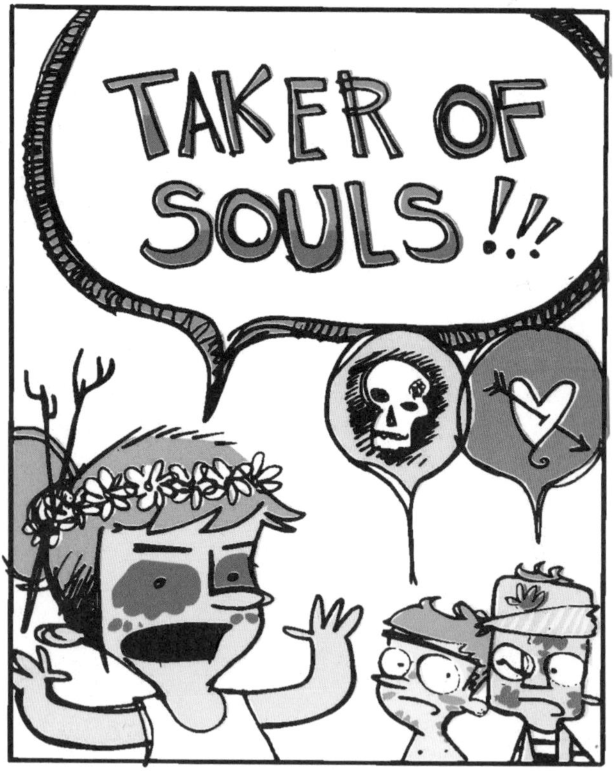
TAKER OF SOULS!!!

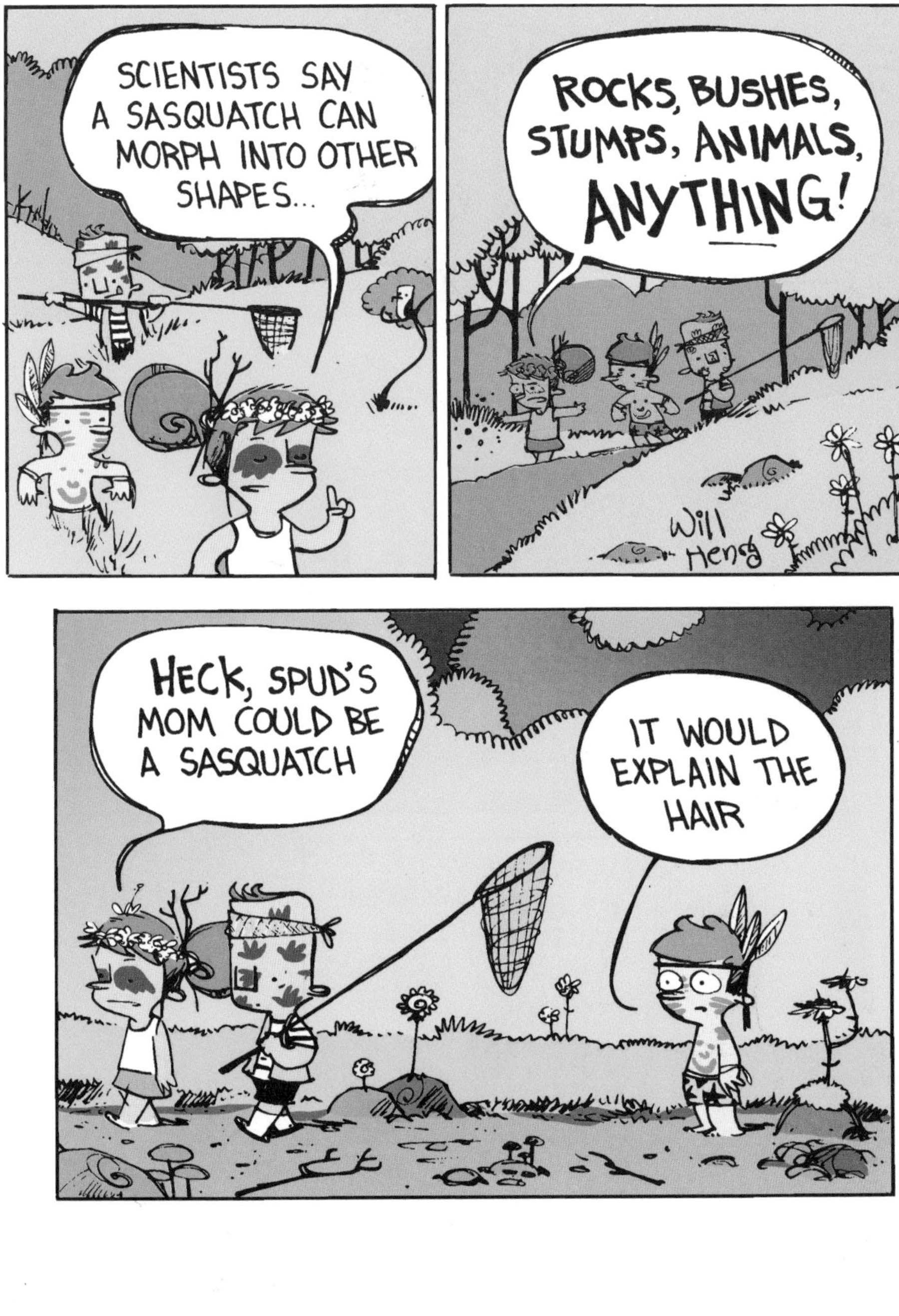
SCIENTISTS SAY A SASQUATCH CAN MORPH INTO OTHER SHAPES...
ROCKS, BUSHES, STUMPS, ANIMALS, ANYTHING!
Will Heng
HECK, SPUD'S MOM COULD BE A SASQUATCH
IT WOULD EXPLAIN THE HAIR

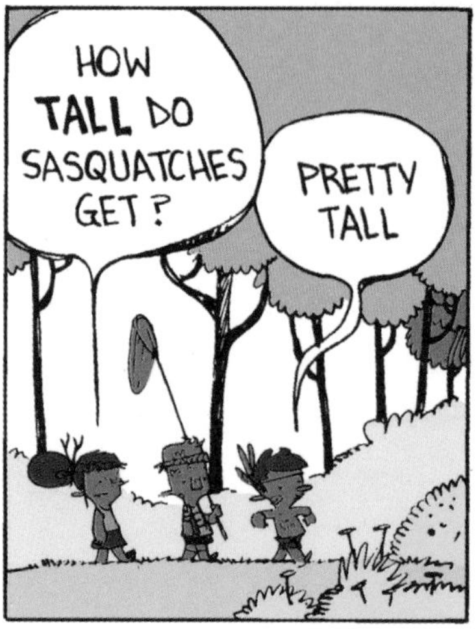
HOW TALL DO SASQUATCHES GET?
PRETTY TALL

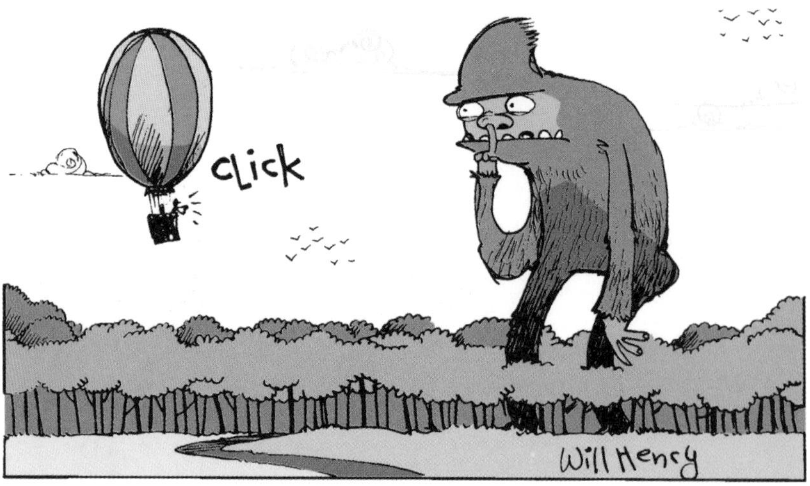
CLICK
Will Henry

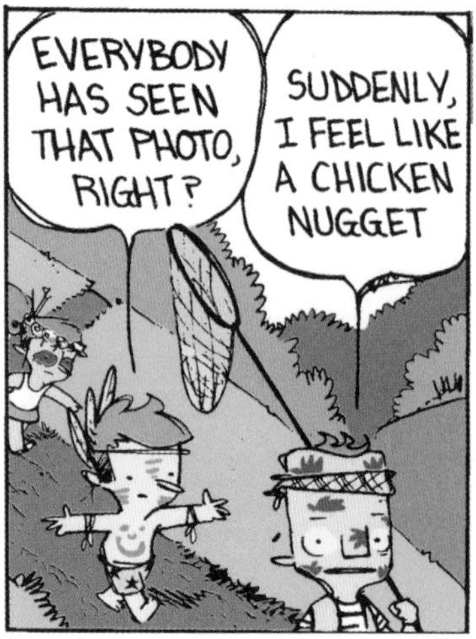
EVERYBODY HAS SEEN THAT PHOTO, RIGHT?
SUDDENLY, I FEEL LIKE A CHICKEN NUGGET

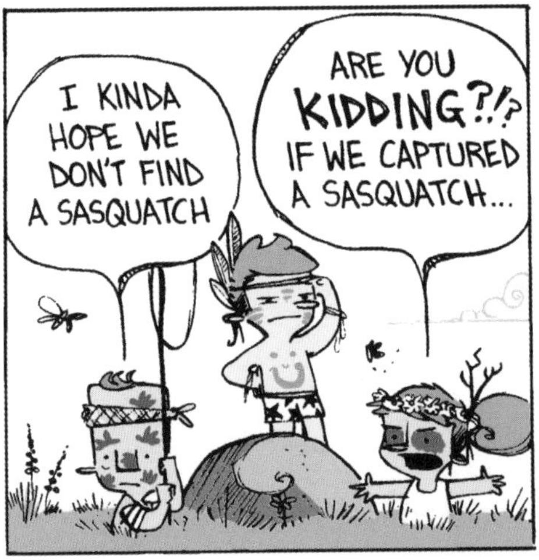
I KINDA HOPE WE DON'T FIND A SASQUATCH
ARE YOU KIDDING?!? IF WE CAPTURED A SASQUATCH...

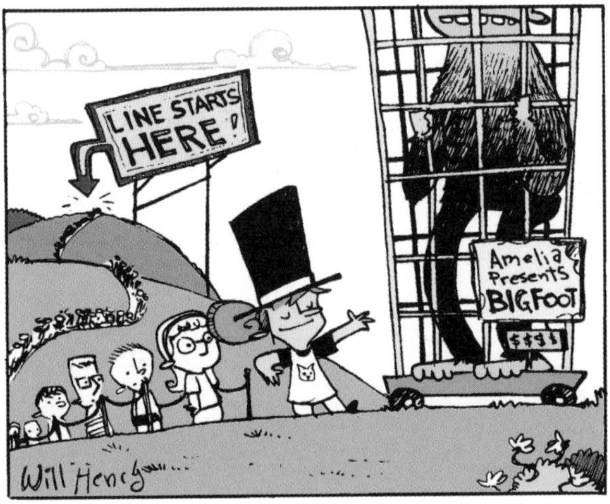
LINE STARTS HERE!
Amelia Presents BIGFOOT
$$$$
Will Henry

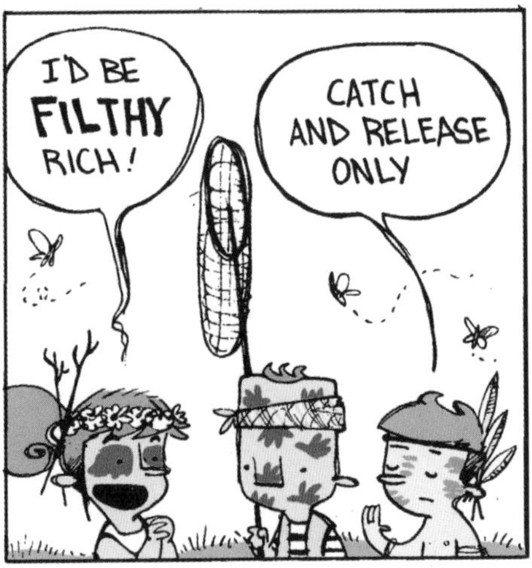
I'D BE FILTHY RICH!
CATCH AND RELEASE ONLY

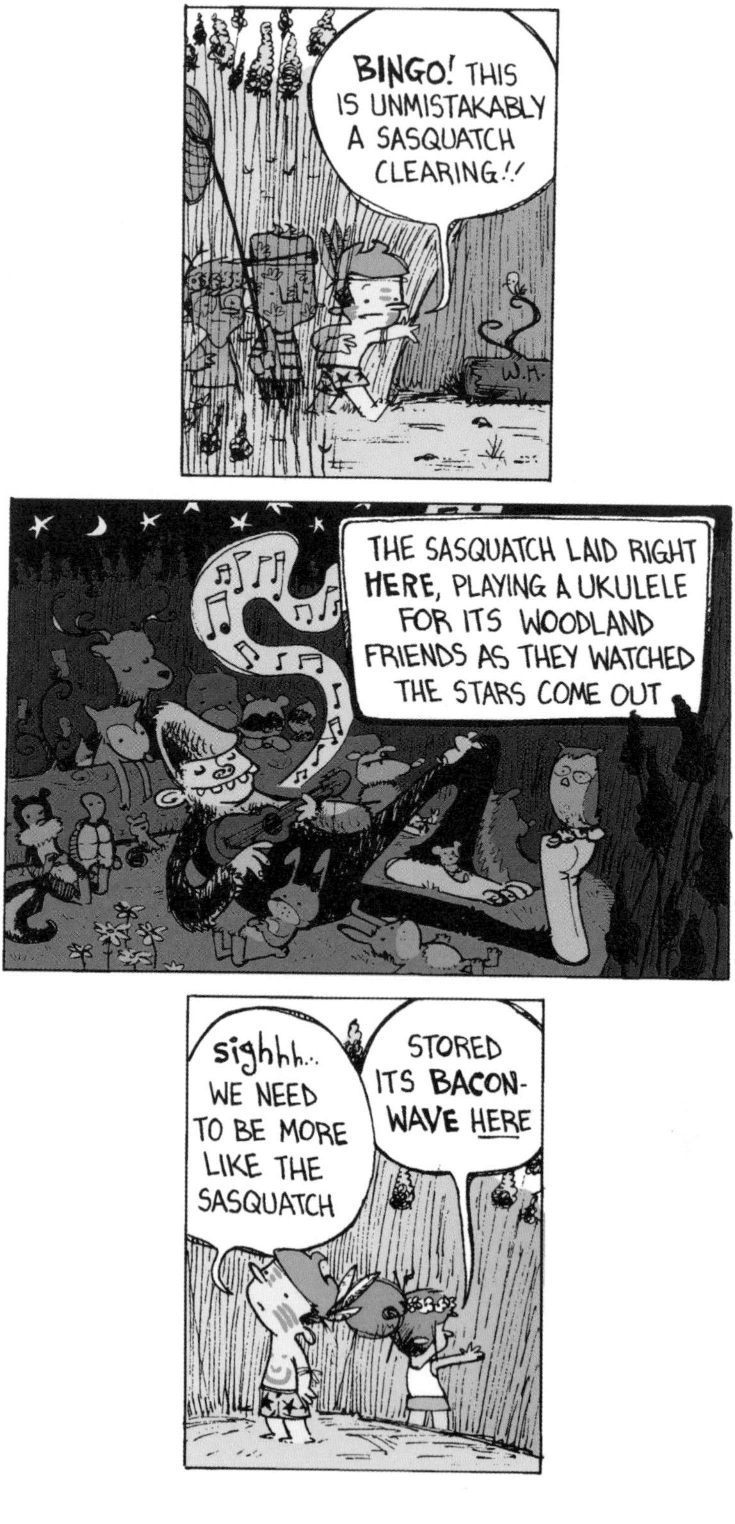
BINGO! THIS IS UNMISTAKABLY A SASQUATCH CLEARING!!
W.H.
THE SASQUATCH LAID RIGHT HERE, PLAYING A UKULELE FOR ITS WOODLAND FRIENDS AS THEY WATCHED THE STARS COME OUT
sighhh... WE NEED TO BE MORE LIKE THE SASQUATCH
STORED ITS BACON-WAVE HERE

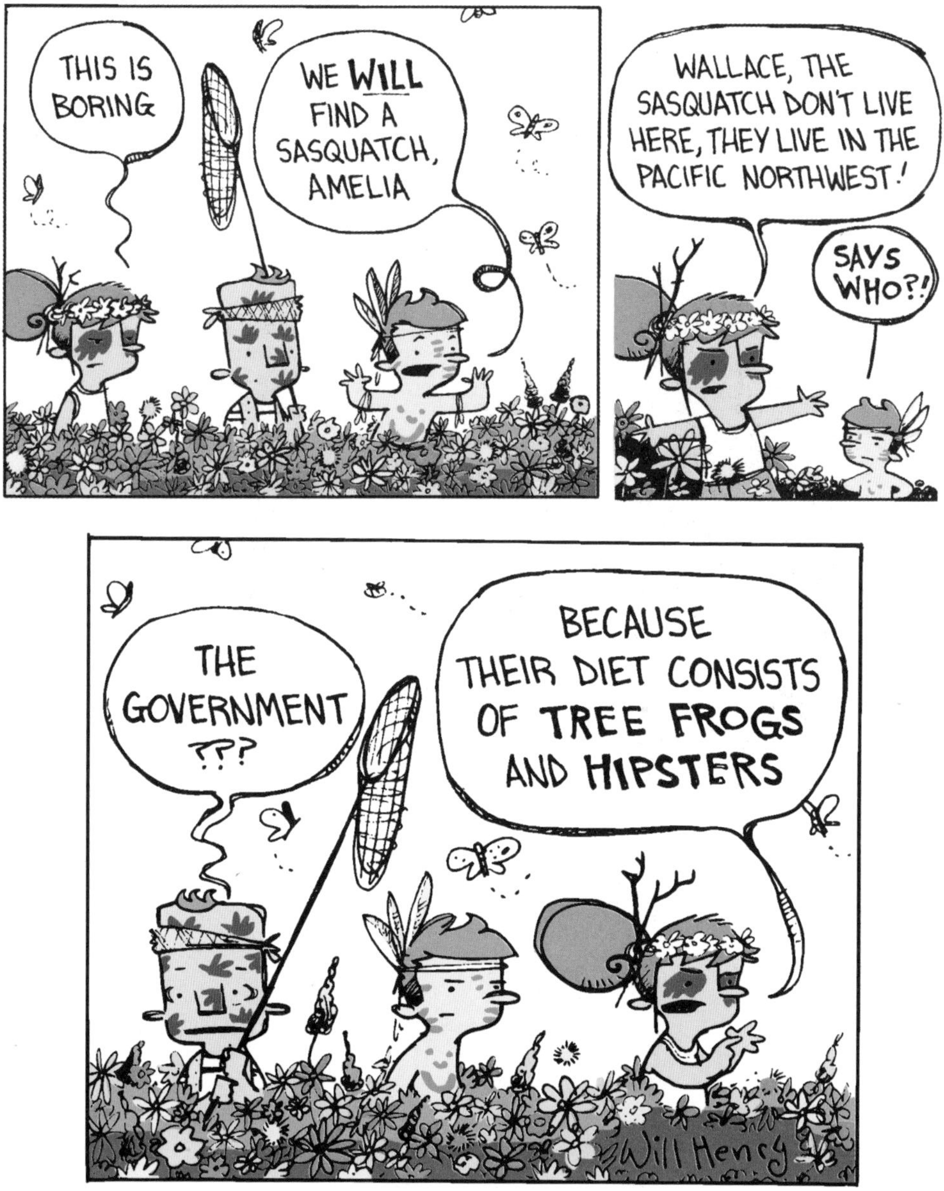
THIS IS BORING
WE WILL FIND A SASQUATCH, AMELIA
WALLACE, THE SASQUATCH DON'T LIVE HERE, THEY LIVE IN THE PACIFIC NORTHWEST!
SAYS WHO?!
THE GOVERNMENT ???
BECAUSE THEIR DIET CONSISTS OF TREE FROGS AND HIPSTERS
Will Henry

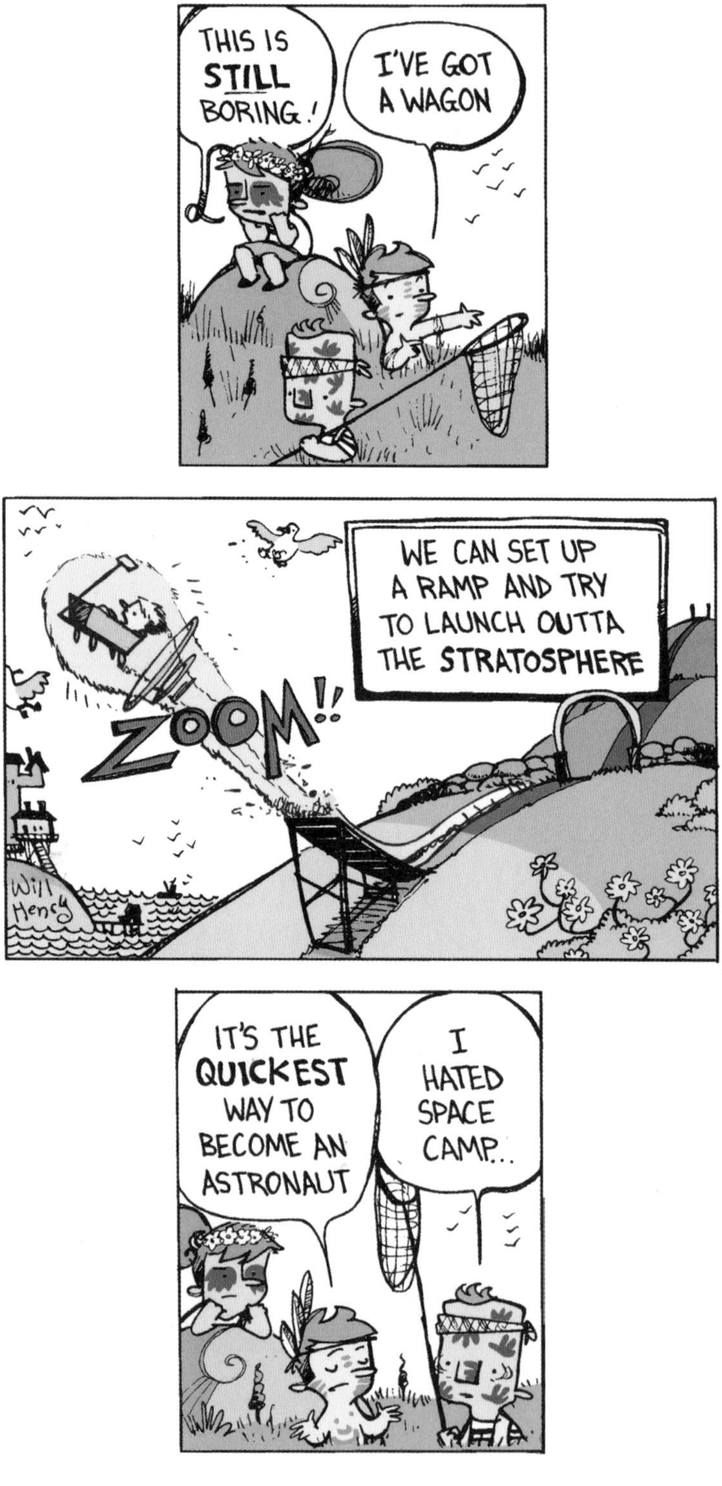
THIS IS STILL BORING!
I'VE GOT A WAGON
WE CAN SET UP A RAMP AND TRY TO LAUNCH OUTTA THE STRATOSPHERE
ZOOM!!
Will Hensy
IT'S THE QUICKEST WAY TO BECOME AN ASTRONAUT
I HATED SPACE CAMP...

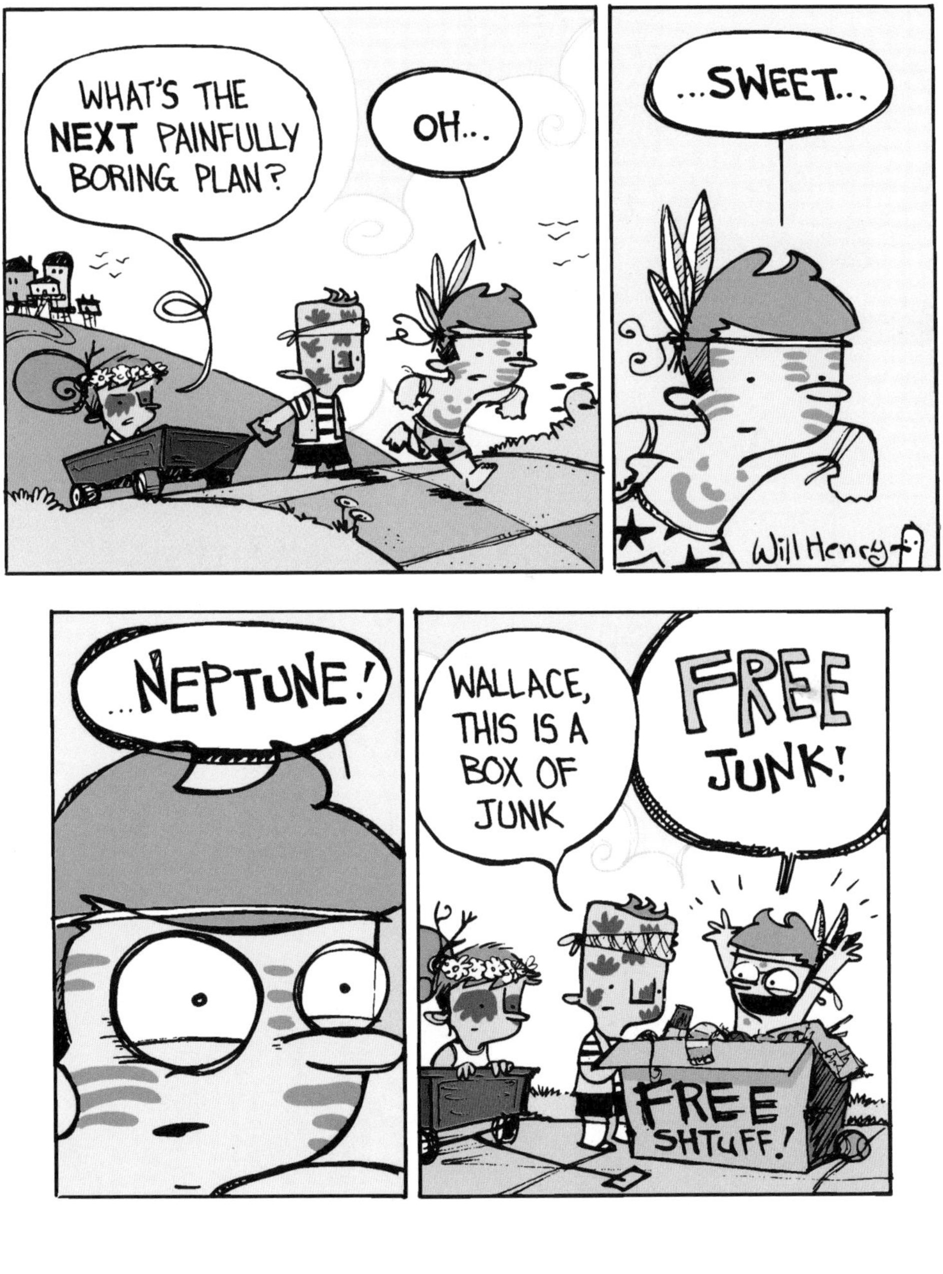

WHAT'S THE NEXT PAINFULLY BORING PLAN?
OH...
...SWEET...
Will Henry
...NEPTUNE!
WALLACE, THIS IS A BOX OF JUNK
FREE JUNK!
FREE SHTUFF!

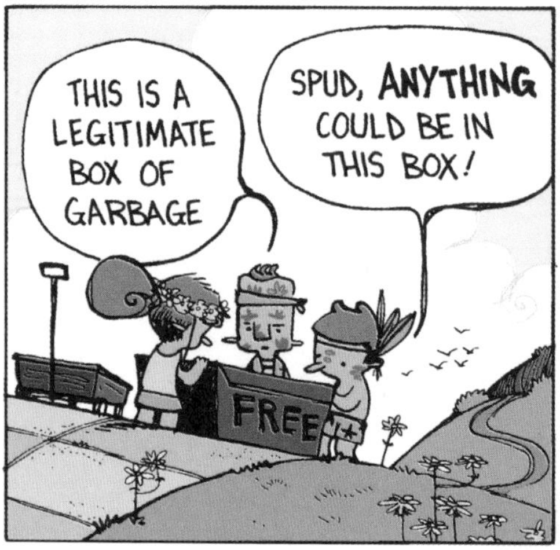
THIS IS A LEGITIMATE BOX OF GARBAGE
SPUD, ANYTHING COULD BE IN THIS BOX!
FREE

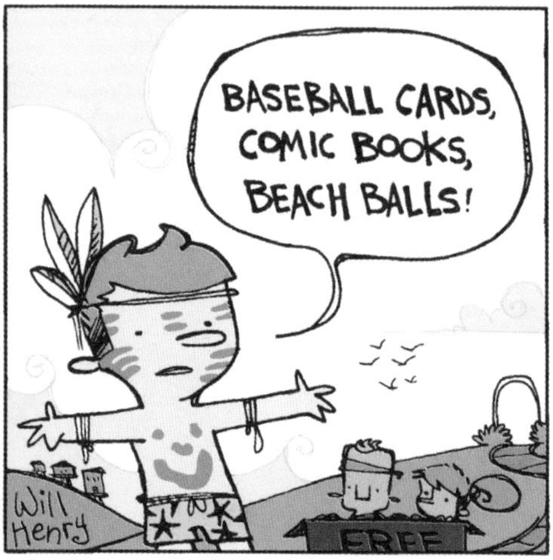
BASEBALL CARDS, COMIC BOOKS, BEACH BALLS!
Will Henry

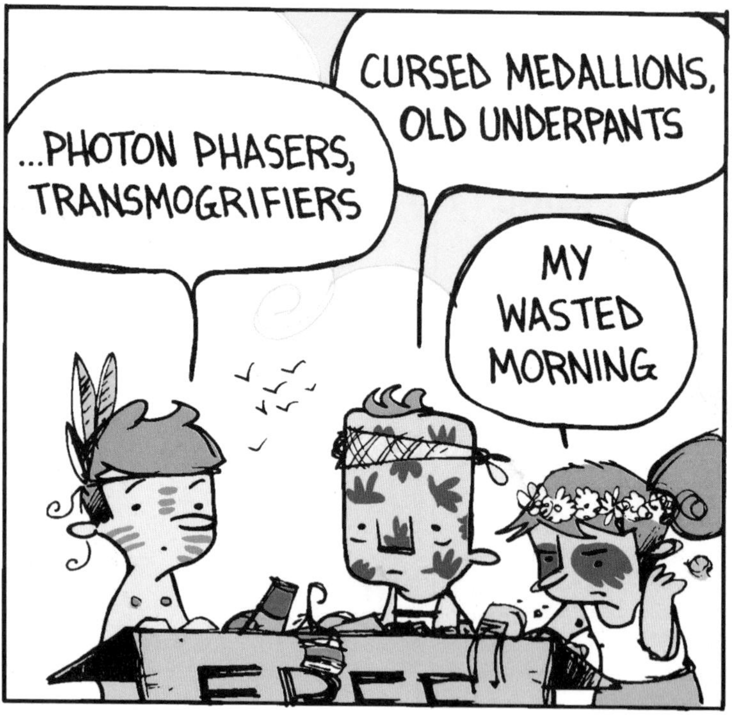
...PHOTON PHASERS, TRANSMOGRIFIERS
CURSED MEDALLIONS, OLD UNDERPANTS
MY WASTED MORNING

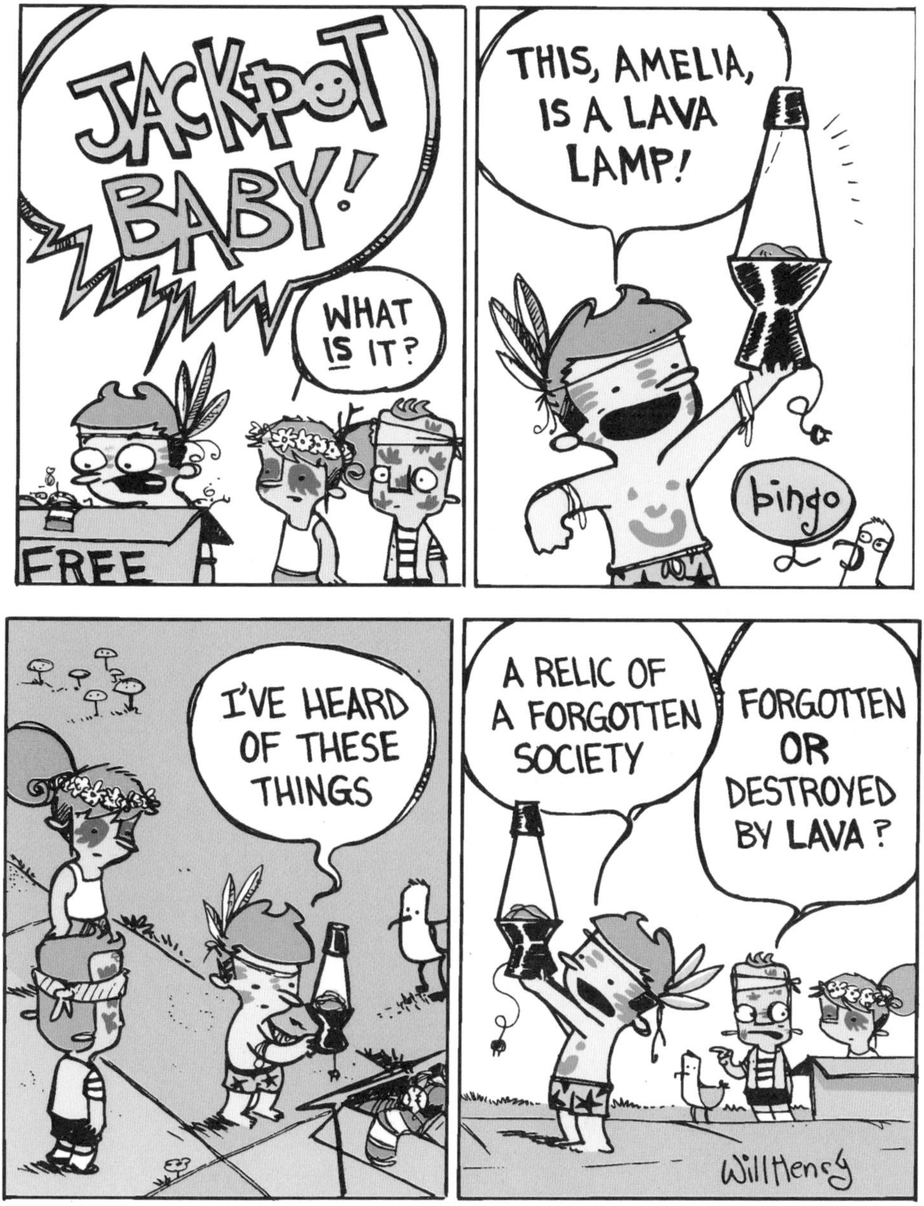
JACKPOT BABY!
WHAT IS IT?
FREE
THIS, AMELIA, IS A LAVA LAMP!
bingo
I'VE HEARD OF THESE THINGS
A RELIC OF A FORGOTTEN SOCIETY
FORGOTTEN OR DESTROYED BY LAVA?
WillHenry

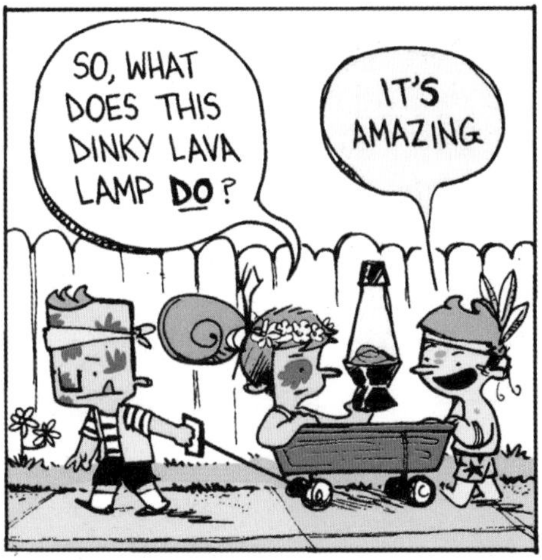
SO, WHAT DOES THIS DINKY LAVA LAMP DO?
IT'S AMAZING

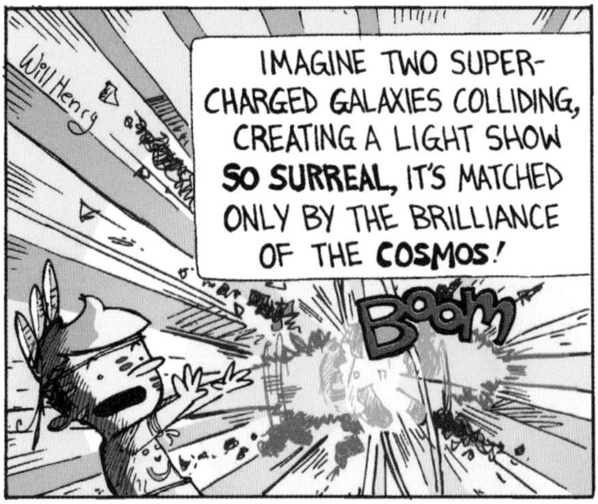
Will Henry
IMAGINE TWO SUPER-CHARGED GALAXIES COLLIDING, CREATING A LIGHT SHOW SO SURREAL, IT'S MATCHED ONLY BY THE BRILLIANCE OF THE COSMOS!
BOOM

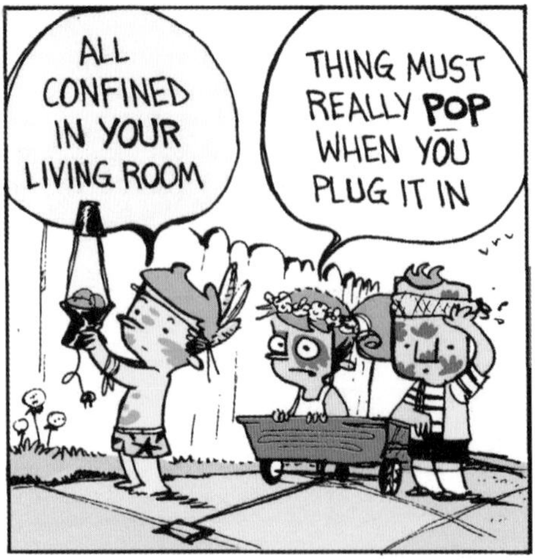
ALL CONFINED IN YOUR LIVING ROOM
THING MUST REALLY POP WHEN YOU PLUG IT IN

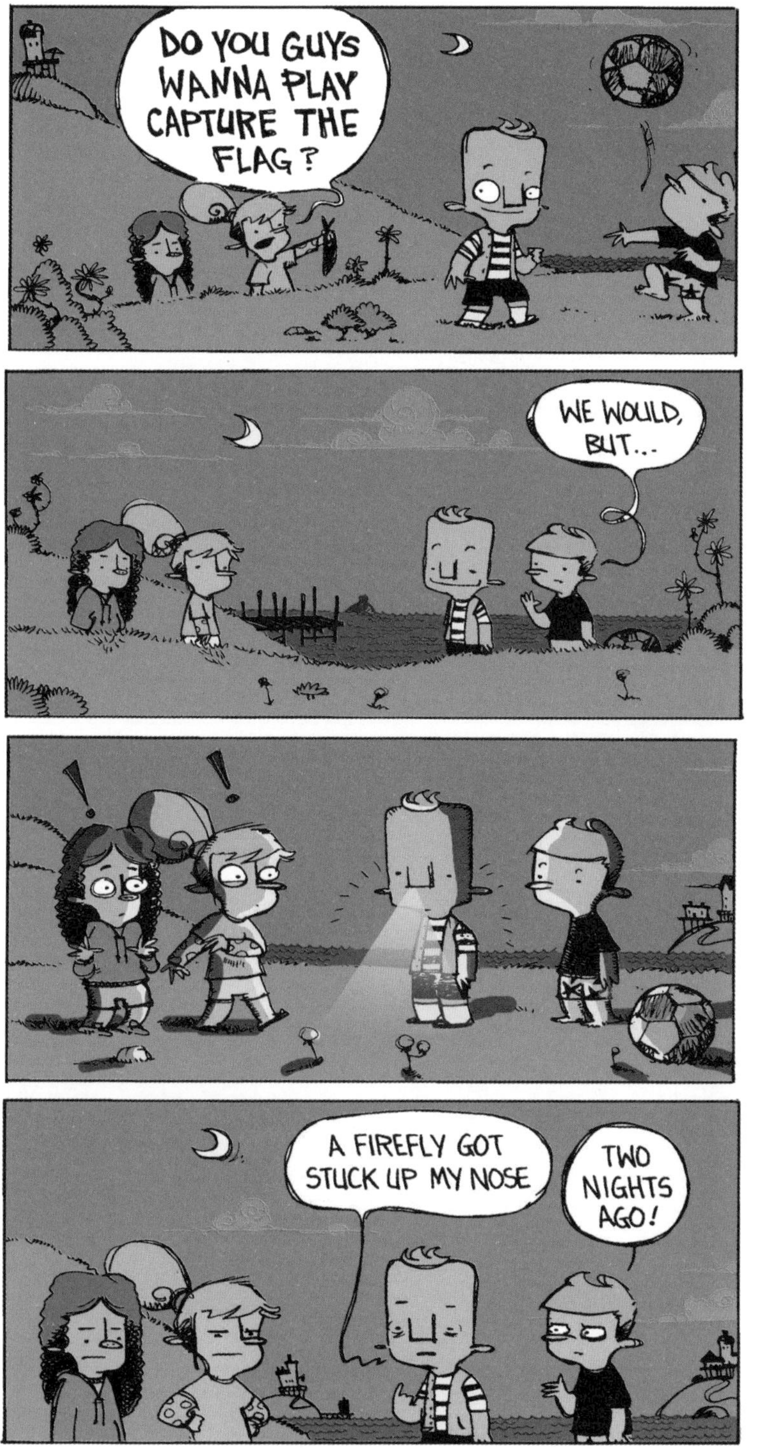
DO YOU GUYS WANNA PLAY CAPTURE THE FLAG?
WE WOULD, BUT...
A FIREFLY GOT STUCK UP MY NOSE
TWO NIGHTS AGO!

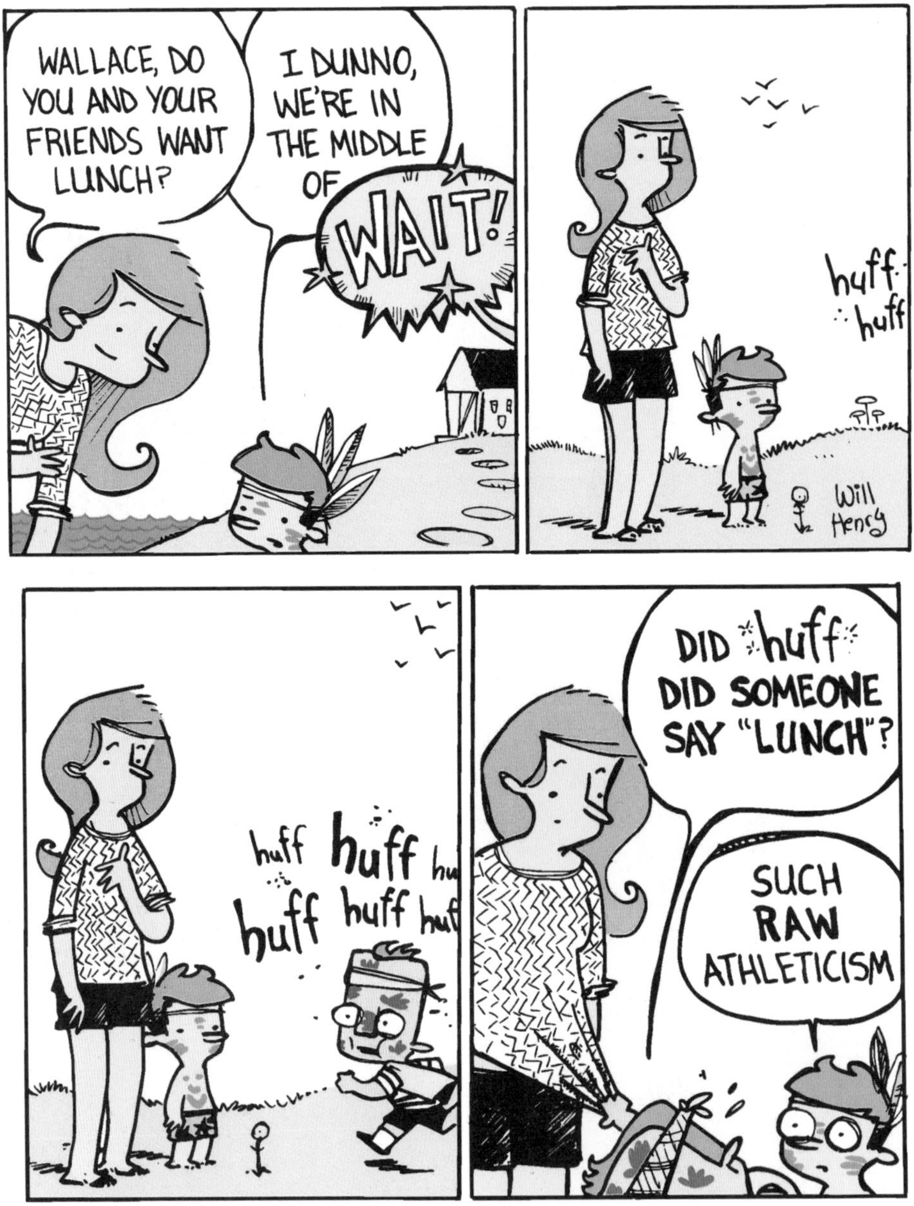
WALLACE, DO YOU AND YOUR FRIENDS WANT LUNCH?
I DUNNO, WE'RE IN THE MIDDLE OF
WAIT!
huff huff
Will Henry
huff huff huff
huff huff
DID huff DID SOMEONE SAY "LUNCH"?
SUCH RAW ATHLETICISM

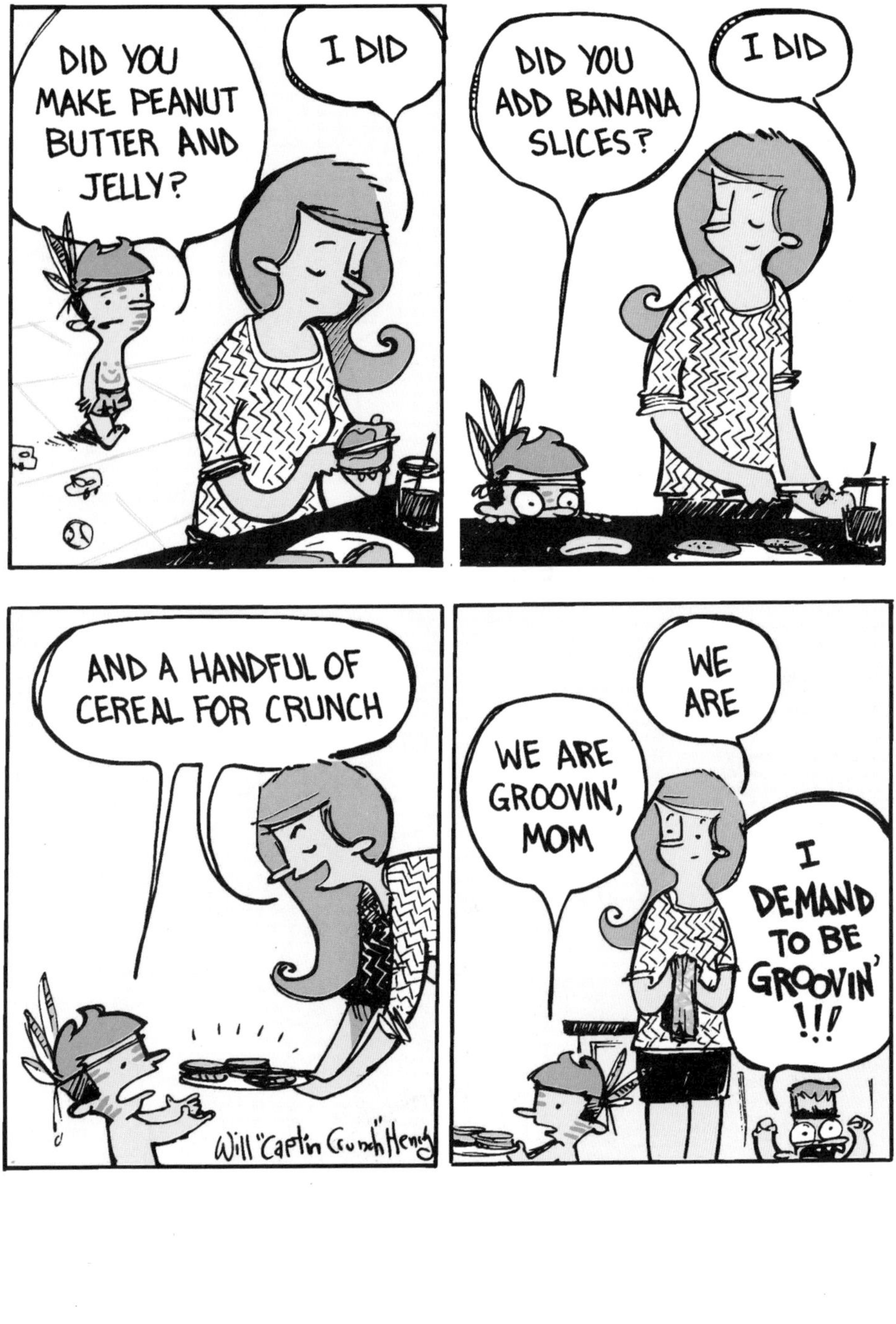
DID YOU MAKE PEANUT BUTTER AND JELLY?
I DID
DID YOU ADD BANANA SLICES?
I DID
AND A HANDFUL OF CEREAL FOR CRUNCH
Will "Captin Crunch" Henry
WE ARE GROOVIN', MOM
WE ARE
I DEMAND TO BE GROOVIN' !!!

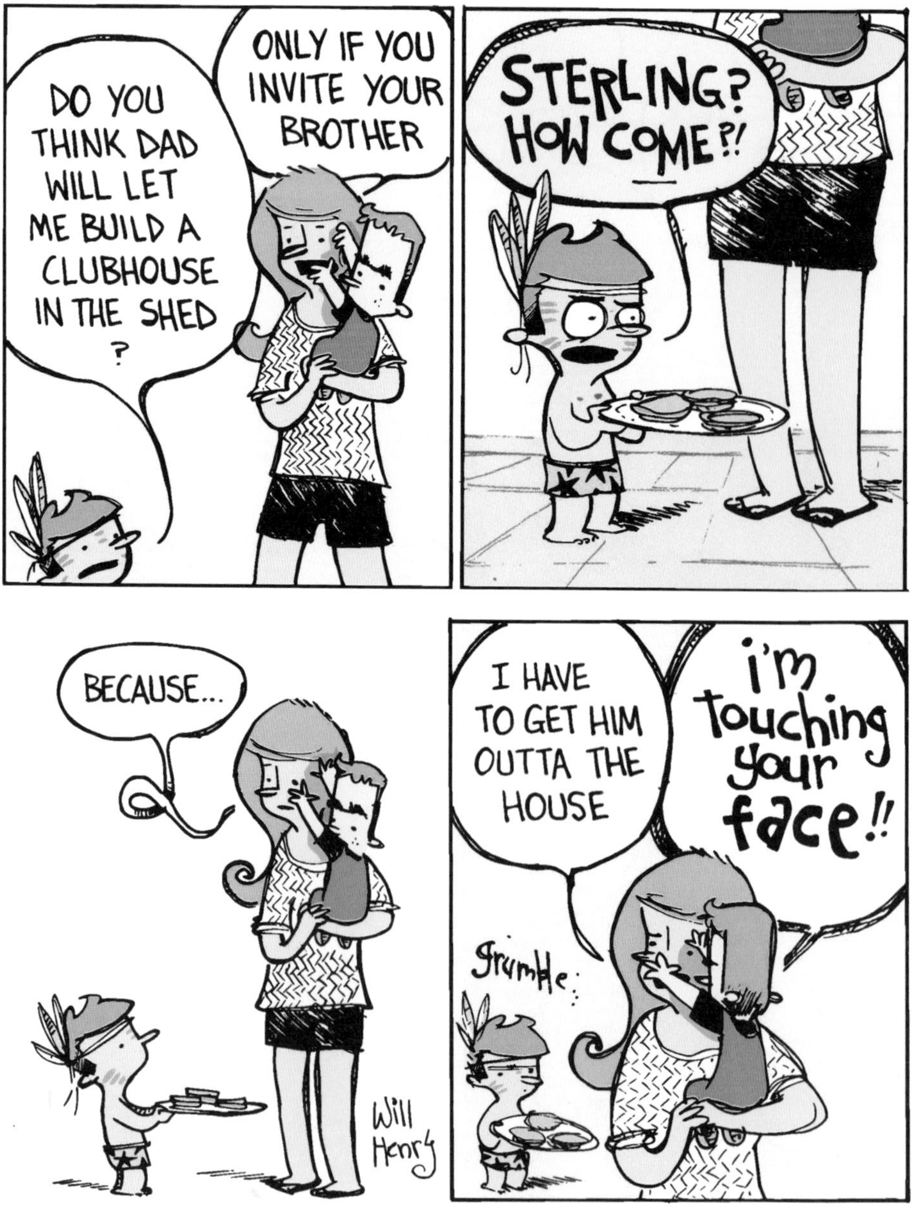
DO YOU THINK DAD WILL LET ME BUILD A CLUBHOUSE IN THE SHED ?
ONLY IF YOU INVITE YOUR BROTHER
STERLING? HOW COME?!
BECAUSE...
Will Henry
I HAVE TO GET HIM OUTTA THE HOUSE
i'm touching your face!!
grumble

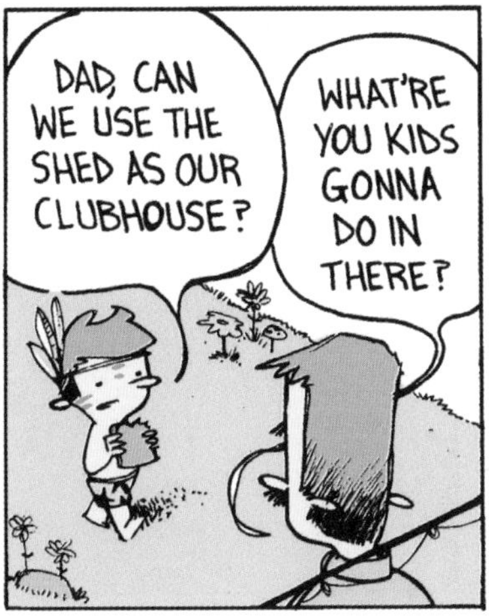
DAD, CAN WE USE THE SHED AS OUR CLUBHOUSE?
WHAT'RE YOU KIDS GONNA DO IN THERE?

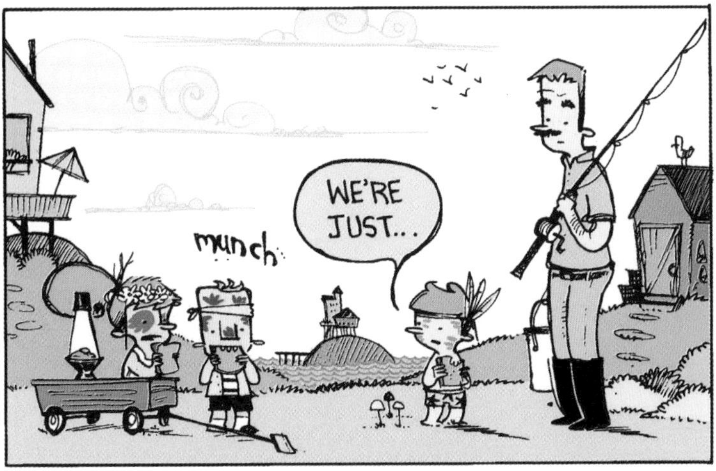
munch
WE'RE JUST...

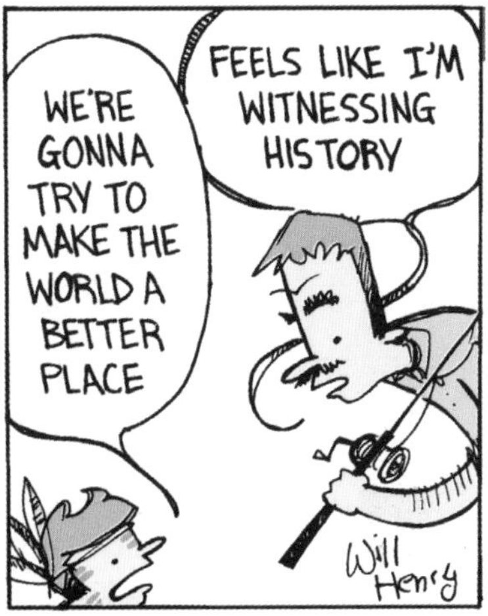
WE'RE GONNA TRY TO MAKE THE WORLD A BETTER PLACE
FEELS LIKE I'M WITNESSING HISTORY
Will Henry

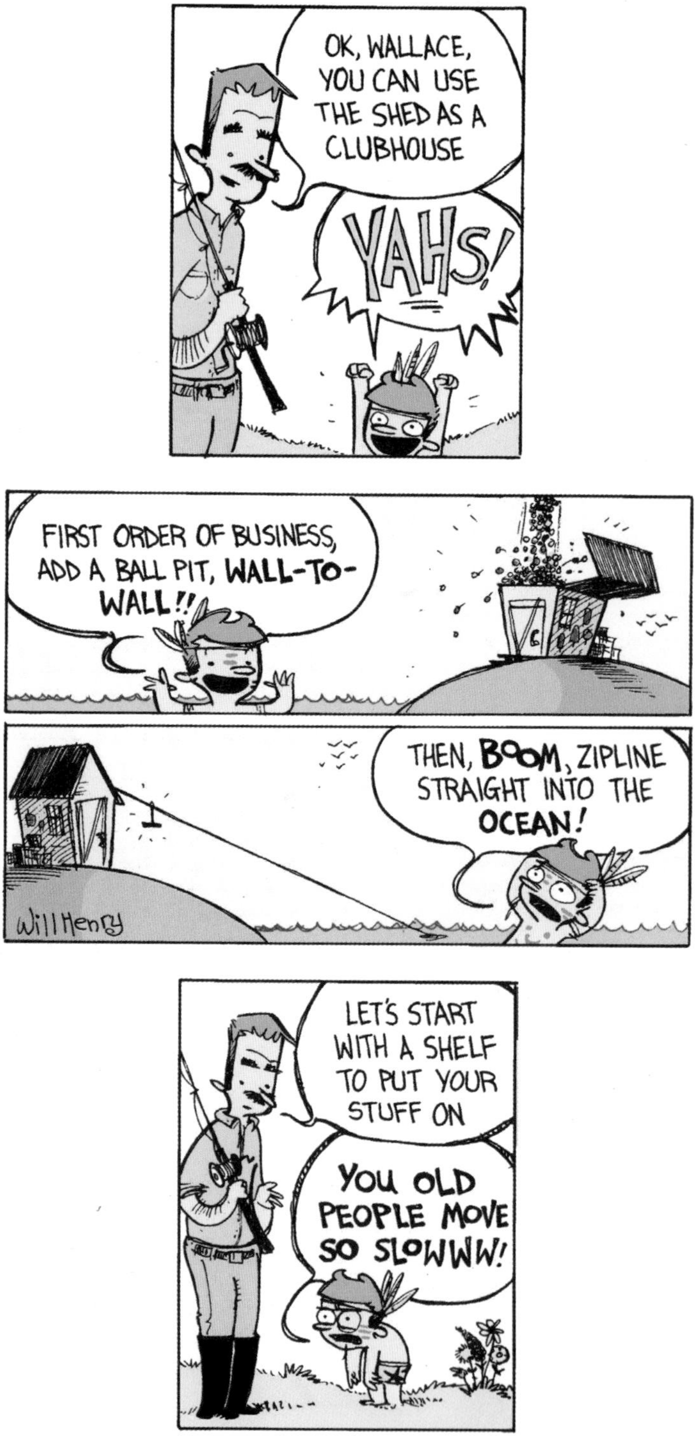
OK, WALLACE, YOU CAN USE THE SHED AS A CLUBHOUSE
YAHS!
FIRST ORDER OF BUSINESS, ADD A BALL PIT, WALL-TO-WALL!!
THEN, BOOM, ZIPLINE STRAIGHT INTO THE OCEAN!
Will Henry
LET'S START WITH A SHELF TO PUT YOUR STUFF ON
YOU OLD PEOPLE MOVE SO SLOWWW!

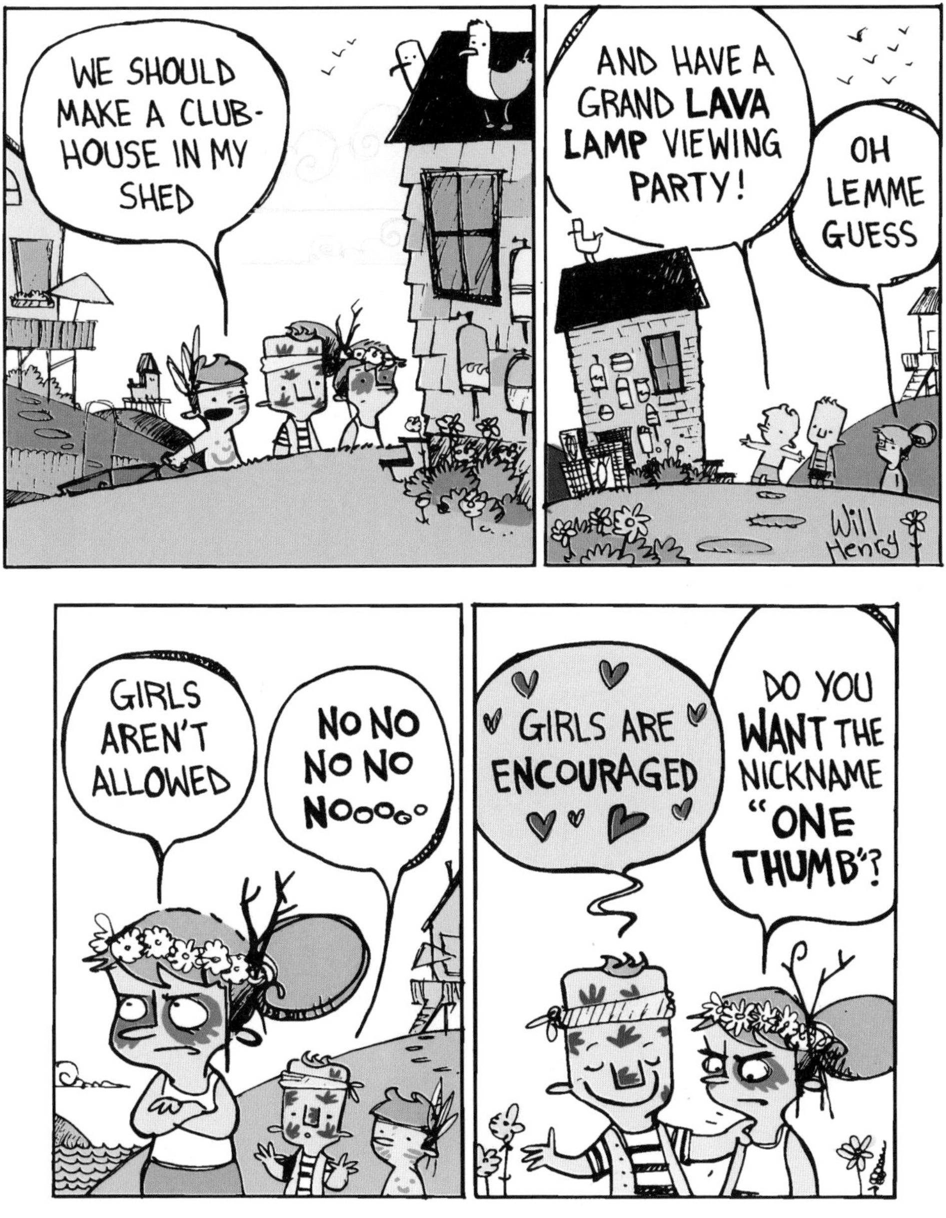
WE SHOULD MAKE A CLUB-HOUSE IN MY SHED
AND HAVE A GRAND LAVA LAMP VIEWING PARTY!
OH LEMME GUESS
Will Henry
GIRLS AREN'T ALLOWED
NO NO NO NO NOoooo
GIRLS ARE ENCOURAGED
DO YOU WANT THE NICKNAME "ONE THUMB"?

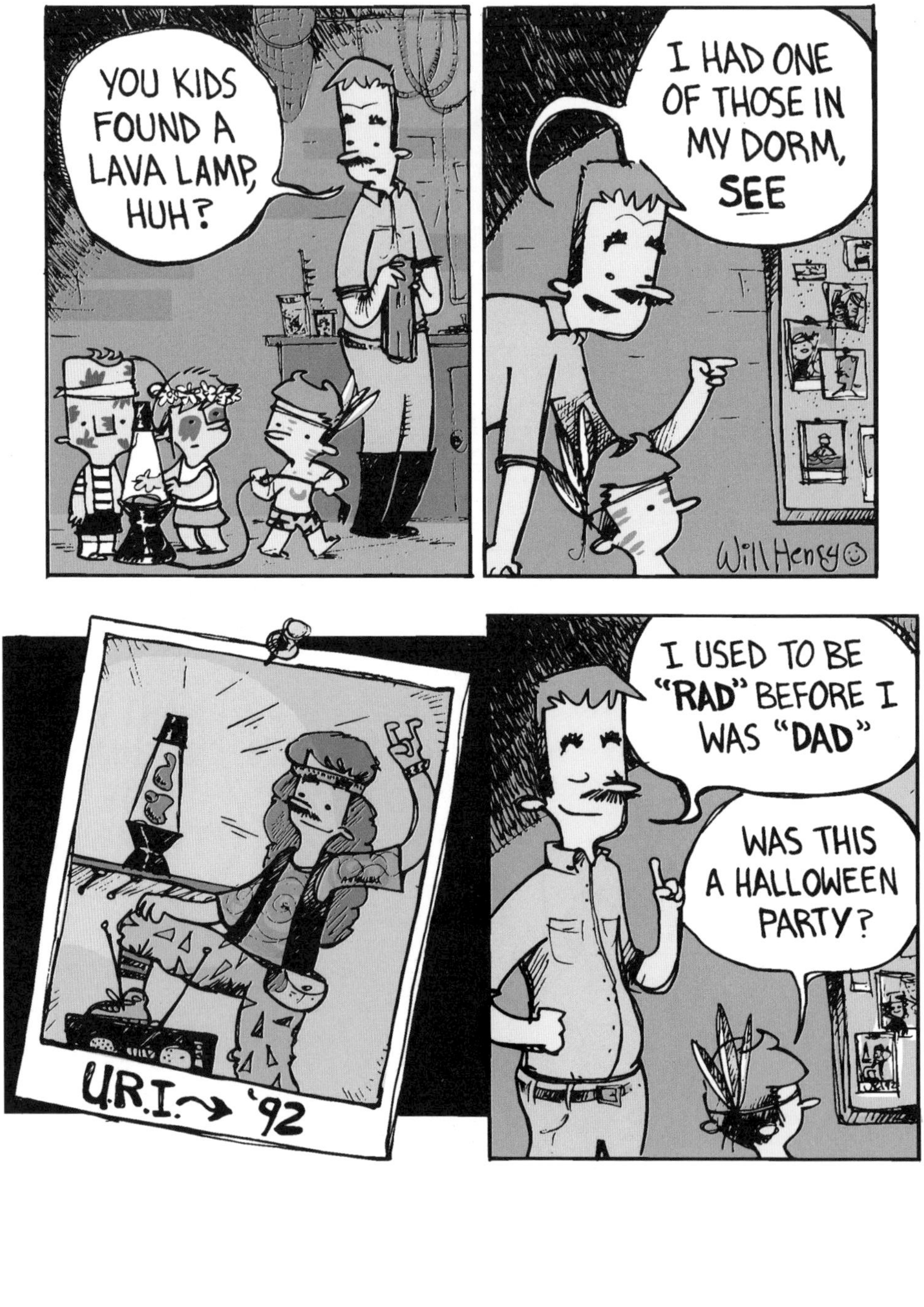
YOU KIDS FOUND A LAVA LAMP, HUH?
I HAD ONE OF THOSE IN MY DORM, SEE
Will Henry
U.R.I. → '92
I USED TO BE "RAD" BEFORE I WAS "DAD"
WAS THIS A HALLOWEEN PARTY?

AND NOW, THE MAIN EVENT!
CLIK
WHHHOOAAAA!!!
W. Henry
hello.

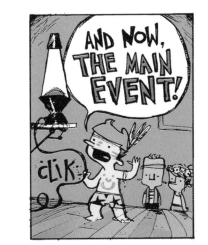

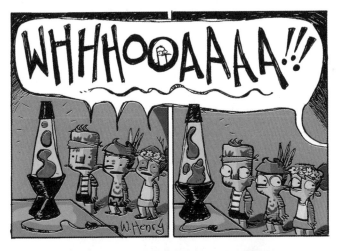

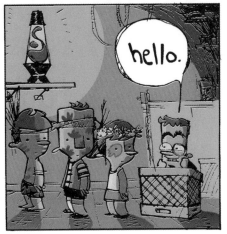

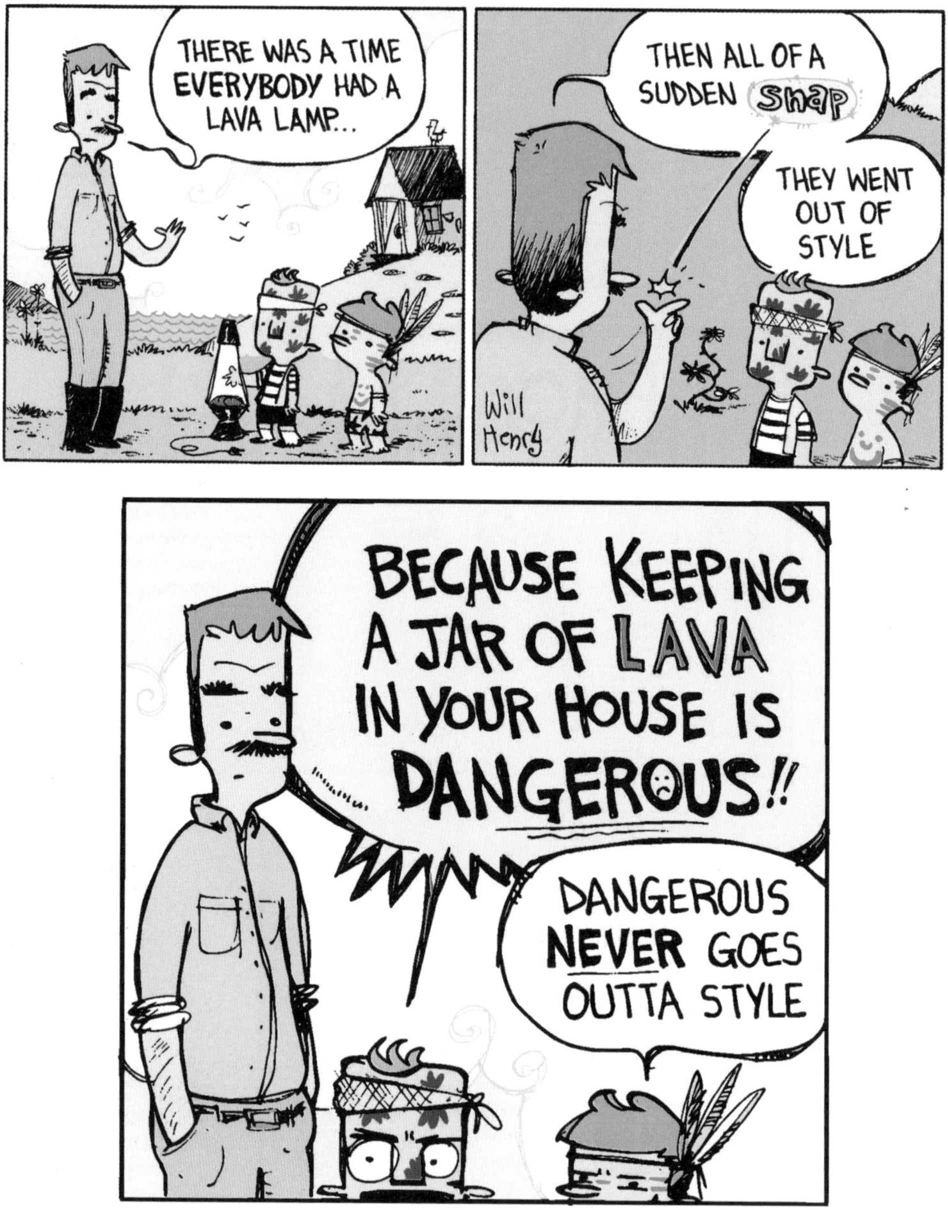
THERE WAS A TIME EVERYBODY HAD A LAVA LAMP...
THEN ALL OF A SUDDEN SNAP
THEY WENT OUT OF STYLE
Will Henry
BECAUSE KEEPING A JAR OF LAVA IN YOUR HOUSE IS DANGEROUS!!
DANGEROUS NEVER GOES OUTTA STYLE

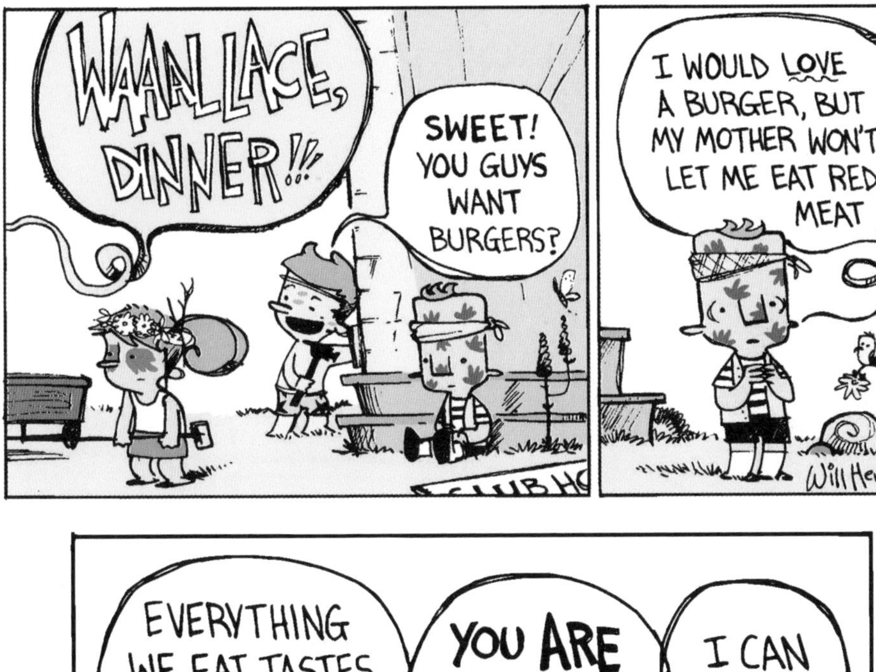
WAAALLACE, DINNER!!!
SWEET! YOU GUYS WANT BURGERS?
I WOULD LOVE A BURGER, BUT MY MOTHER WON'T LET ME EAT RED MEAT
Will Henry
EVERYTHING WE EAT TASTES LIKE A PIECE OF WET CARD-BOARD!
YOU ARE WHAT YOU EAT...
I CAN SEE IT

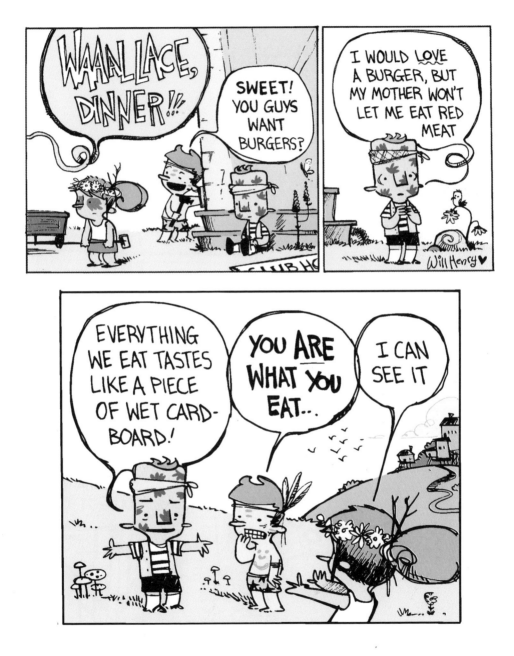

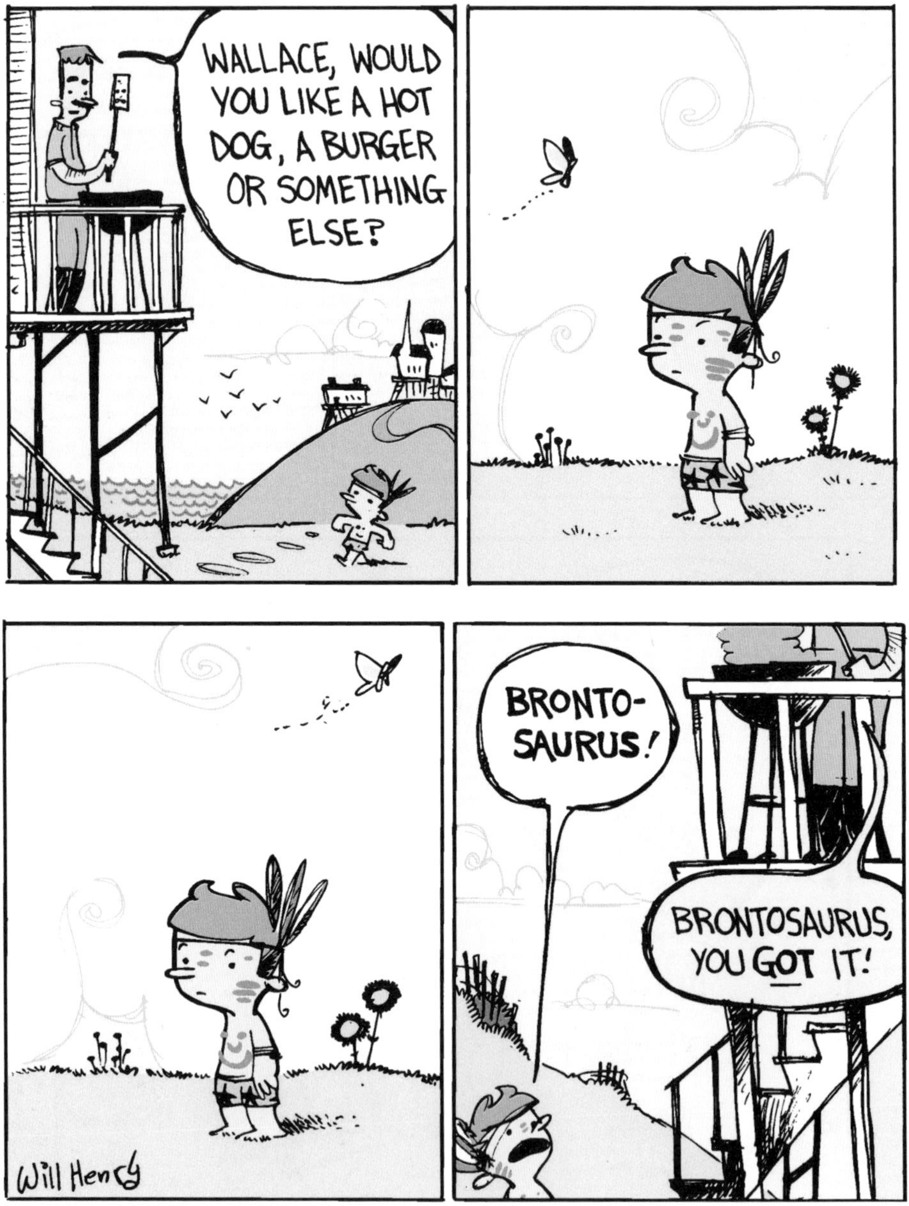
WALLACE, WOULD YOU LIKE A HOT DOG, A BURGER OR SOMETHING ELSE?
BRONTO-SAURUS!
BRONTOSAURUS, YOU GOT IT!
Will Henry

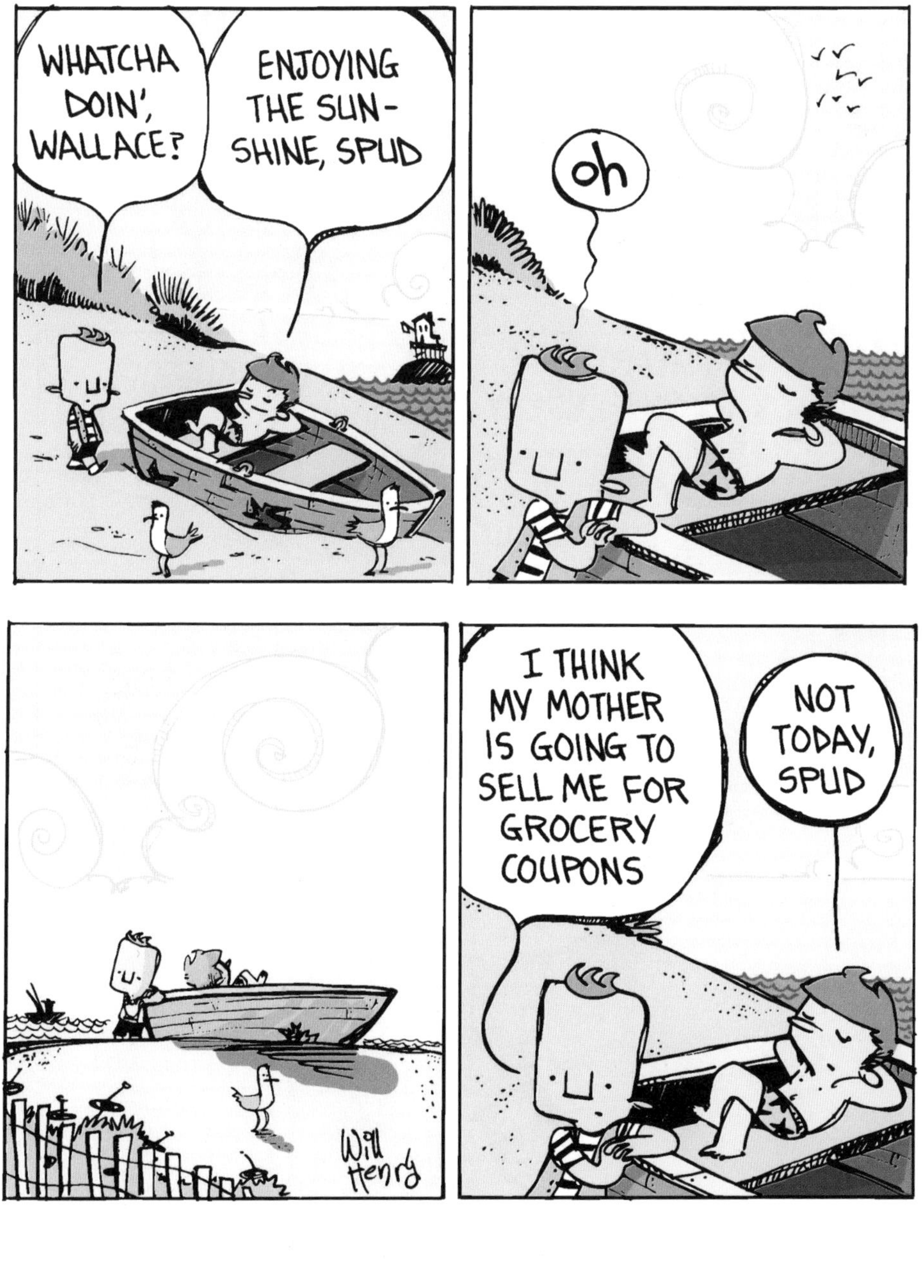
WHATCHA DOIN', WALLACE?
ENJOYING THE SUN-SHINE, SPUD
oh
I THINK MY MOTHER IS GOING TO SELL ME FOR GROCERY COUPONS
NOT TODAY, SPUD
Will Henry

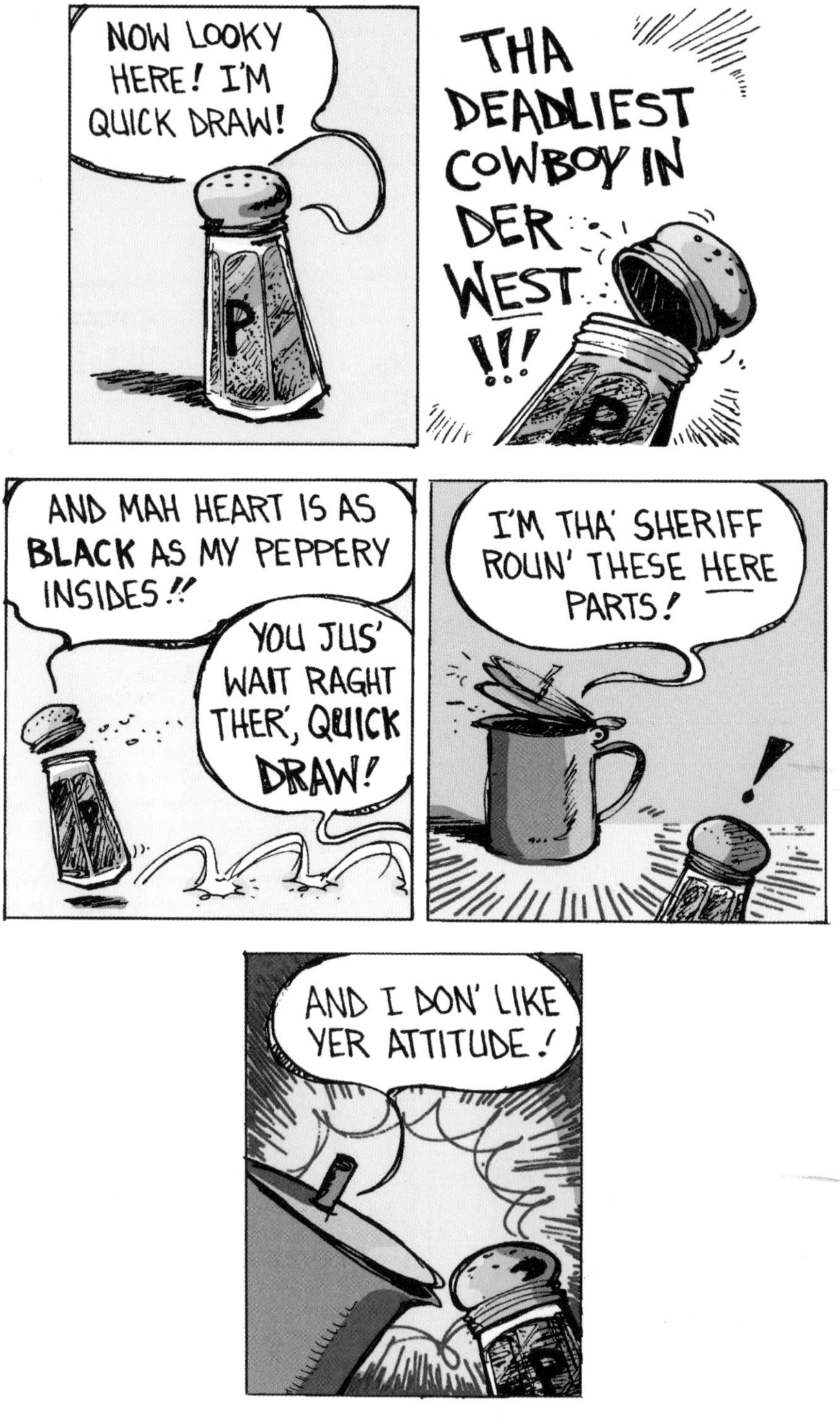
NOW LOOKY HERE! I'M QUICK DRAW!
THA DEADLIEST COWBOY IN DER WEST !!!
AND MAH HEART IS AS BLACK AS MY PEPPERY INSIDES!!
YOU JUS' WAIT RAGHT THER', QUICK DRAW!
I'M THA' SHERIFF ROUN' THESE HERE PARTS!
!
AND I DON' LIKE YER ATTITUDE!

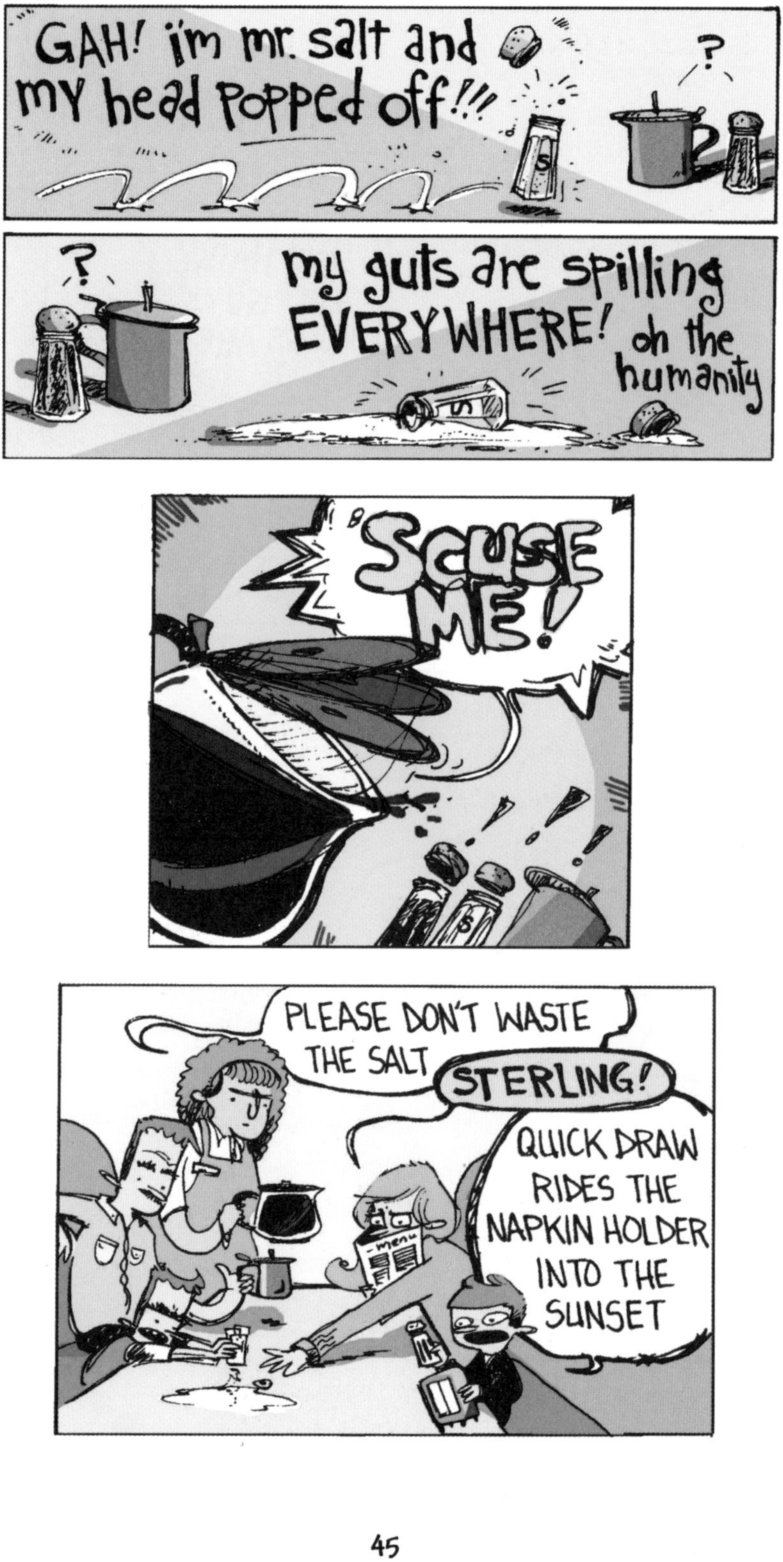
GAH! i'm mr. salt and my head popped off!!!
?
S
?
my guts are spilling EVERYWHERE!
oh the humanity
S
SCUSE ME!
S
PLEASE DON'T WASTE THE SALT
STERLING!
QUICK DRAW RIDES THE NAPKIN HOLDER INTO THE SUNSET
menu

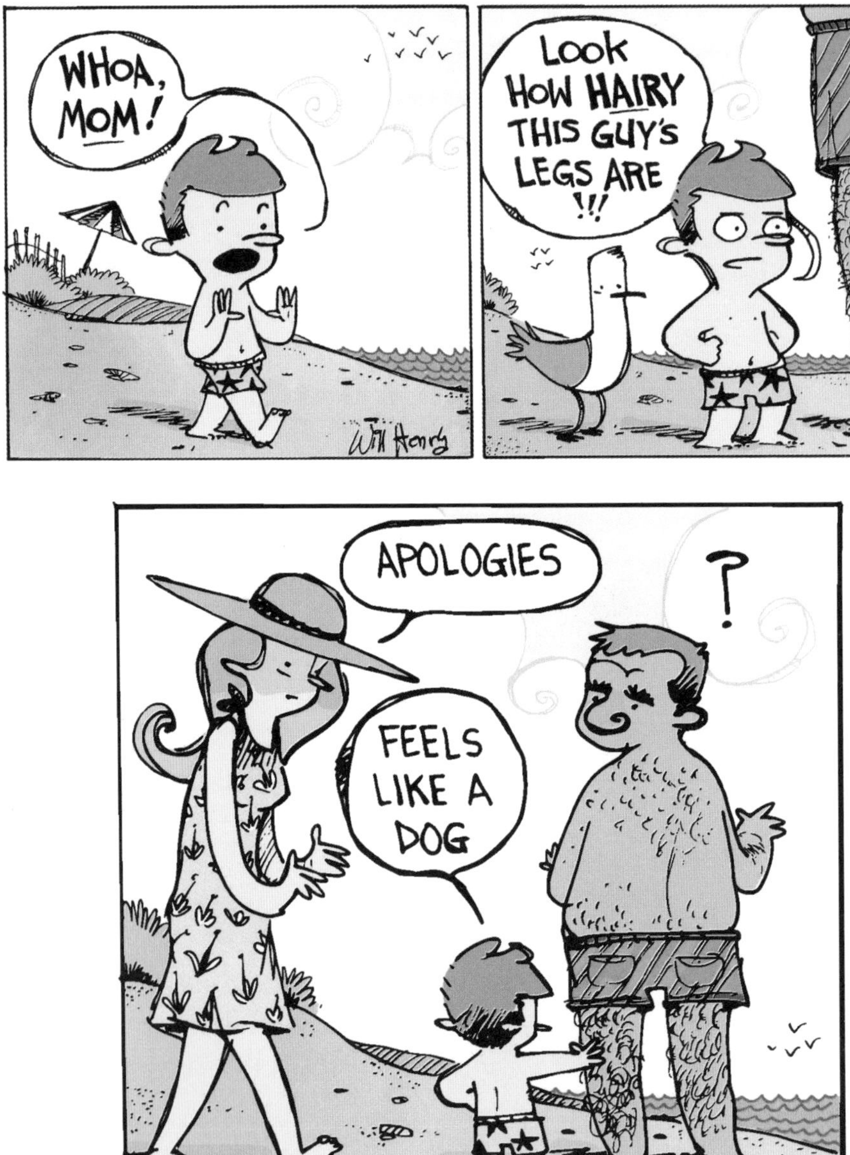
WHOA, MOM!
Will Henry
LOOK HOW HAIRY THIS GUY'S LEGS ARE !!!
APOLOGIES
?
FEELS LIKE A DOG

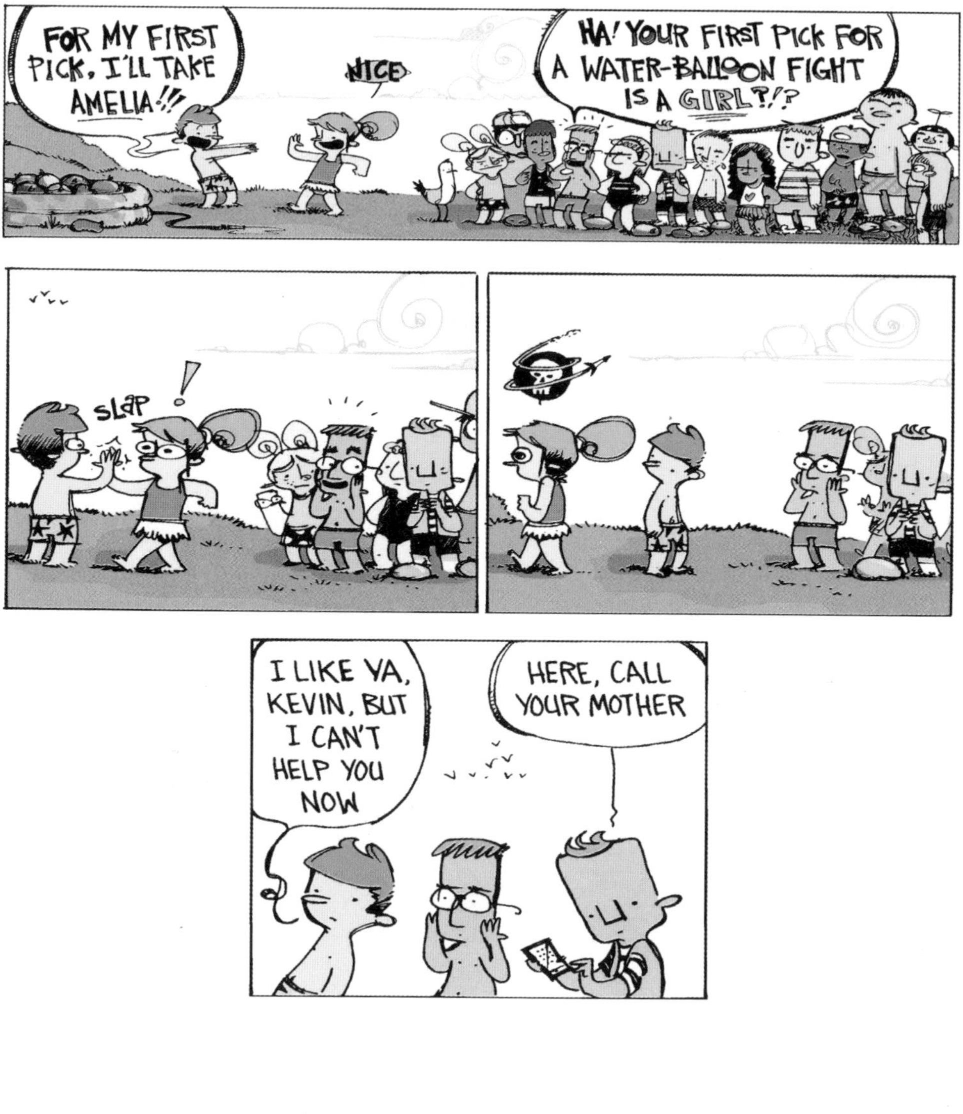
FOR MY FIRST PICK, I'LL TAKE AMELIA!!!
NICE
HA! YOUR FIRST PICK FOR A WATER-BALLOON FIGHT IS A GIRL?!?
SLAP
!
I LIKE YA, KEVIN, BUT I CAN'T HELP YOU NOW
HERE, CALL YOUR MOTHER

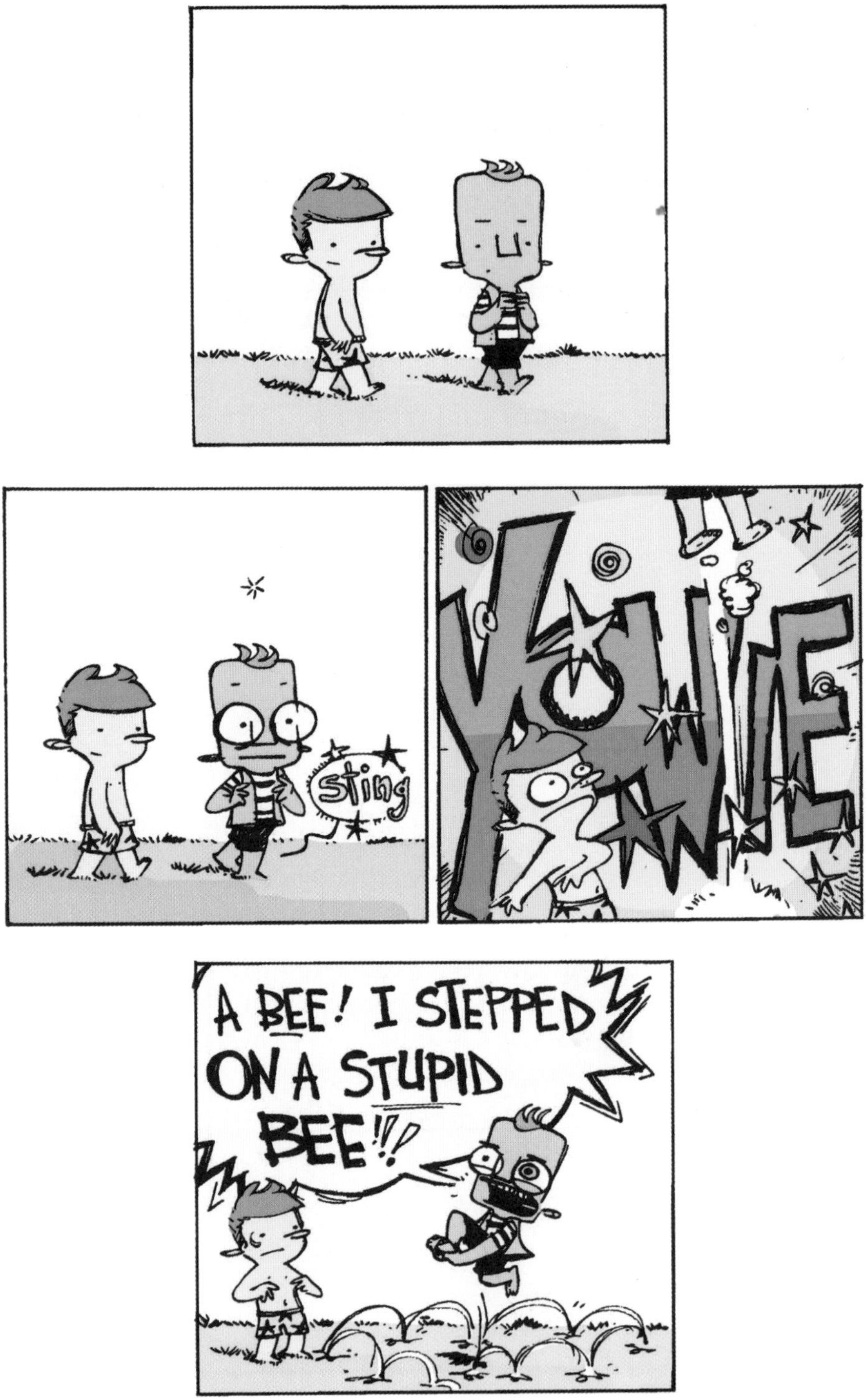
sting
YOWIE
A BEE! I STEPPED ON A STUPID BEE!!!

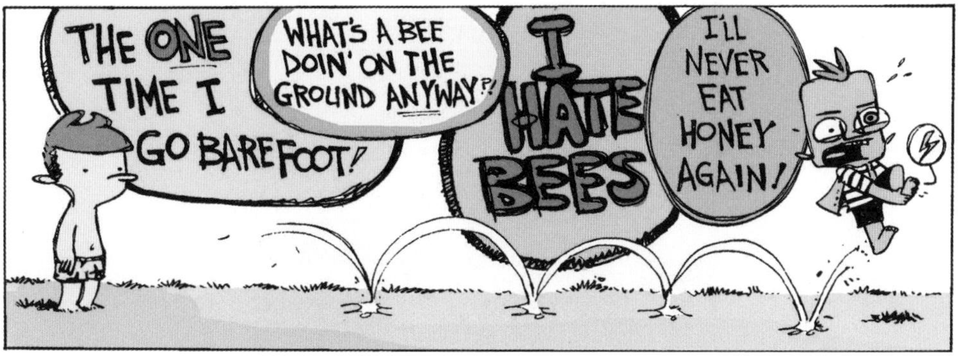
THE ONE TIME I GO BAREFOOT!
WHAT'S A BEE DOIN' ON THE GROUND ANYWAY?!
I HATE BEES
I'LL NEVER EAT HONEY AGAIN!

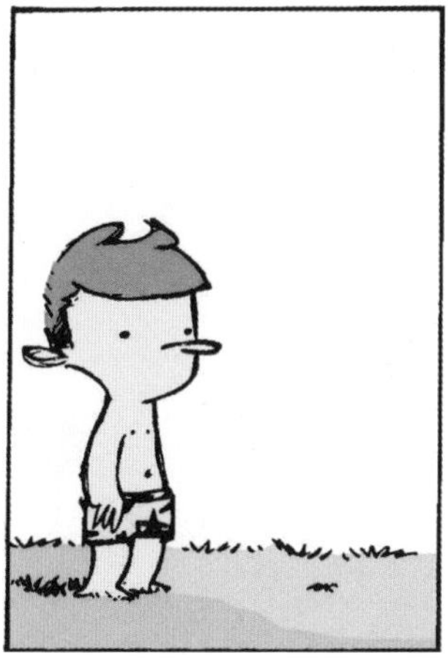

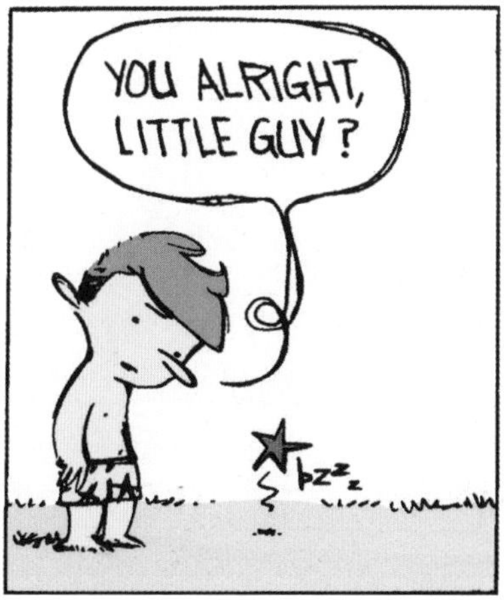
YOU ALRIGHT, LITTLE GUY?
bzzz

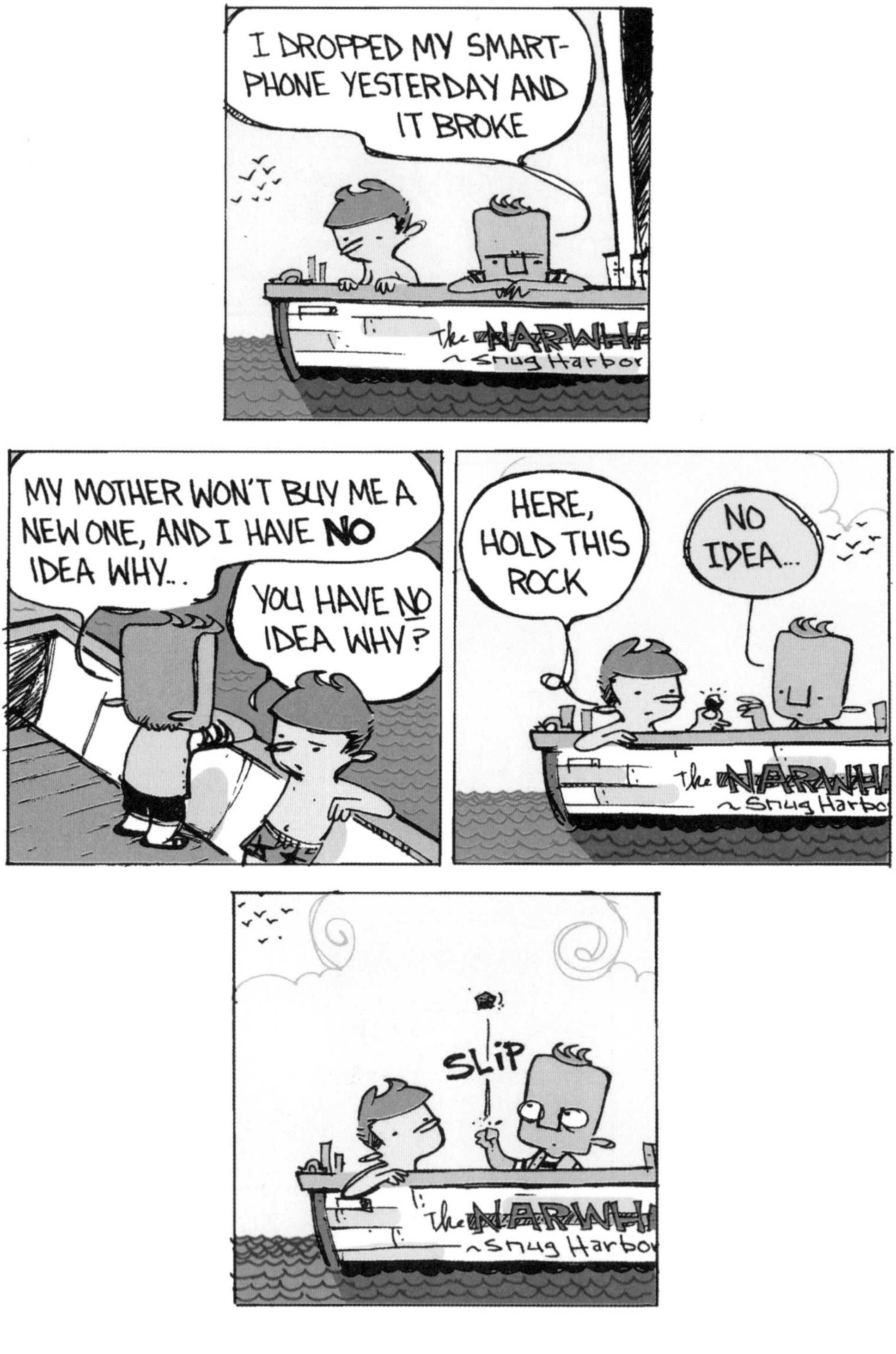
I DROPPED MY SMART-PHONE YESTERDAY AND IT BROKE
The NARWHA
Snug Harbor
MY MOTHER WON'T BUY ME A NEW ONE, AND I HAVE **NO** IDEA WHY...
YOU HAVE NO IDEA WHY?
HERE, HOLD THIS ROCK
NO IDEA...
SLIP

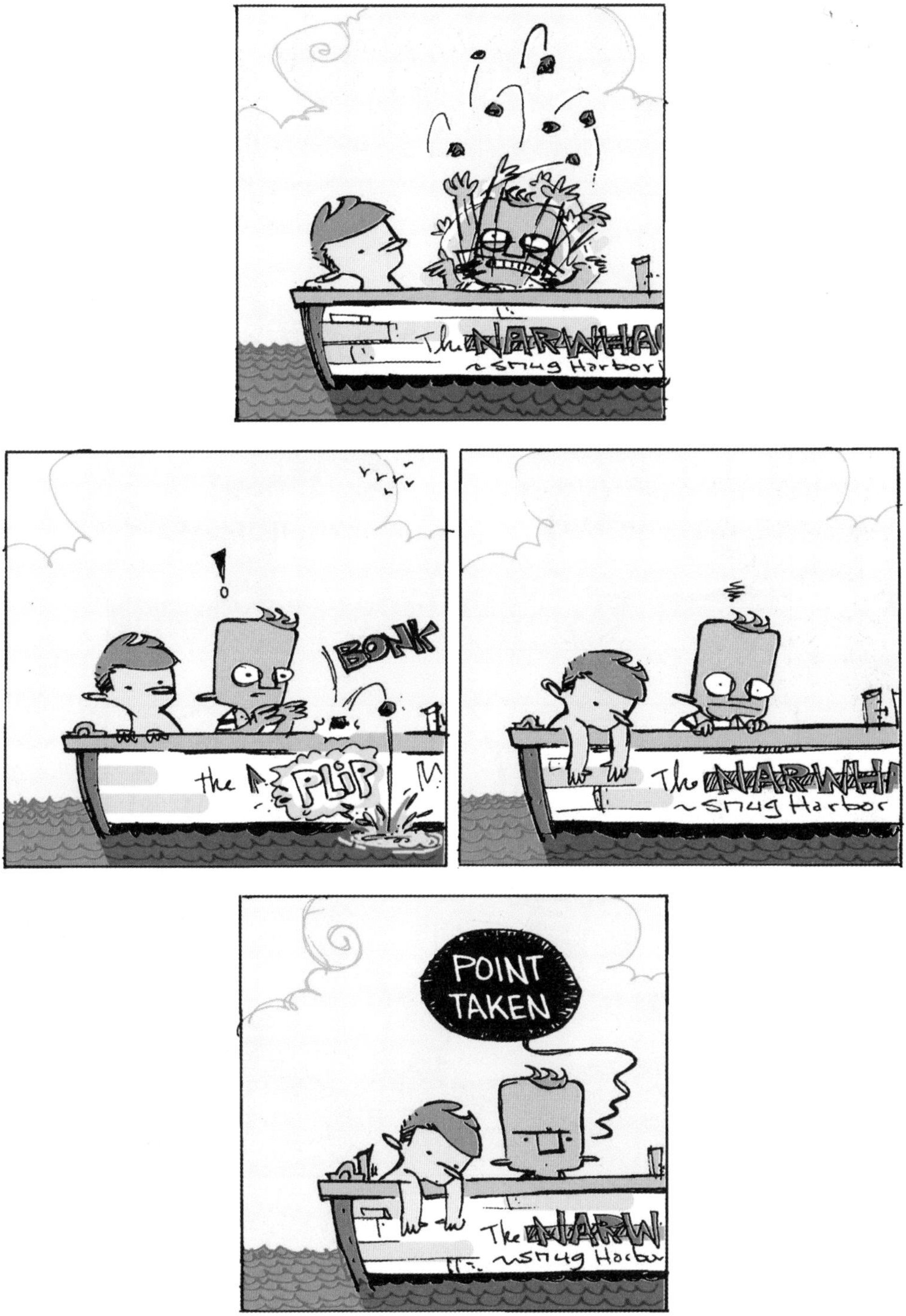
BONK
PLIP
POINT TAKEN

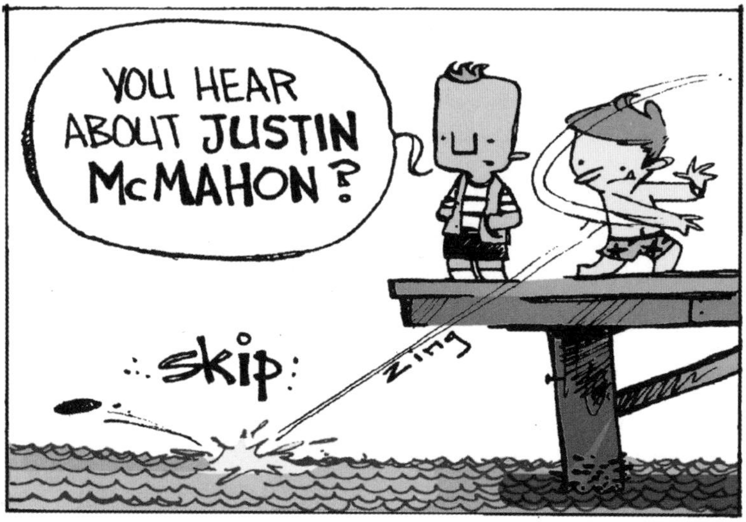
YOU HEAR ABOUT JUSTIN McMAHON?
zing
skip

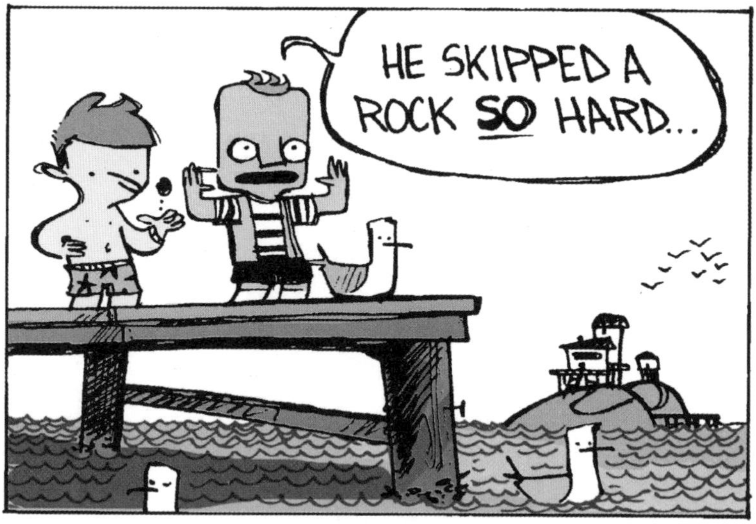
HE SKIPPED A ROCK SO HARD...

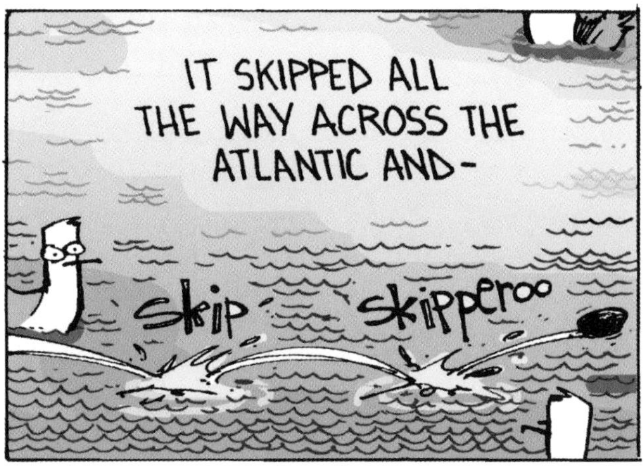
IT SKIPPED ALL THE WAY ACROSS THE ATLANTIC AND-
skip
skipperoo

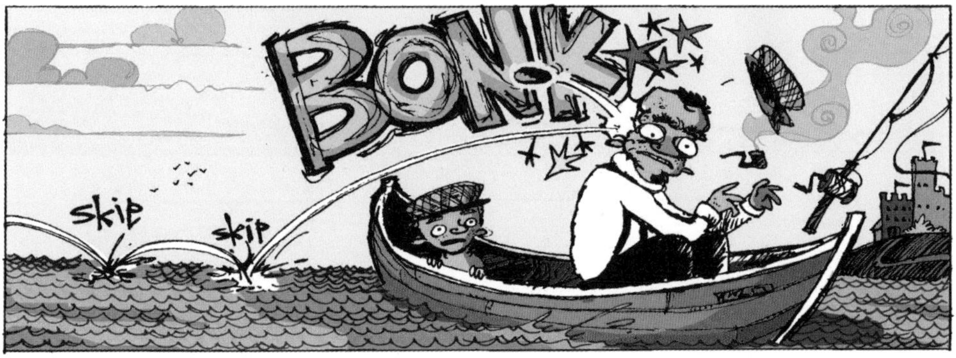
BONK
skip
skip

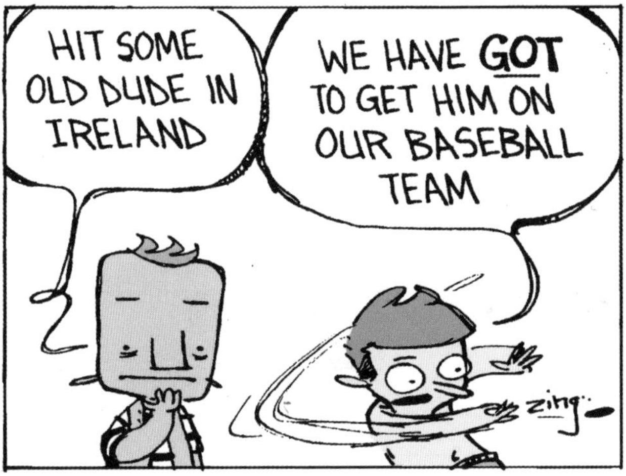
HIT SOME OLD DUDE IN IRELAND
WE HAVE **GOT** TO GET HIM ON OUR BASEBALL TEAM
zing

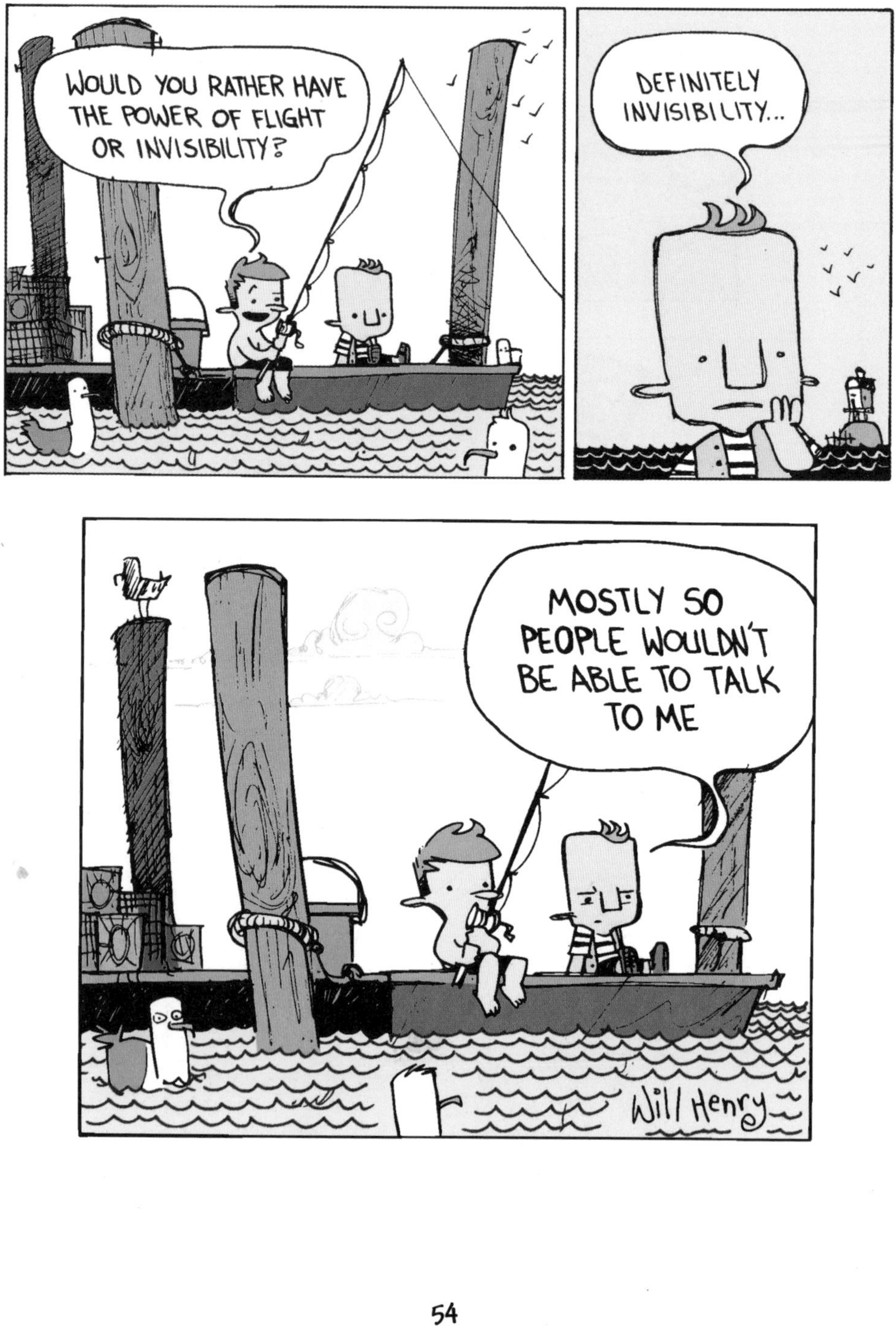
WOULD YOU RATHER HAVE THE POWER OF FLIGHT OR INVISIBILITY?
DEFINITELY INVISIBILITY...
MOSTLY SO PEOPLE WOULDN'T BE ABLE TO TALK TO ME
Will Henry

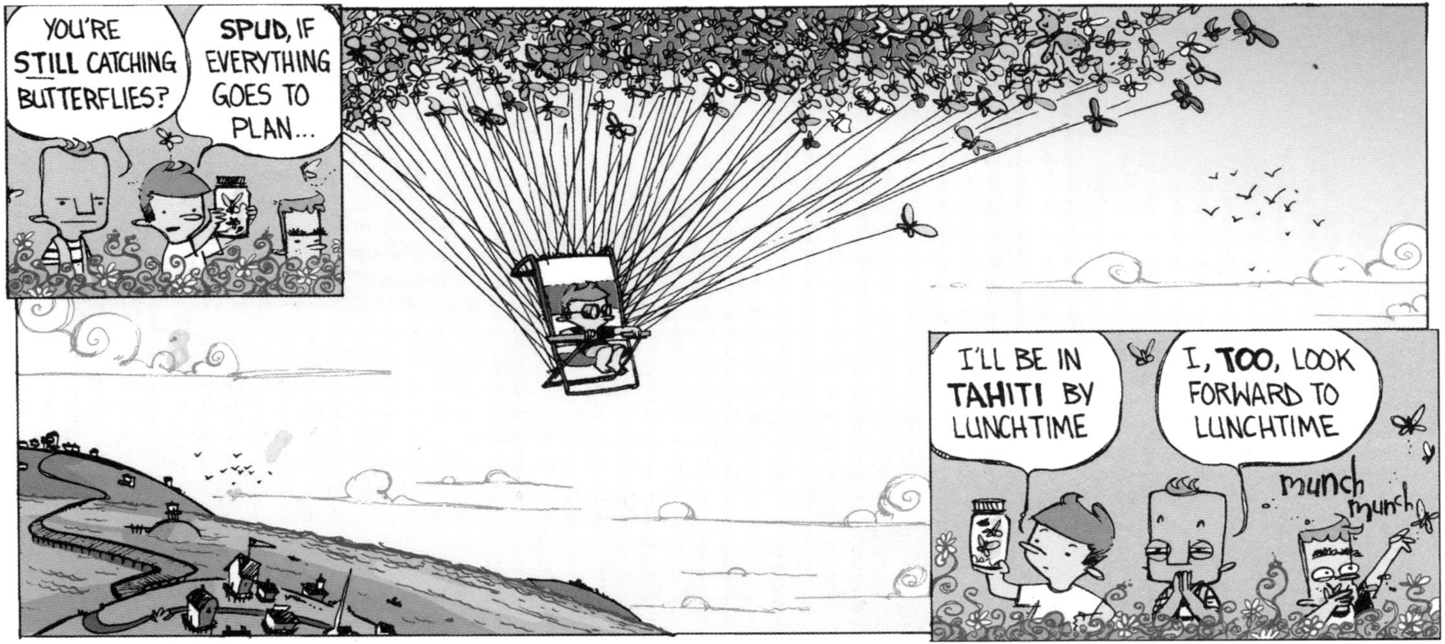
YOU'RE STILL CATCHING BUTTERFLIES?
SPUD, IF EVERYTHING GOES TO PLAN...
I'LL BE IN TAHITI BY LUNCHTIME
I, TOO, LOOK FORWARD TO LUNCHTIME
munch munch

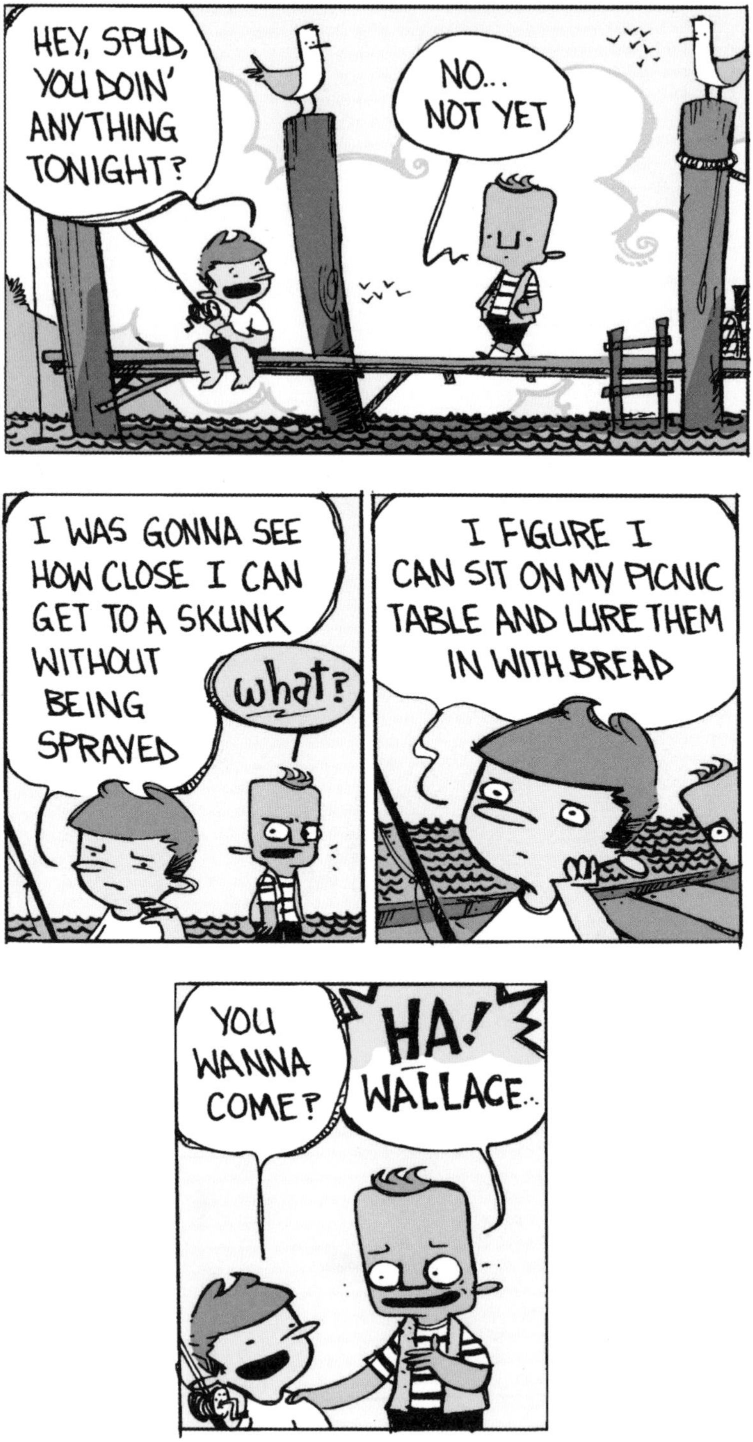
HEY, SPUD, YOU DOIN' ANYTHING TONIGHT?
NO... NOT YET
I WAS GONNA SEE HOW CLOSE I CAN GET TO A SKUNK WITHOUT BEING SPRAYED
what?
I FIGURE I CAN SIT ON MY PICNIC TABLE AND LURE THEM IN WITH BREAD
YOU WANNA COME?
HA! WALLACE..

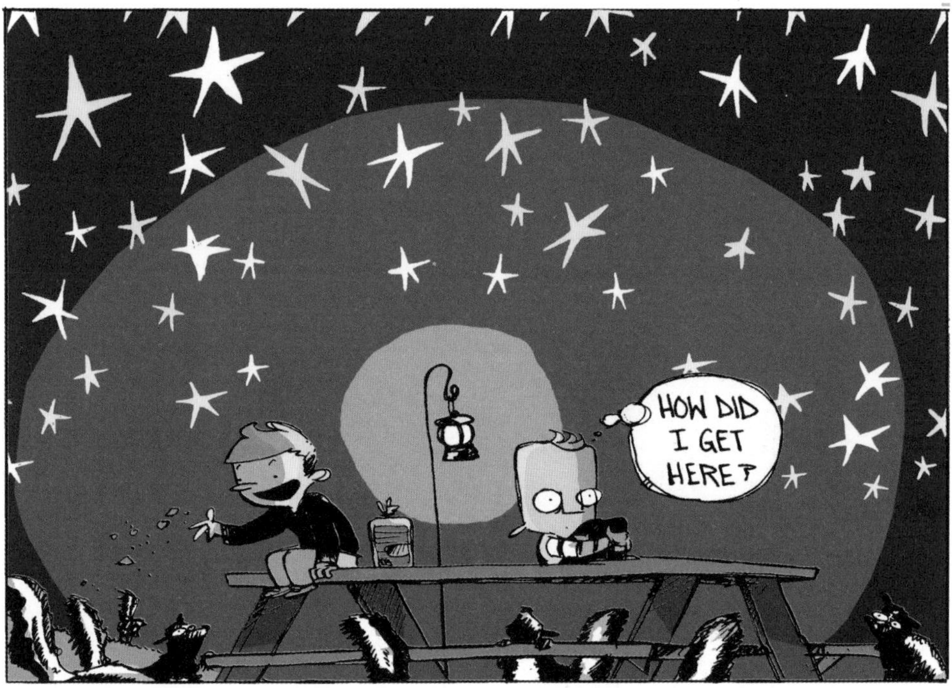
HOW DID I GET HERE?

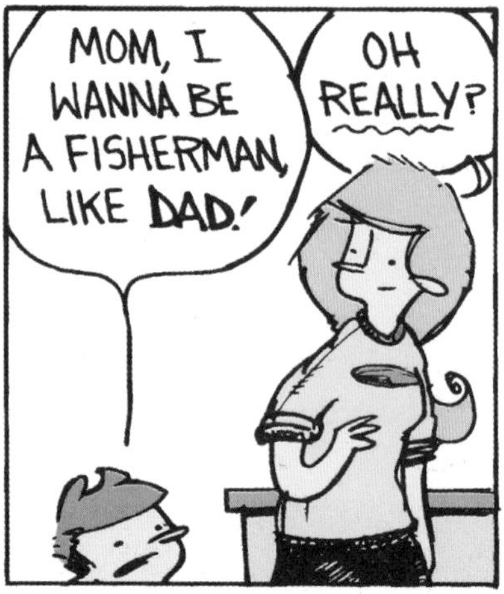
MOM, I WANNA BE A FISHERMAN, LIKE DAD!
OH REALLY?

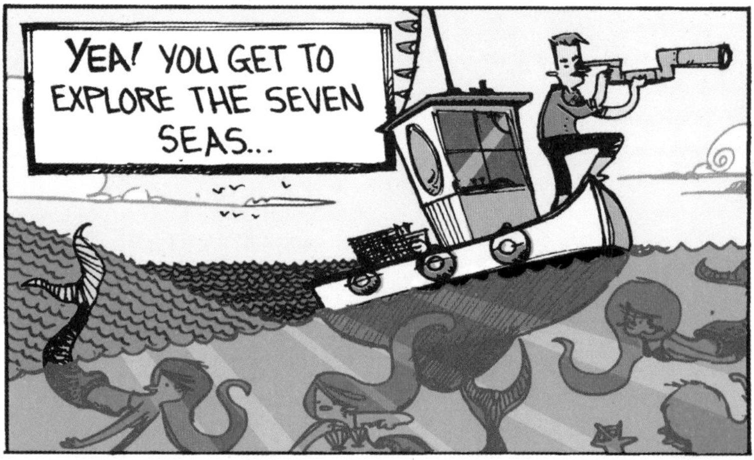
YEA! YOU GET TO EXPLORE THE SEVEN SEAS...

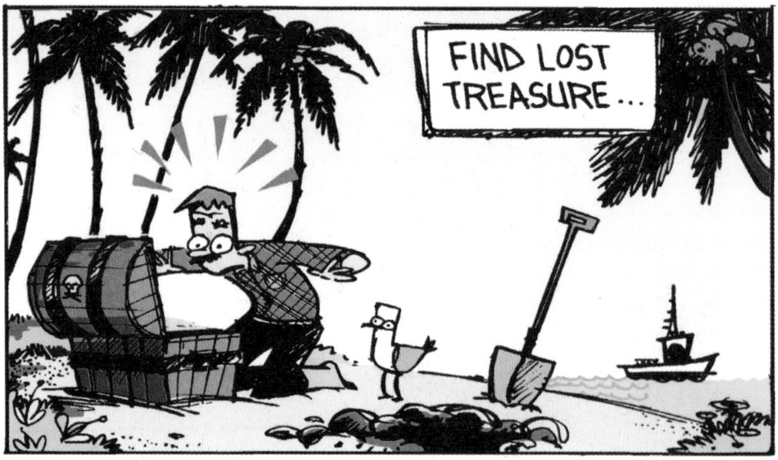
FIND LOST TREASURE...

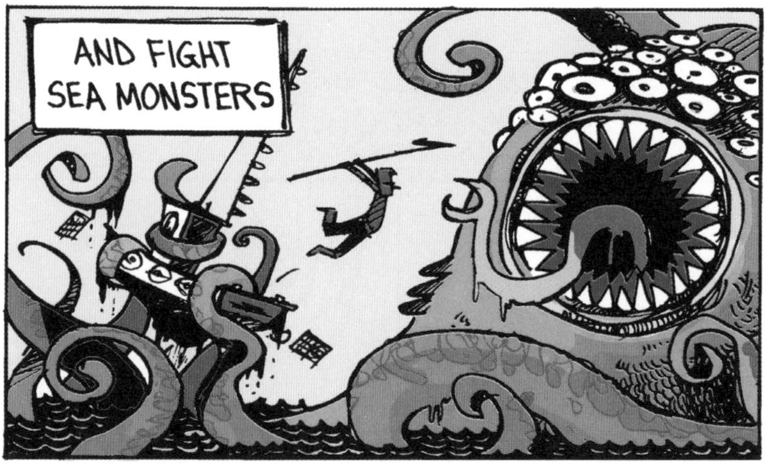
AND FIGHT SEA MONSTERS

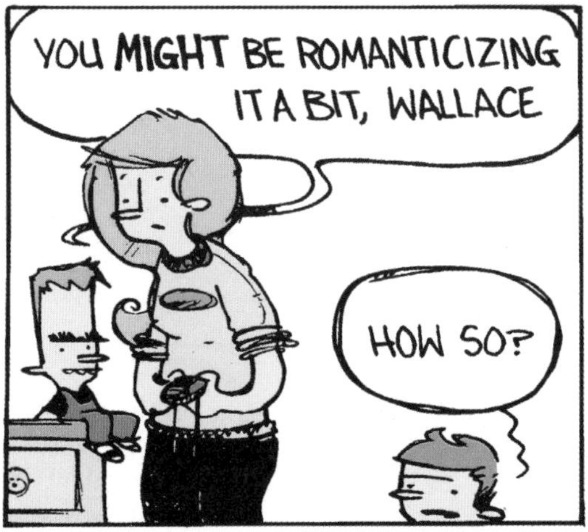
YOU **MIGHT** BE ROMANTICIZING IT A BIT, WALLACE
HOW SO?

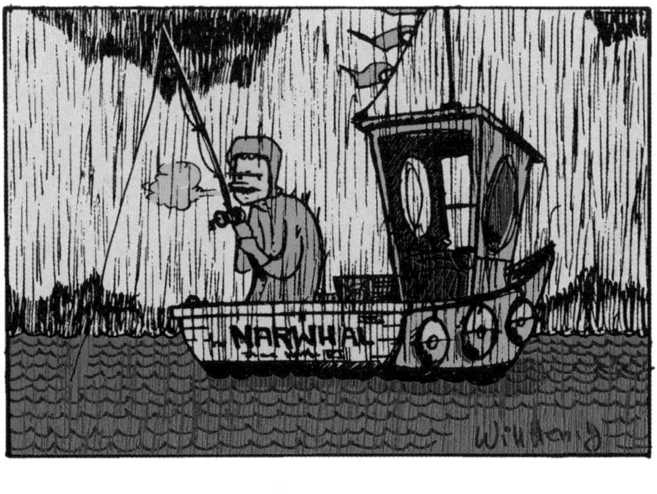
NARWHAL

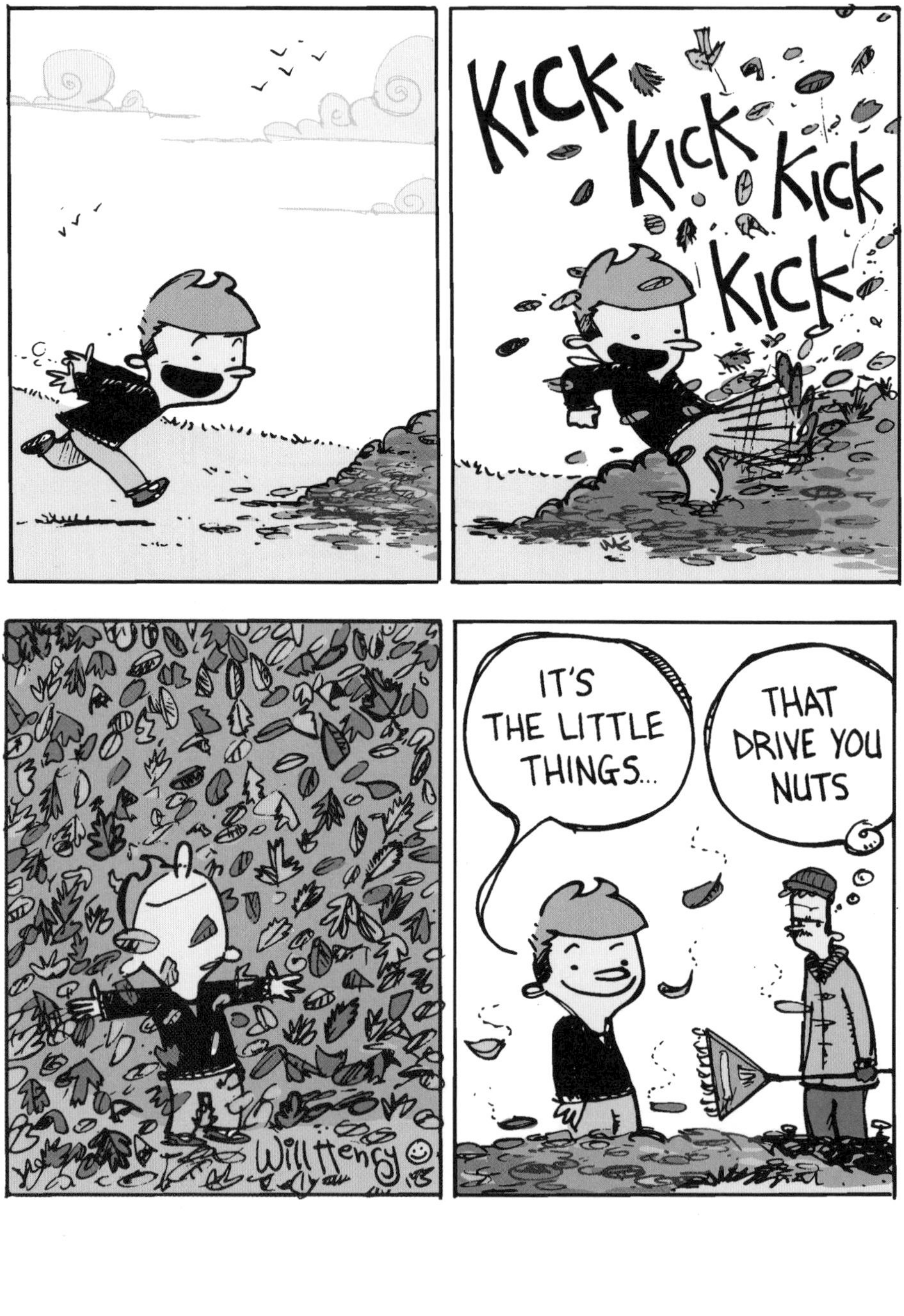
KICK
KICK KICK
KICK
IT'S THE LITTLE THINGS...
THAT DRIVE YOU NUTS
Will Henry

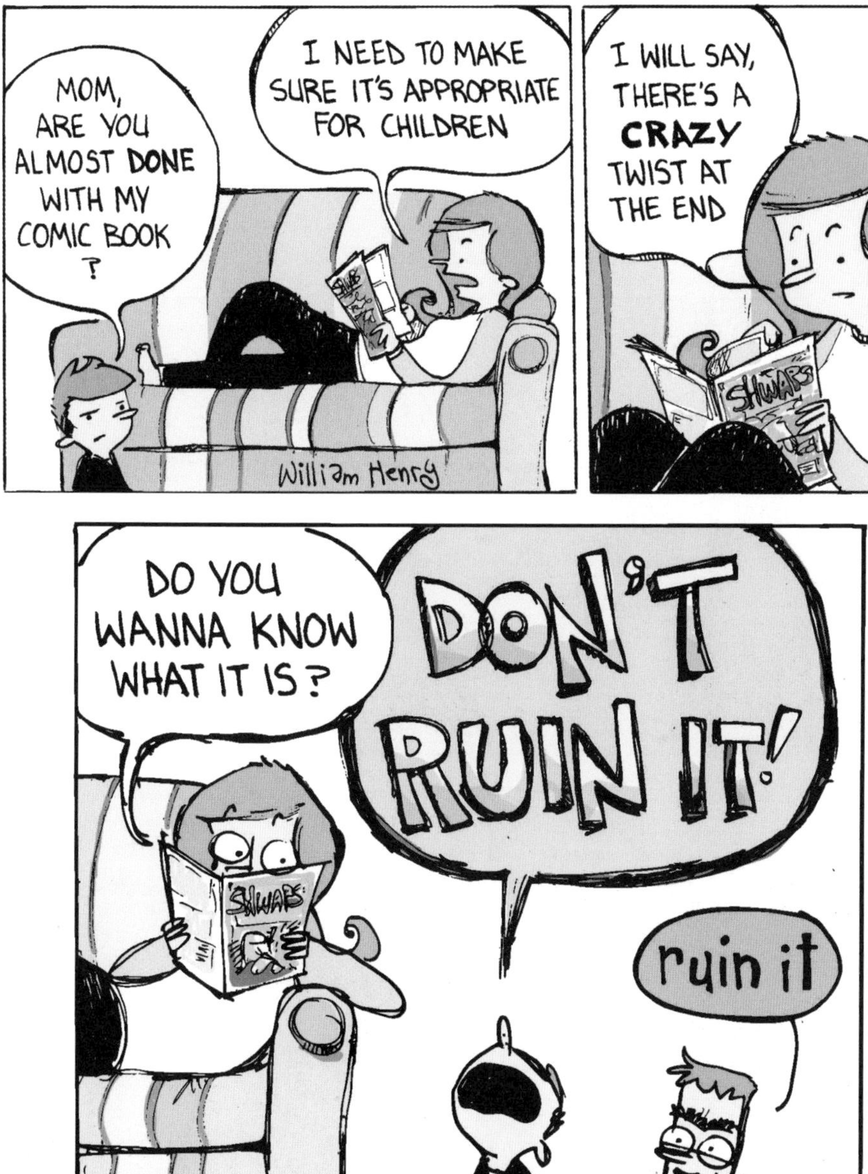
MOM, ARE YOU ALMOST DONE WITH MY COMIC BOOK ?
I NEED TO MAKE SURE IT'S APPROPRIATE FOR CHILDREN
William Henry
I WILL SAY, THERE'S A CRAZY TWIST AT THE END
DO YOU WANNA KNOW WHAT IT IS?
DON'T RUIN IT!
ruin it

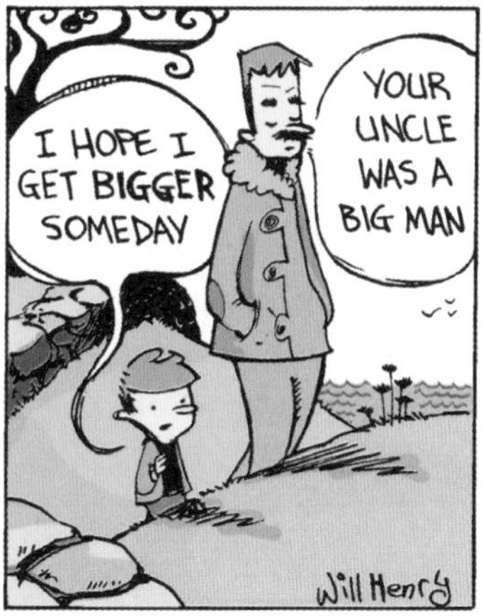
I HOPE I GET BIGGER SOMEDAY
YOUR UNCLE WAS A BIG MAN
Will Henry

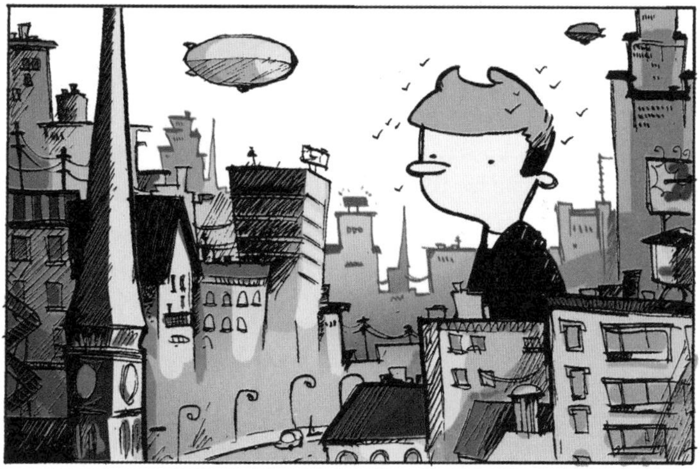

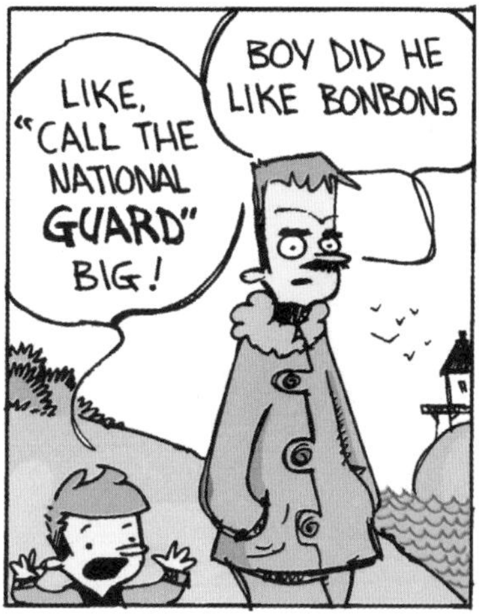
BOY DID HE LIKE BONBONS
LIKE, "CALL THE NATIONAL GUARD" BIG!

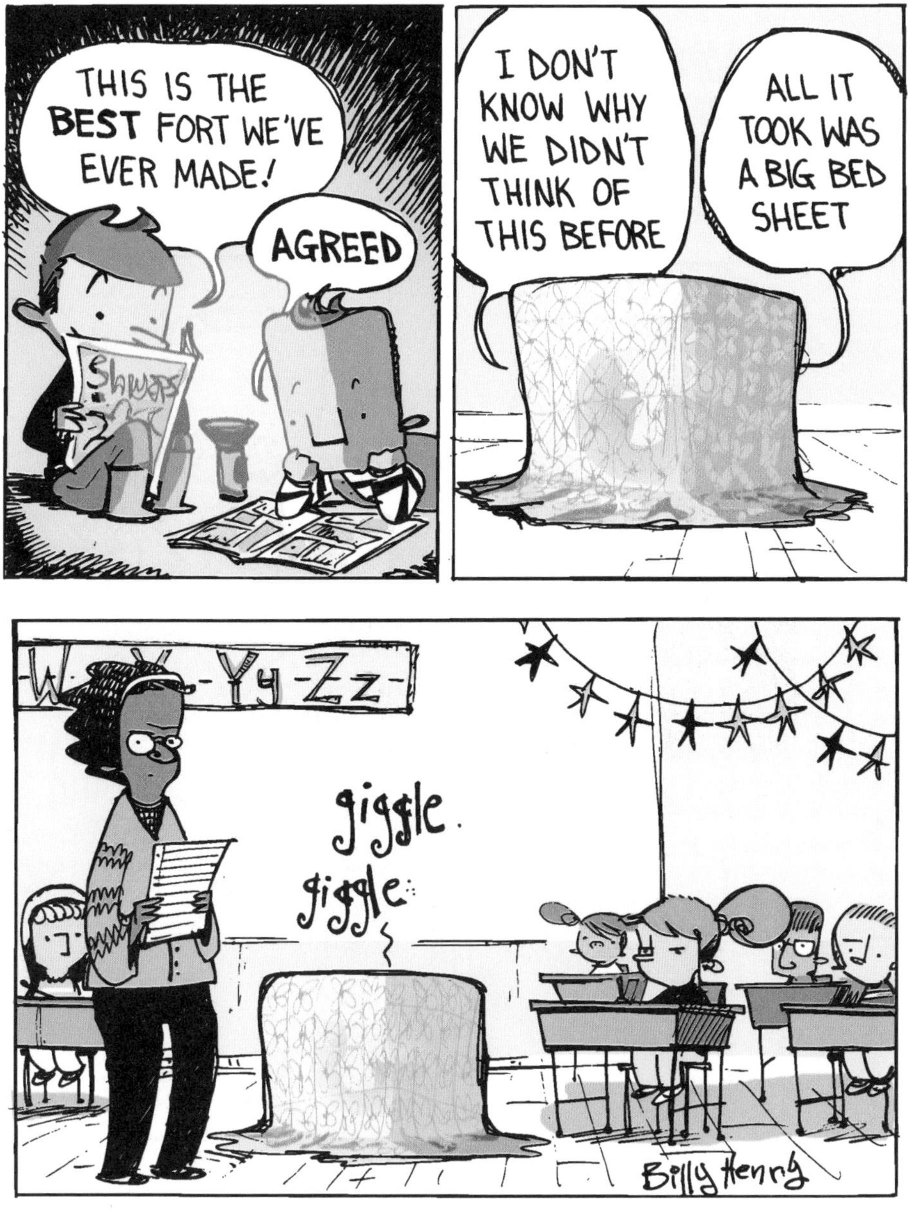
THIS IS THE **BEST** FORT WE'VE EVER MADE!
AGREED
I DON'T KNOW WHY WE DIDN'T THINK OF THIS BEFORE
ALL IT TOOK WAS A BIG BED SHEET
giggle.
giggle
Billy Henry

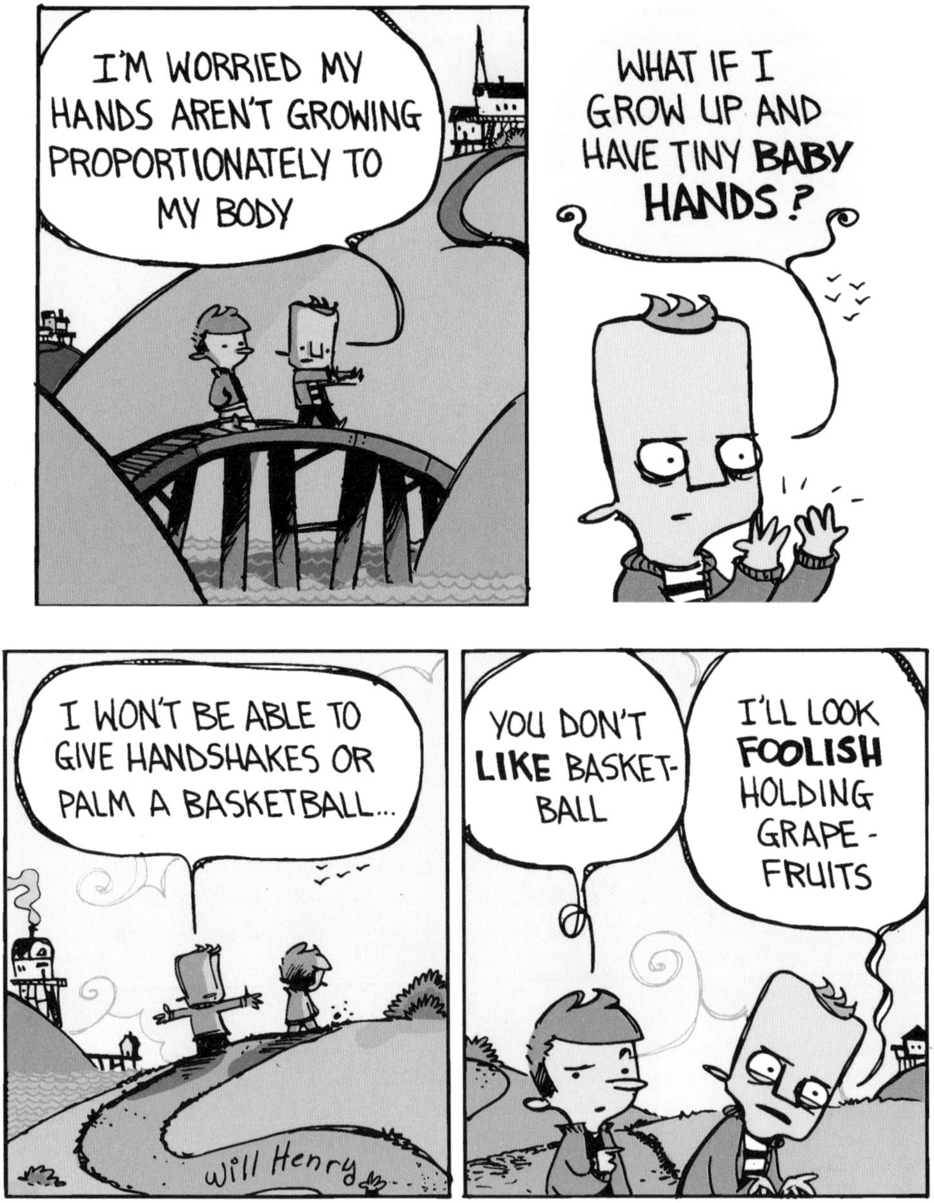
I'M WORRIED MY HANDS AREN'T GROWING PROPORTIONATELY TO MY BODY
WHAT IF I GROW UP AND HAVE TINY **BABY HANDS**?
I WON'T BE ABLE TO GIVE HANDSHAKES OR PALM A BASKETBALL...
Will Henry
YOU DON'T **LIKE** BASKET-BALL
I'LL LOOK **FOOLISH** HOLDING GRAPE-FRUITS

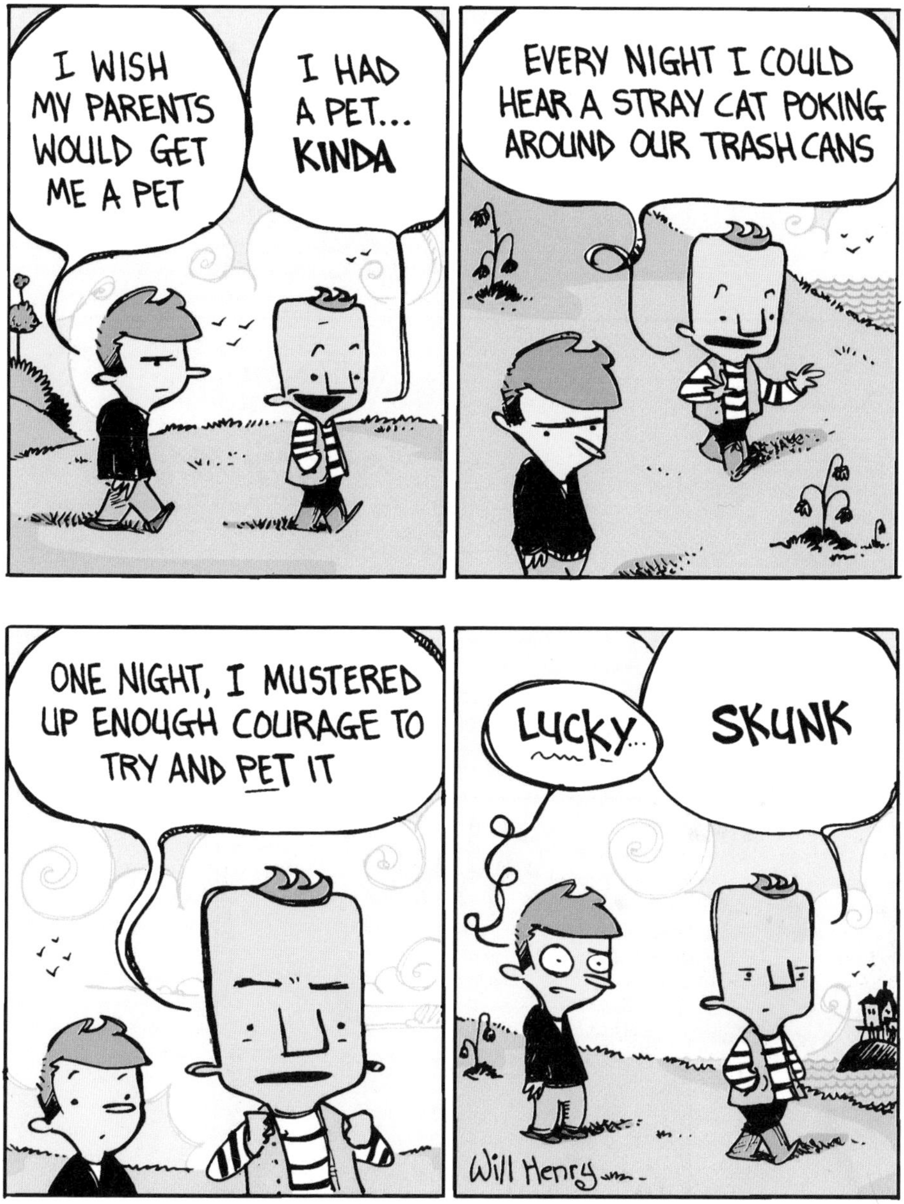
I WISH MY PARENTS WOULD GET ME A PET
I HAD A PET... KINDA
EVERY NIGHT I COULD HEAR A STRAY CAT POKING AROUND OUR TRASH CANS
ONE NIGHT, I MUSTERED UP ENOUGH COURAGE TO TRY AND PET IT
LUCKY...
SKUNK
Will Henry

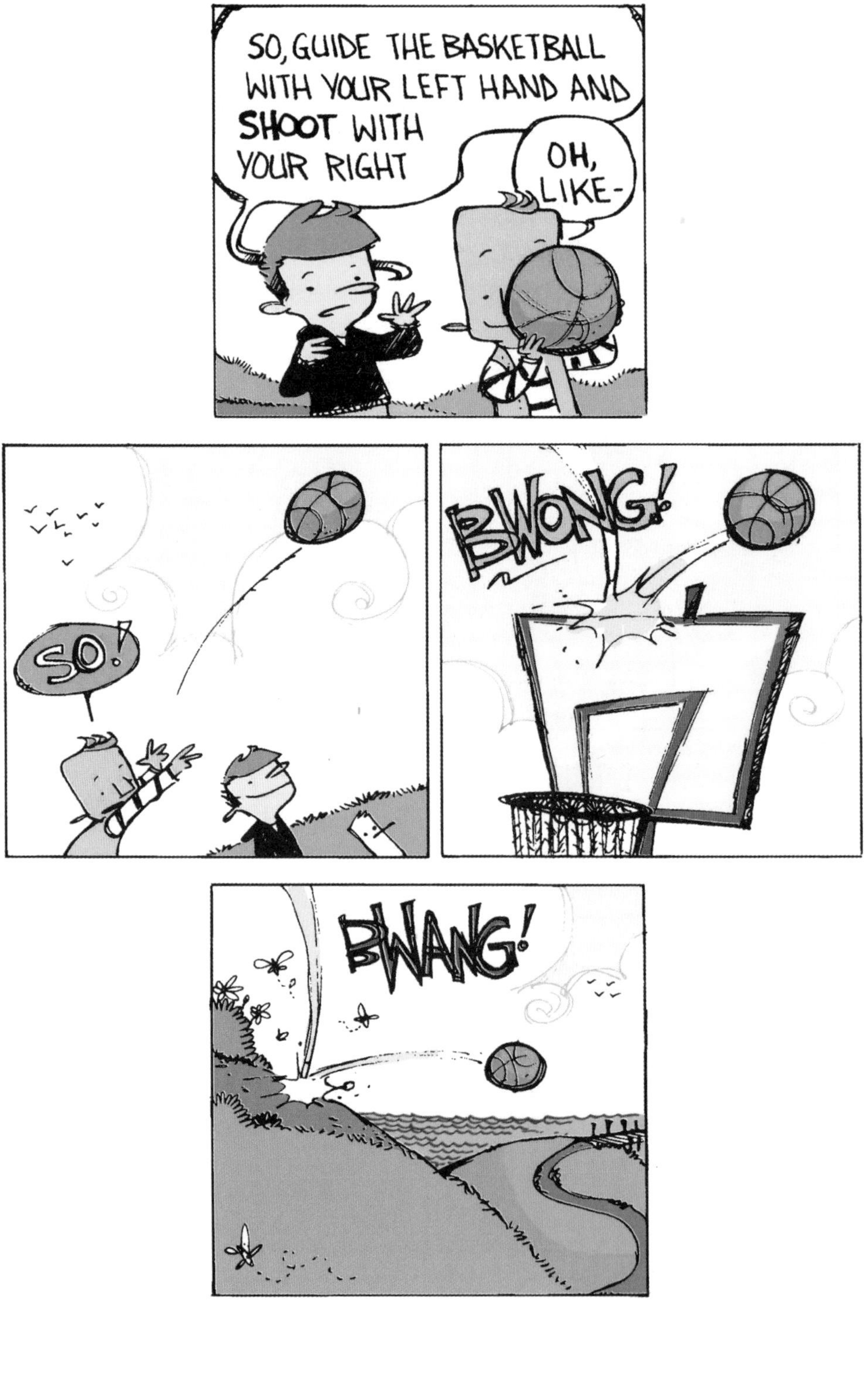
SO, GUIDE THE BASKETBALL WITH YOUR LEFT HAND AND SHOOT WITH YOUR RIGHT
OH, LIKE-
SO!
BWONG!
BWANG!

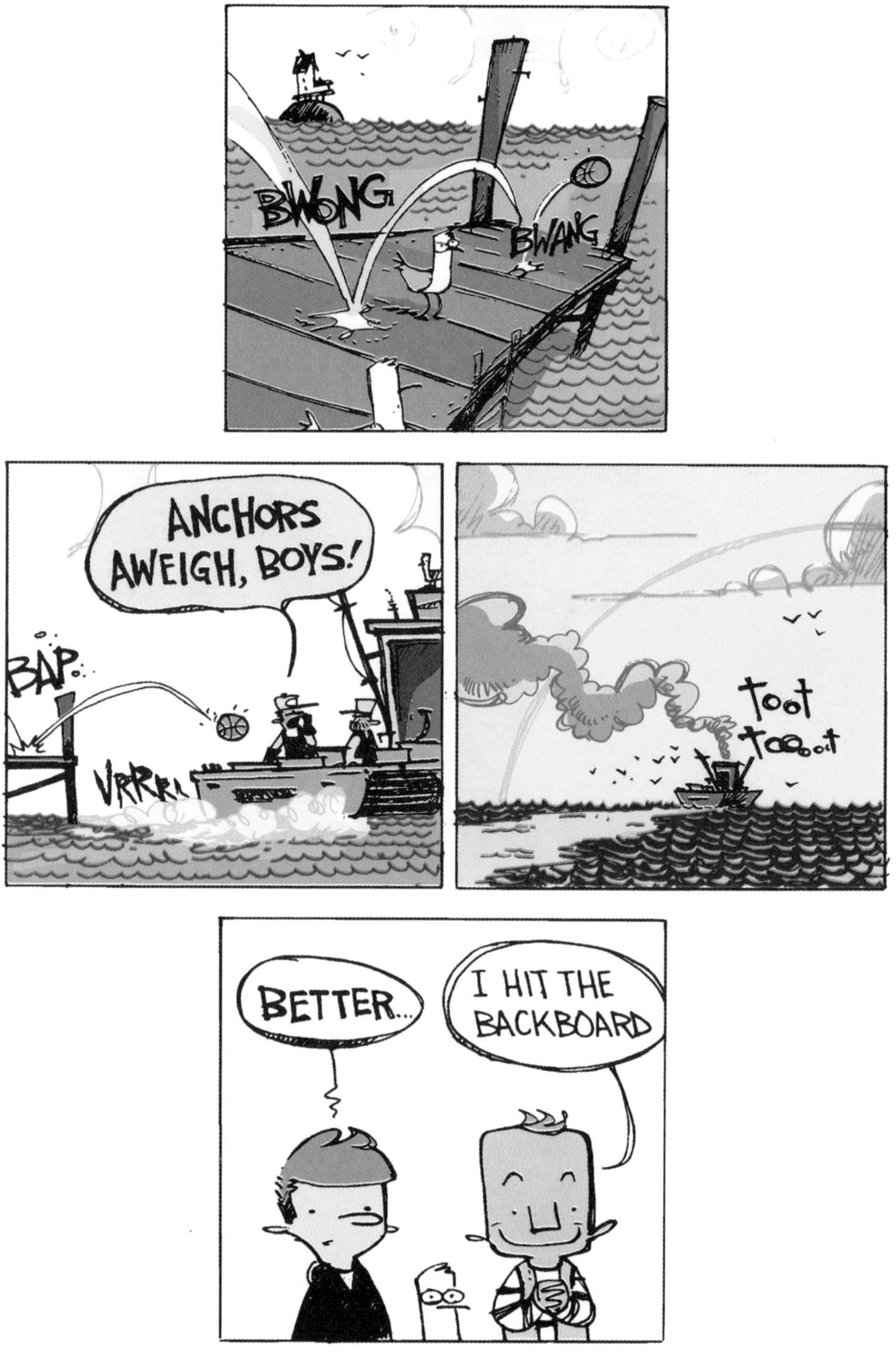
BWONG
BWANG
ANCHORS AWEIGH, BOYS!
BAP
VRRRR
toot
tooooot
BETTER...
I HIT THE BACKBOARD

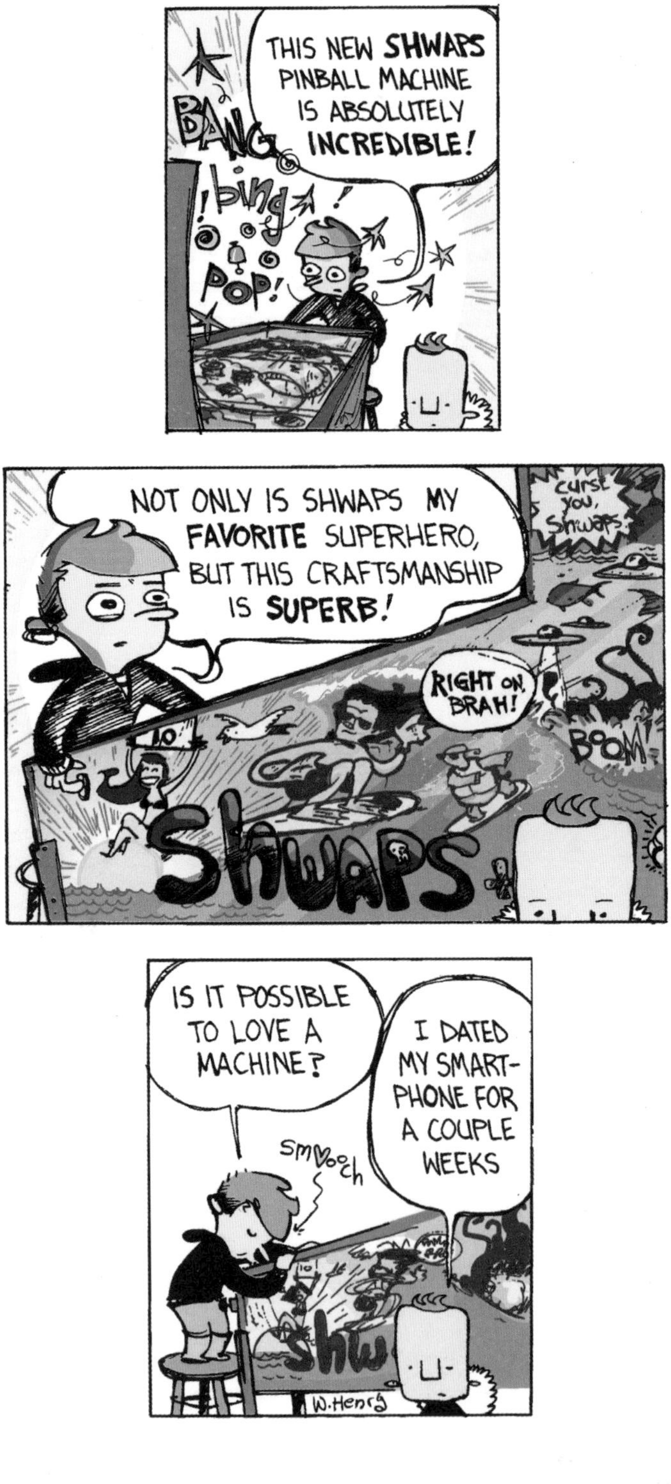
THIS NEW **SHWAPS** PINBALL MACHINE IS ABSOLUTELY **INCREDIBLE!**
BANG
bing
POP!
NOT ONLY IS SHWAPS MY **FAVORITE** SUPERHERO, BUT THIS CRAFTSMANSHIP IS **SUPERB!**
Curse you, Shwaps.
RIGHT ON, BRAH!
BOOM!
SHWAPS
IS IT POSSIBLE TO LOVE A MACHINE?
I DATED MY SMART-PHONE FOR A COUPLE WEEKS
smooch
W.Henry

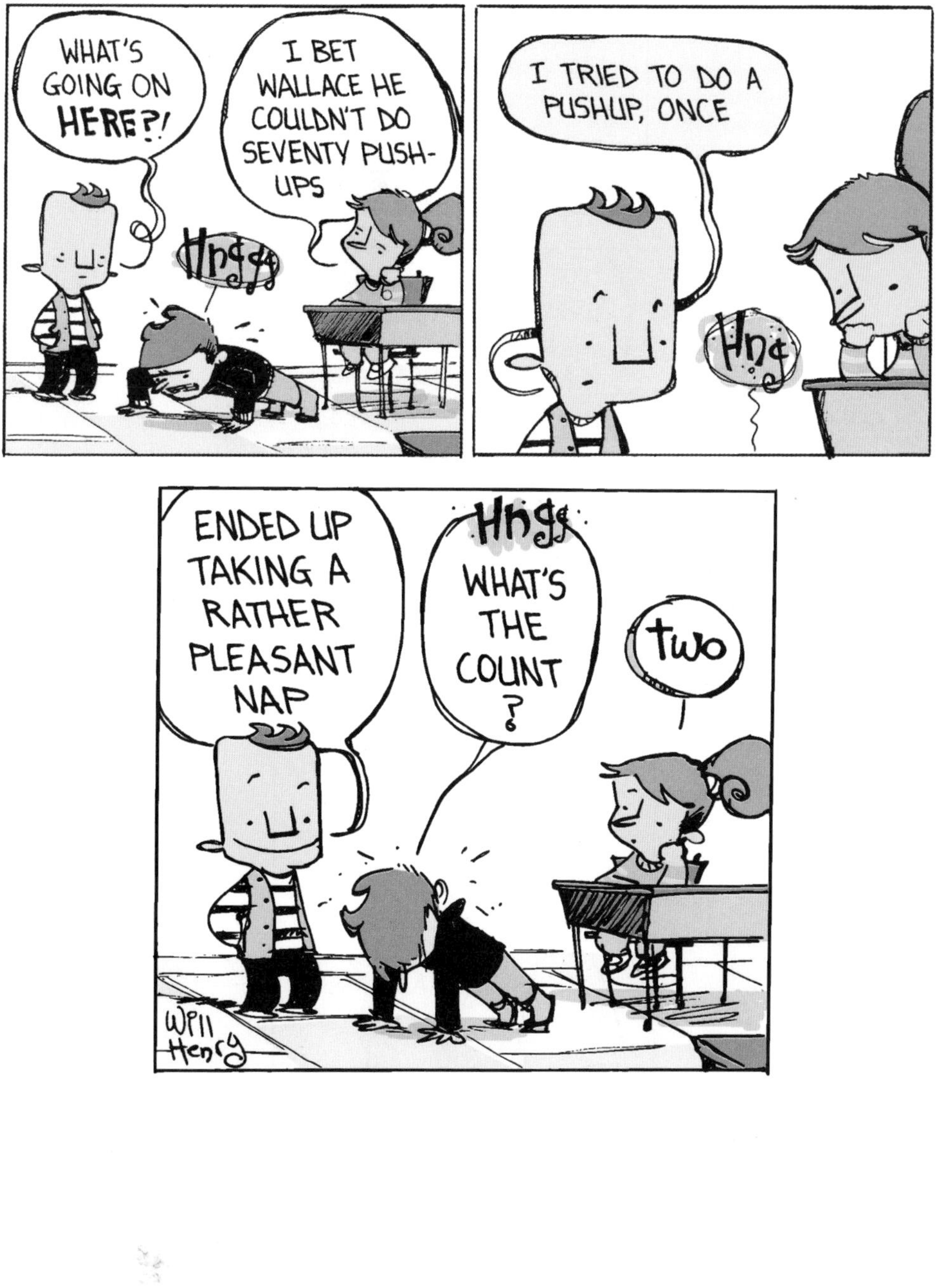
WHAT'S GOING ON HERE?!
I BET WALLACE HE COULDN'T DO SEVENTY PUSH-UPS
Hngg
I TRIED TO DO A PUSHUP, ONCE
Hng
ENDED UP TAKING A RATHER PLEASANT NAP
Hngg
WHAT'S THE COUNT ?
two
Will Henry

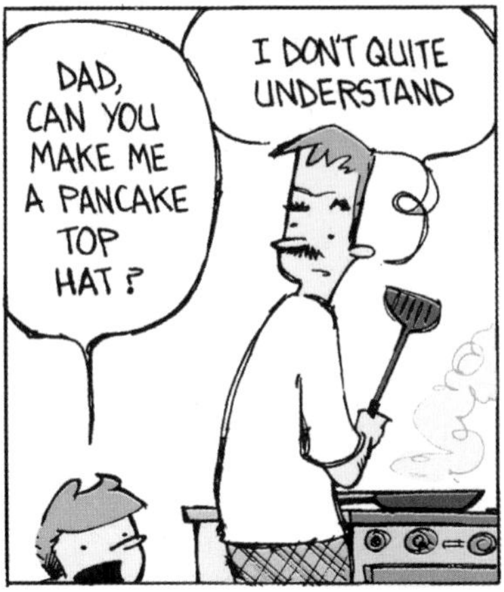
DAD, CAN YOU MAKE ME A PANCAKE TOP HAT?
I DON'T QUITE UNDERSTAND

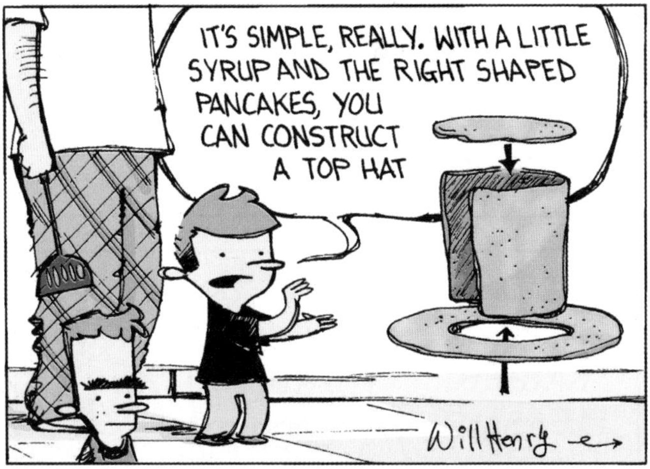
IT'S SIMPLE, REALLY. WITH A LITTLE SYRUP AND THE RIGHT SHAPED PANCAKES, YOU CAN CONSTRUCT A TOP HAT
Will Henry

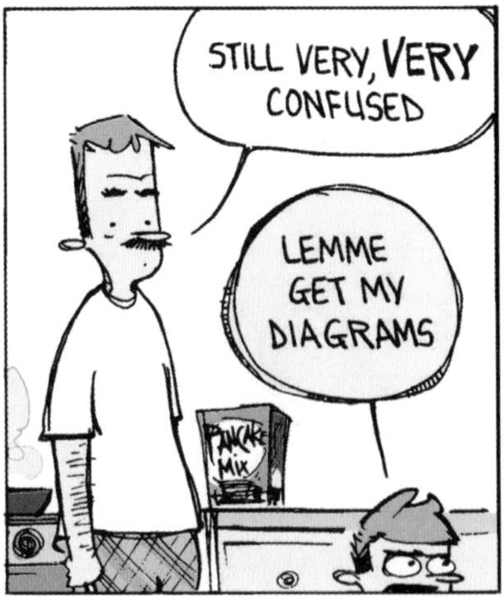
STILL VERY, VERY CONFUSED
LEMME GET MY DIAGRAMS
PANCAKE MIX

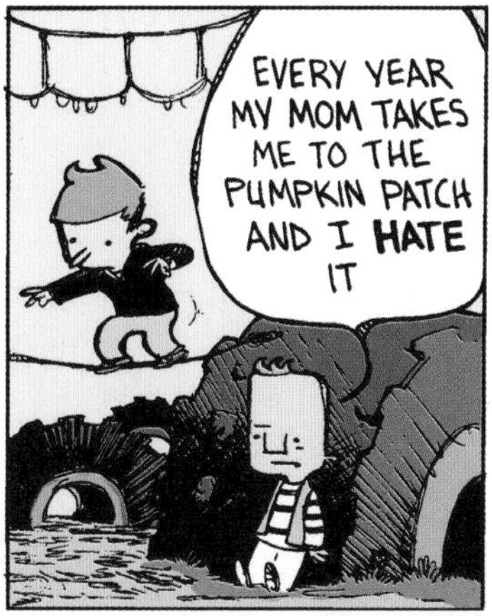
EVERY YEAR MY MOM TAKES ME TO THE PUMPKIN PATCH AND I **HATE** IT

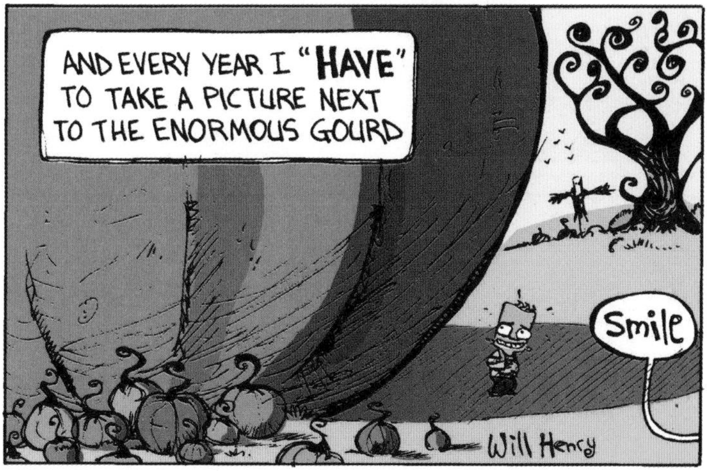
AND EVERY YEAR I "**HAVE**" TO TAKE A PICTURE NEXT TO THE ENORMOUS GOURD
Smile
Will Henry

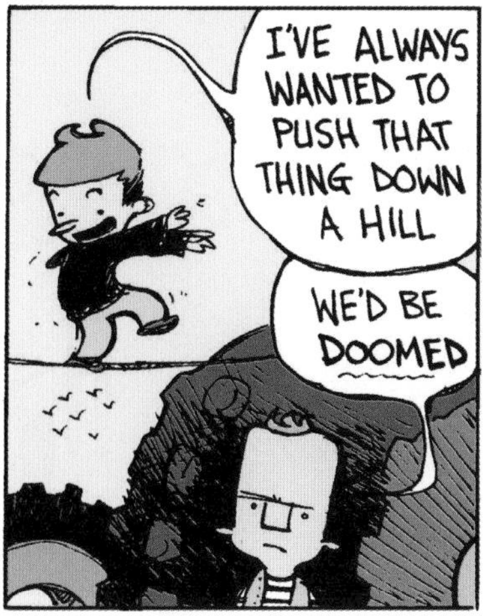
I'VE ALWAYS WANTED TO PUSH THAT THING DOWN A HILL
WE'D BE DOOMED

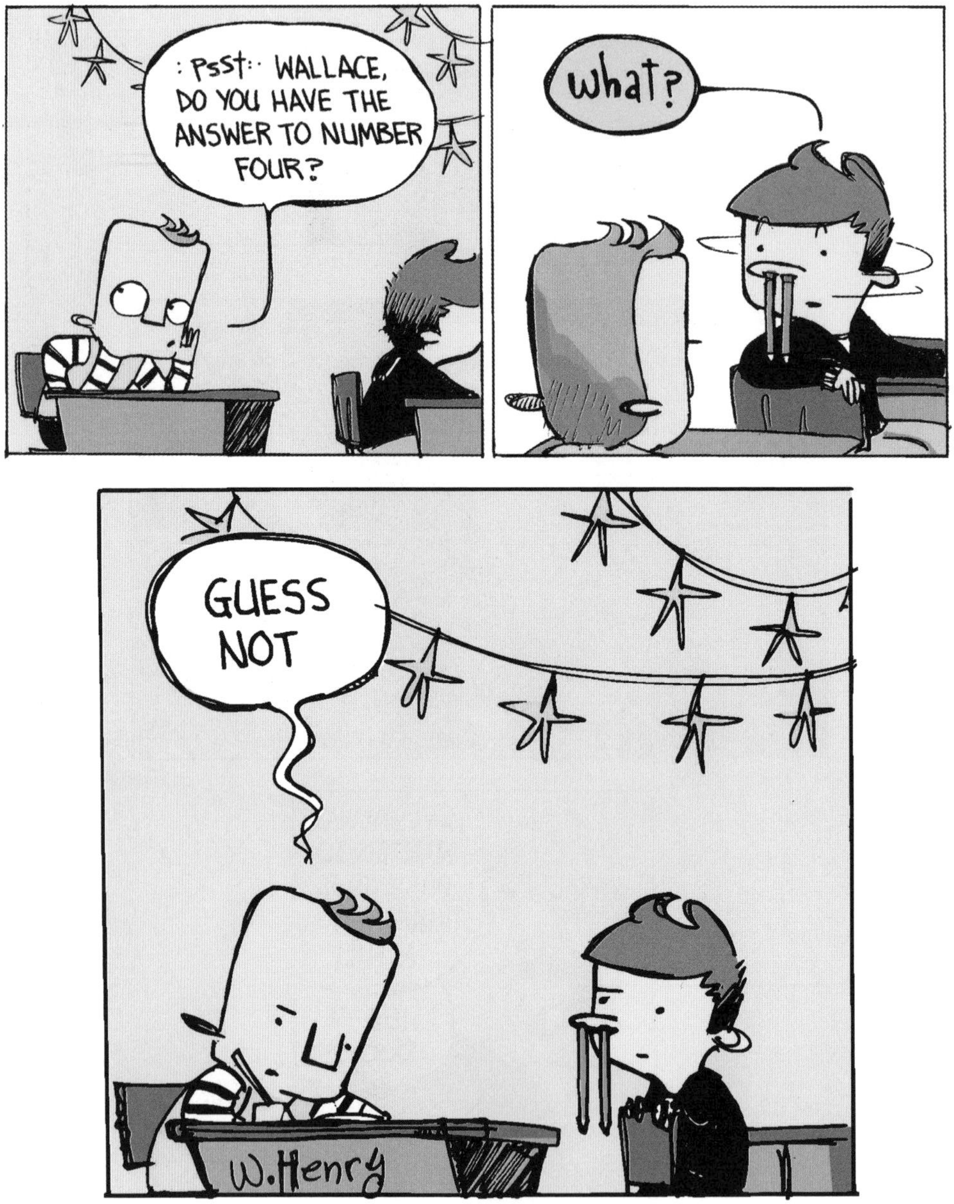
:Psst:: WALLACE, DO YOU HAVE THE ANSWER TO NUMBER FOUR?
what?
GUESS NOT
W.Henry

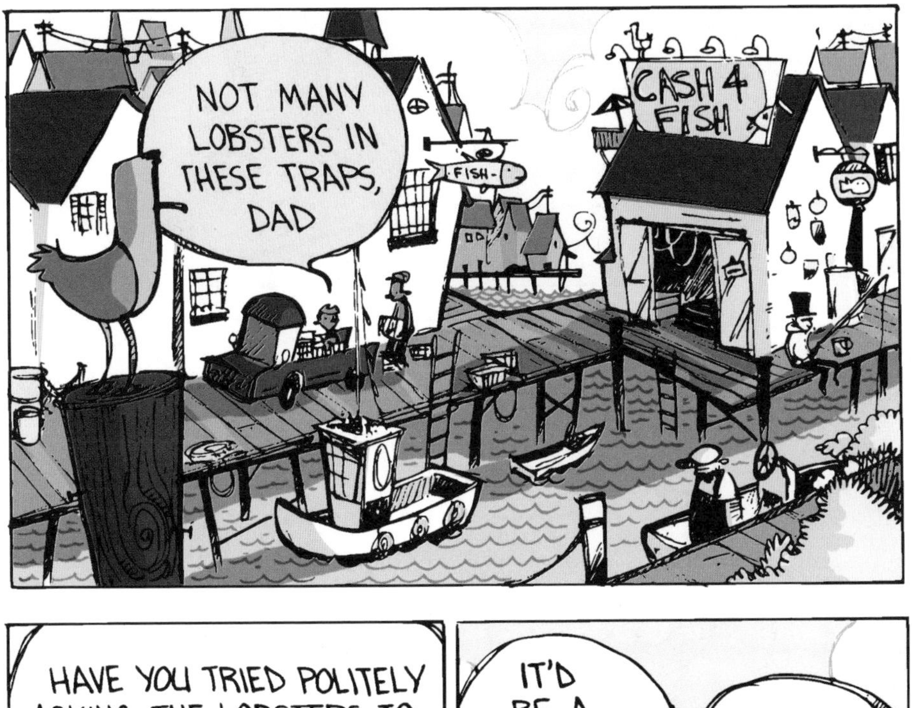
CASH 4 FISH
FISH
NOT MANY LOBSTERS IN THESE TRAPS, DAD
HAVE YOU TRIED POLITELY ASKING THE LOBSTERS TO SWIM INTO THE TRAPS?
Wee Willy Henry
IT'D BE A TOUGH SELL, WALLACE
LEAD WITH A JOKE

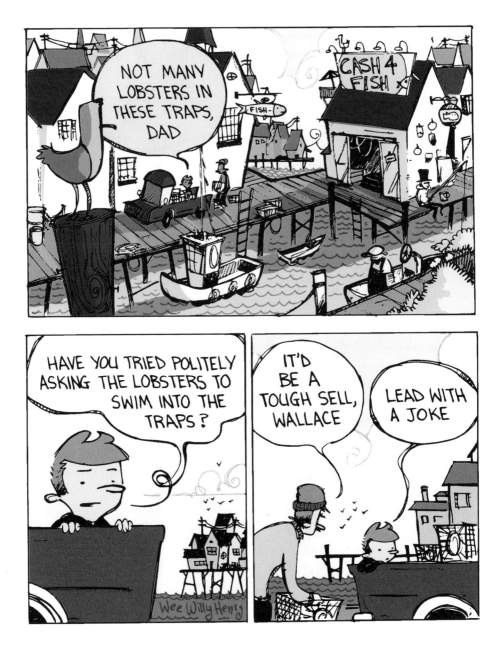

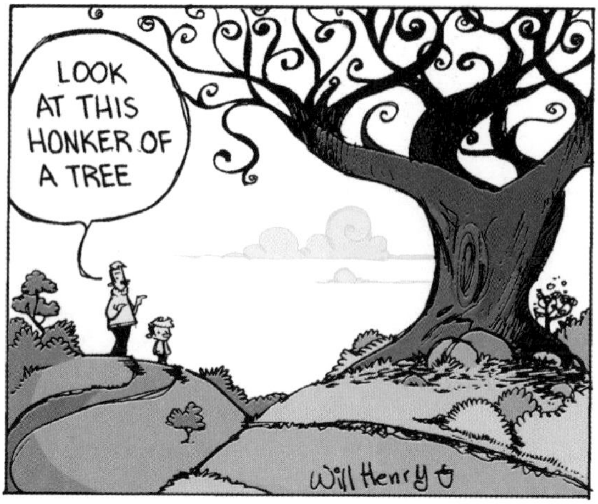
LOOK AT THIS HONKER OF A TREE
Will Henry

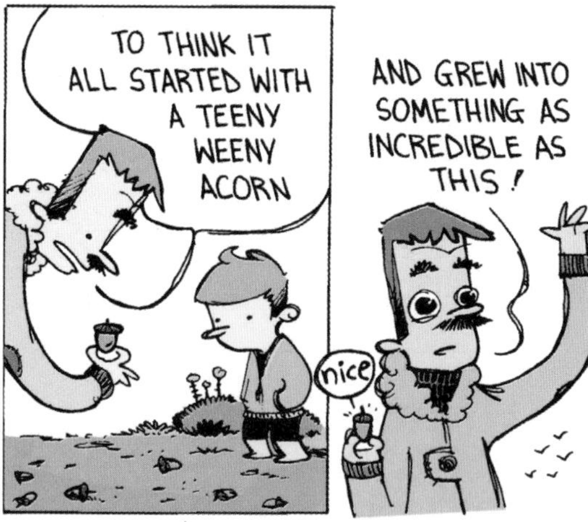
TO THINK IT ALL STARTED WITH A TEENY WEENY ACORN
AND GREW INTO SOMETHING AS INCREDIBLE AS THIS!
nice

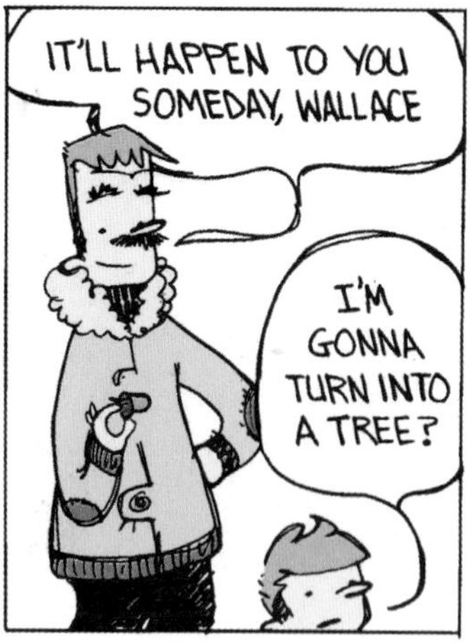
IT'LL HAPPEN TO YOU SOMEDAY, WALLACE
I'M GONNA TURN INTO A TREE?

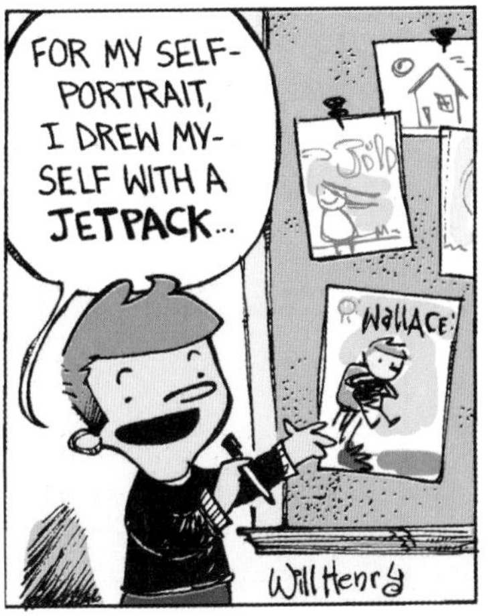
FOR MY SELF-PORTRAIT, I DREW MY-SELF WITH A JETPACK...
Will Henry

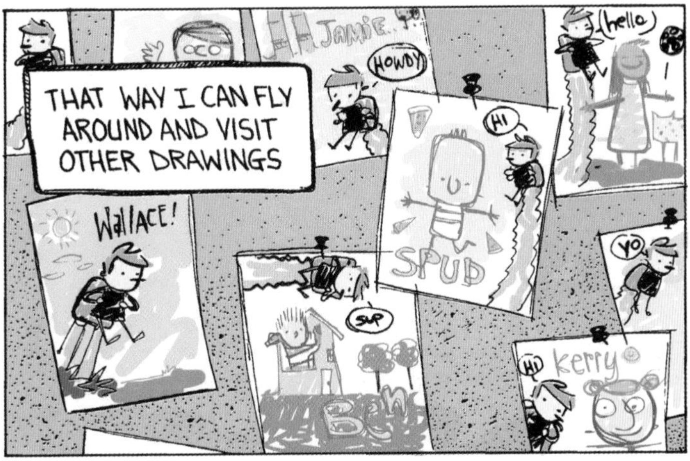
THAT WAY I CAN FLY AROUND AND VISIT OTHER DRAWINGS
JAMIE
HOWDY
hello
HI
WALLACE!
SPUD
YO
SUP
Ben
HI
kerry

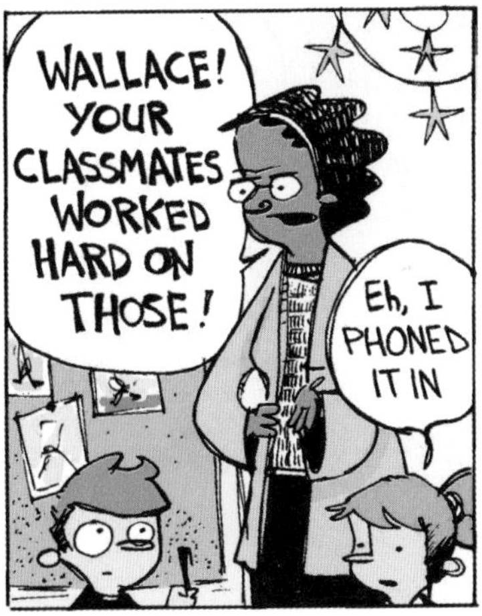
WALLACE! YOUR CLASSMATES WORKED HARD ON THOSE!
Eh, I PHONED IT IN

'SCUSE ME, MA'AM, I'M LOOKING FOR A BOOK
WHAT BOOK, SWEETIE ?
Read
ONE OF THOSE BOOKS WHERE YOU OPEN IT UP AND RAINBOWS AND DRAGONS AND ALL THIS WEIRD STUFF STARTS SPEWING OUT
ZOOM
LIKE IN ALL THE COMMER-CIALS
WE HAVE **POP-UP** BOOKS
Read

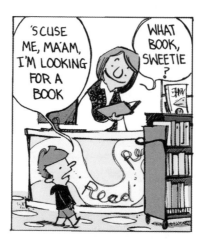

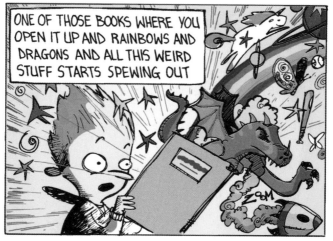

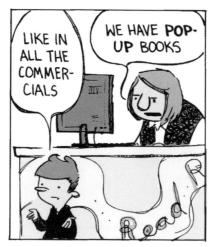

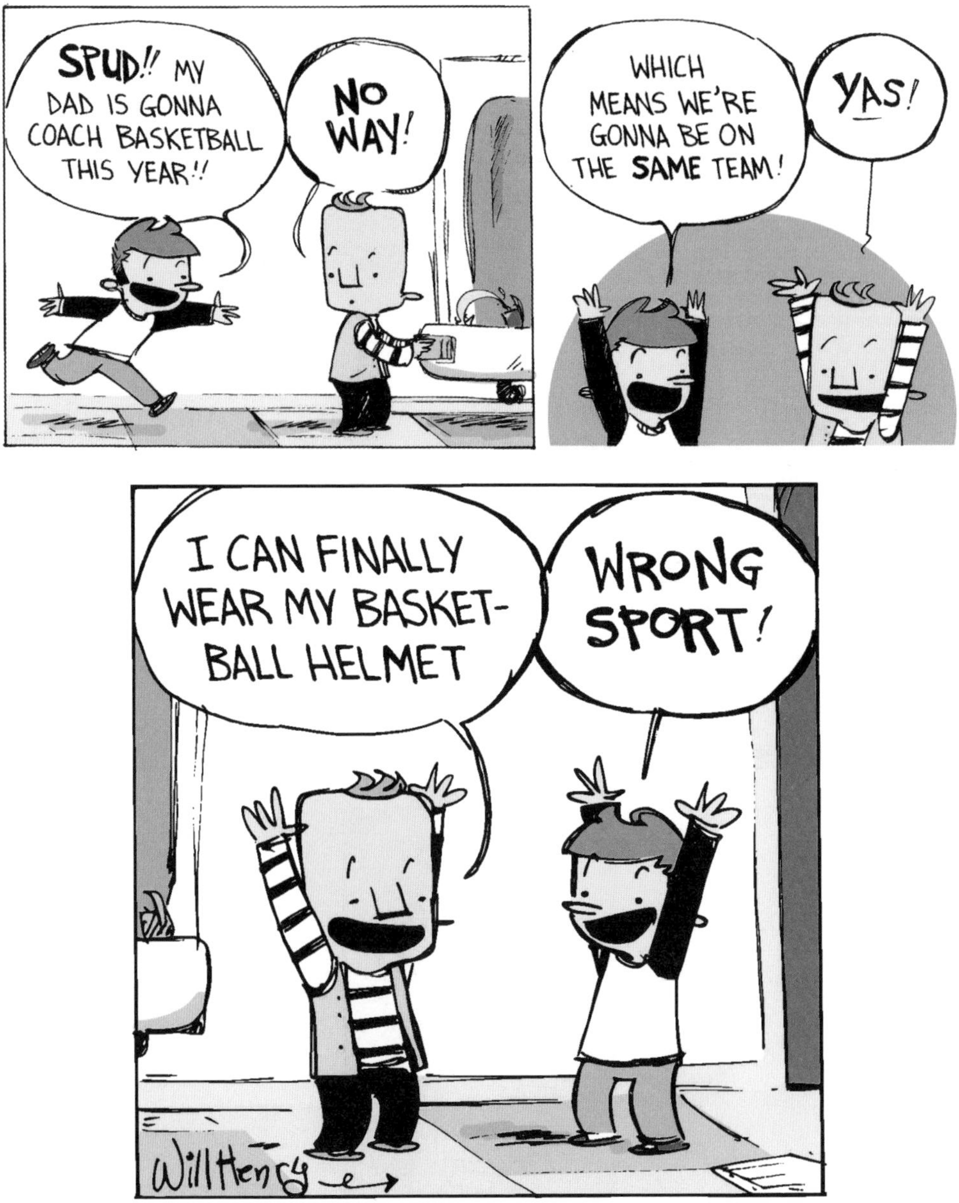
SPUD!! MY DAD IS GONNA COACH BASKETBALL THIS YEAR!!
NO WAY!
WHICH MEANS WE'RE GONNA BE ON THE SAME TEAM!
YAS!
I CAN FINALLY WEAR MY BASKET-BALL HELMET
WRONG SPORT!
Will Henry

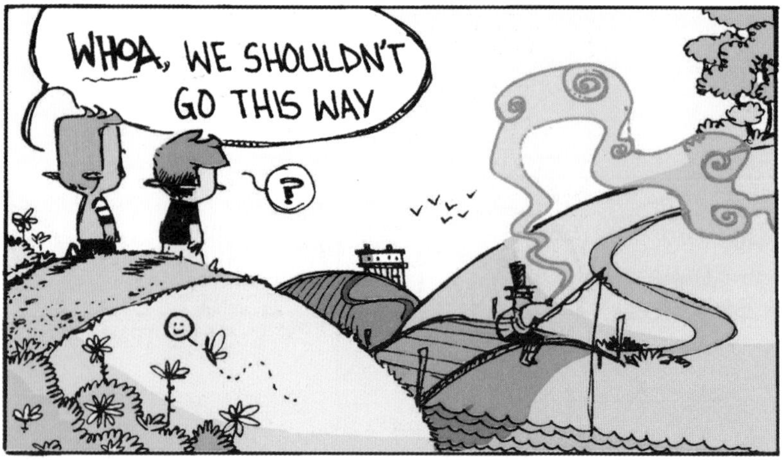
WHOA, WE SHOULDN'T GO THIS WAY
?

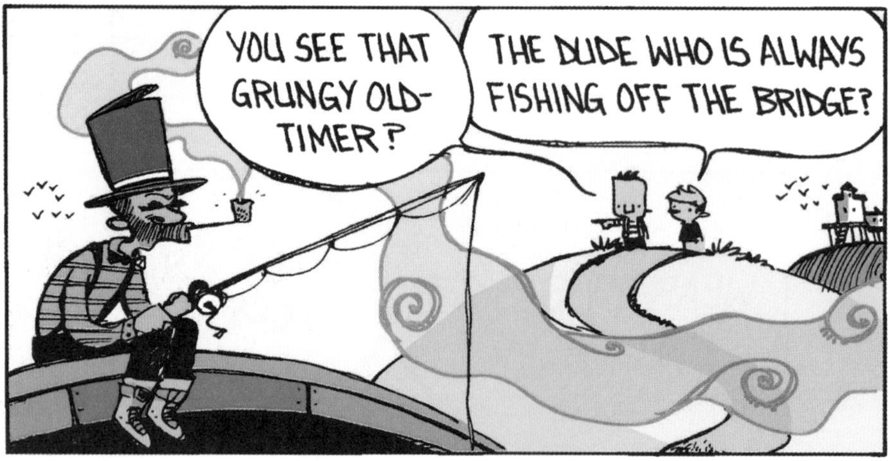
YOU SEE THAT GRUNGY OLD-TIMER?
THE DUDE WHO IS ALWAYS FISHING OFF THE BRIDGE?

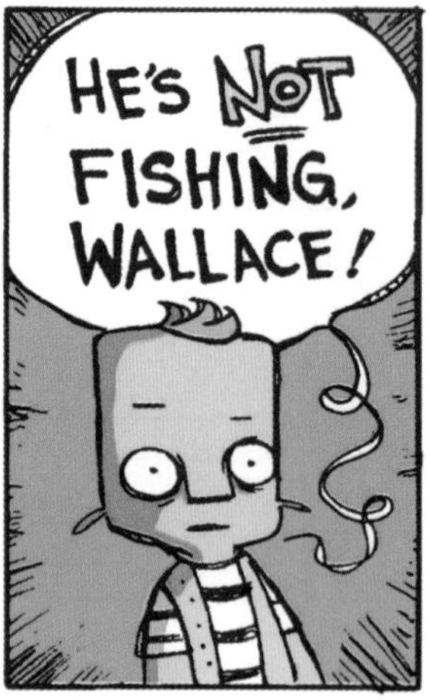
HE'S NOT FISHING, WALLACE!

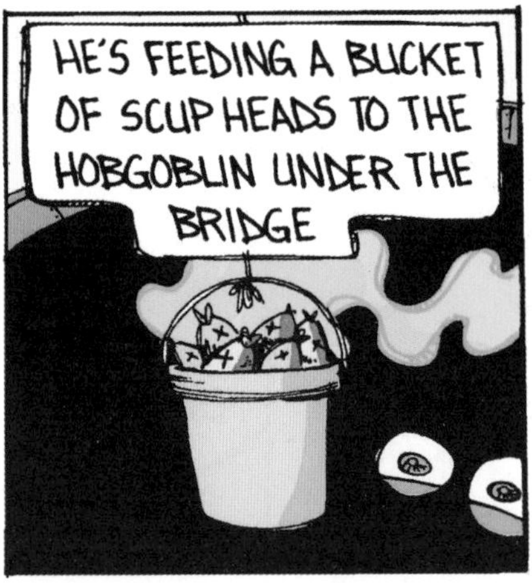
HE'S FEEDING A BUCKET OF SCUP HEADS TO THE HOBGOBLIN UNDER THE BRIDGE

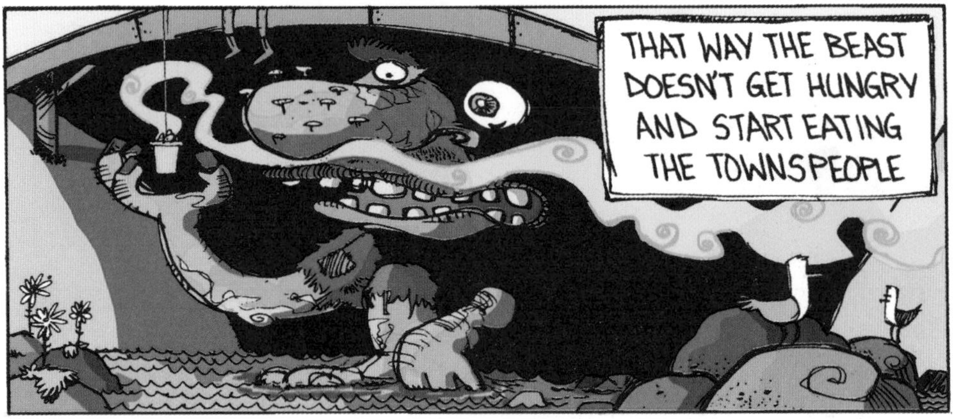
THAT WAY THE BEAST DOESN'T GET HUNGRY AND START EATING THE TOWNSPEOPLE

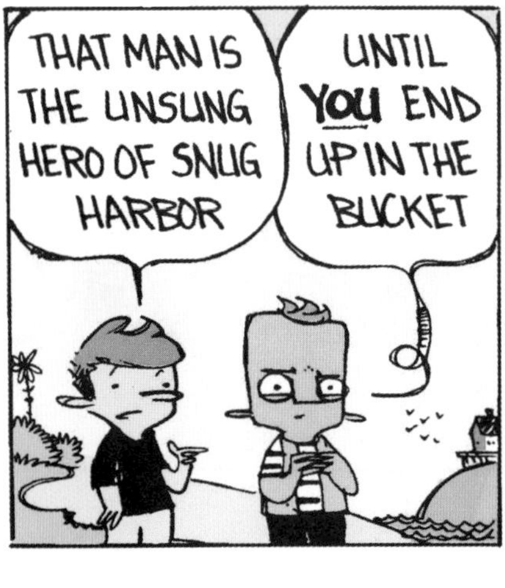
THAT MAN IS THE UNSUNG HERO OF SNUG HARBOR
UNTIL YOU END UP IN THE BUCKET

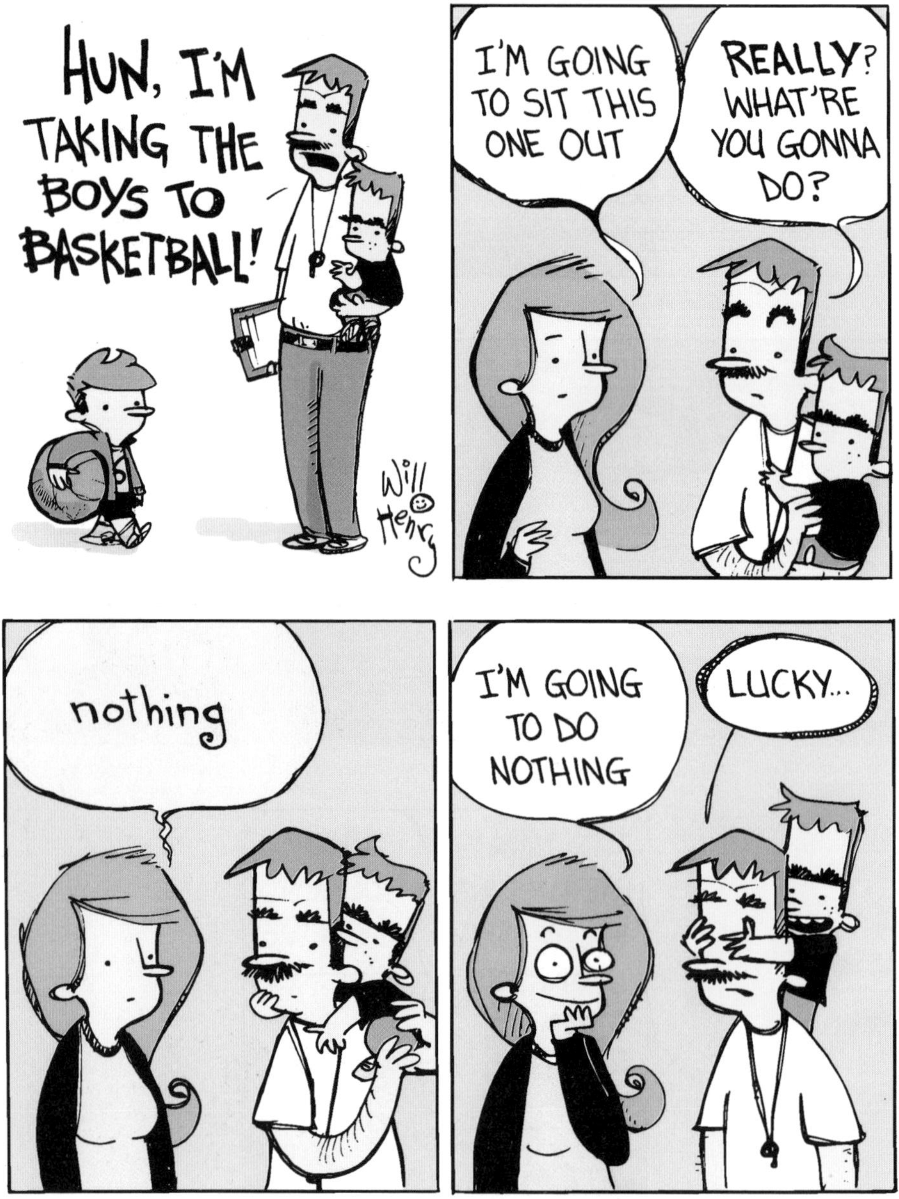
HUN, I'M TAKING THE BOYS TO BASKETBALL!
Will Henry
I'M GOING TO SIT THIS ONE OUT
REALLY? WHAT'RE YOU GONNA DO?
nothing
I'M GOING TO DO NOTHING
LUCKY...

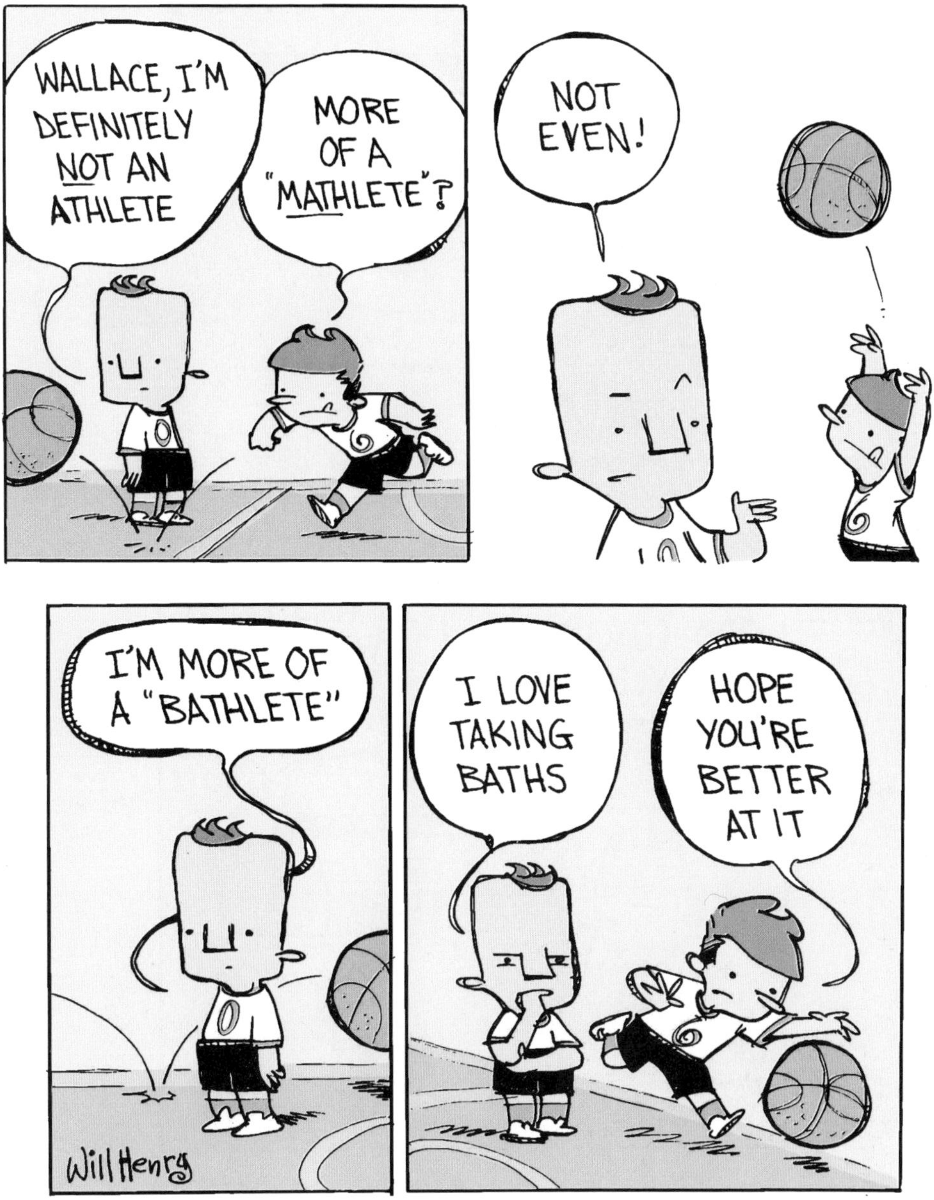
WALLACE, I'M DEFINITELY NOT AN ATHLETE
MORE OF A "MATHLETE"?
NOT EVEN!
I'M MORE OF A "BATHLETE"
I LOVE TAKING BATHS
HOPE YOU'RE BETTER AT IT
Will Henry

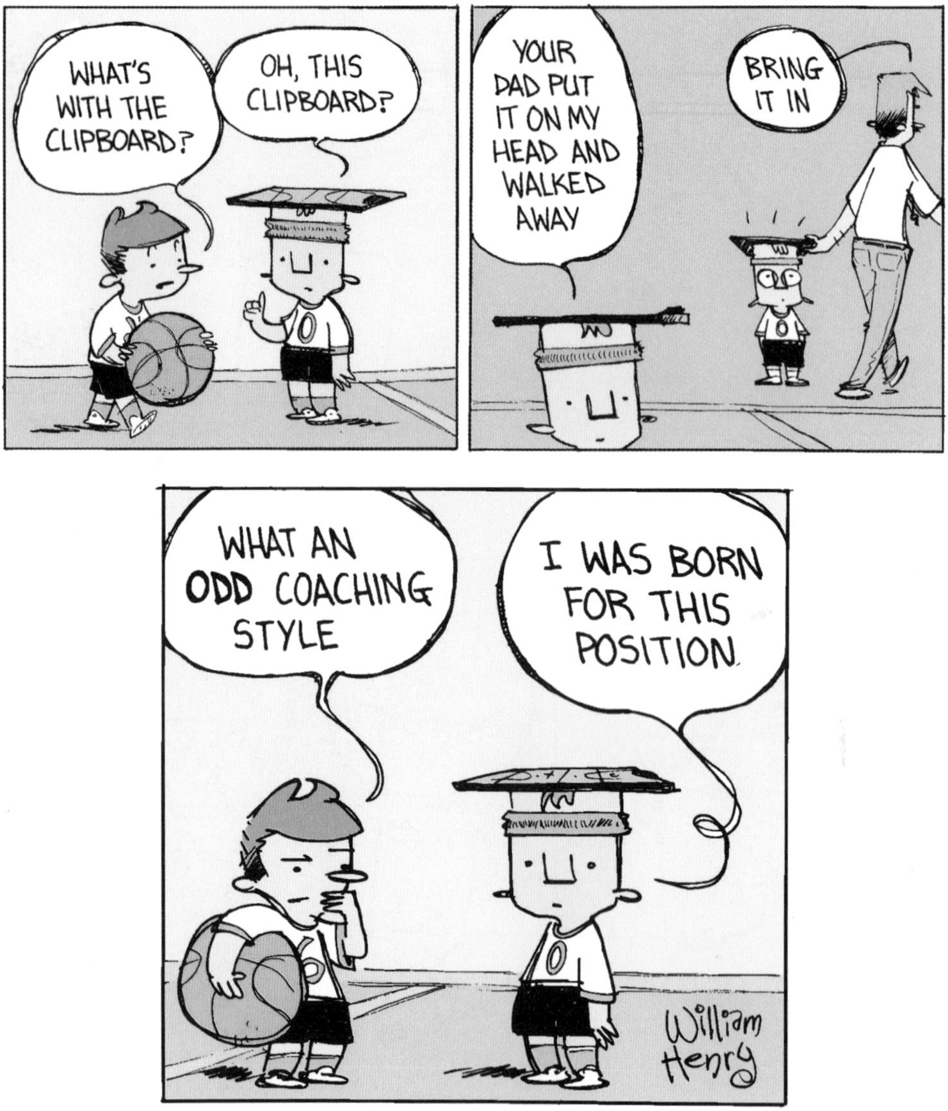
WHAT'S WITH THE CLIPBOARD?
OH, THIS CLIPBOARD?
YOUR DAD PUT IT ON MY HEAD AND WALKED AWAY
BRING IT IN
WHAT AN ODD COACHING STYLE
I WAS BORN FOR THIS POSITION
William Henry

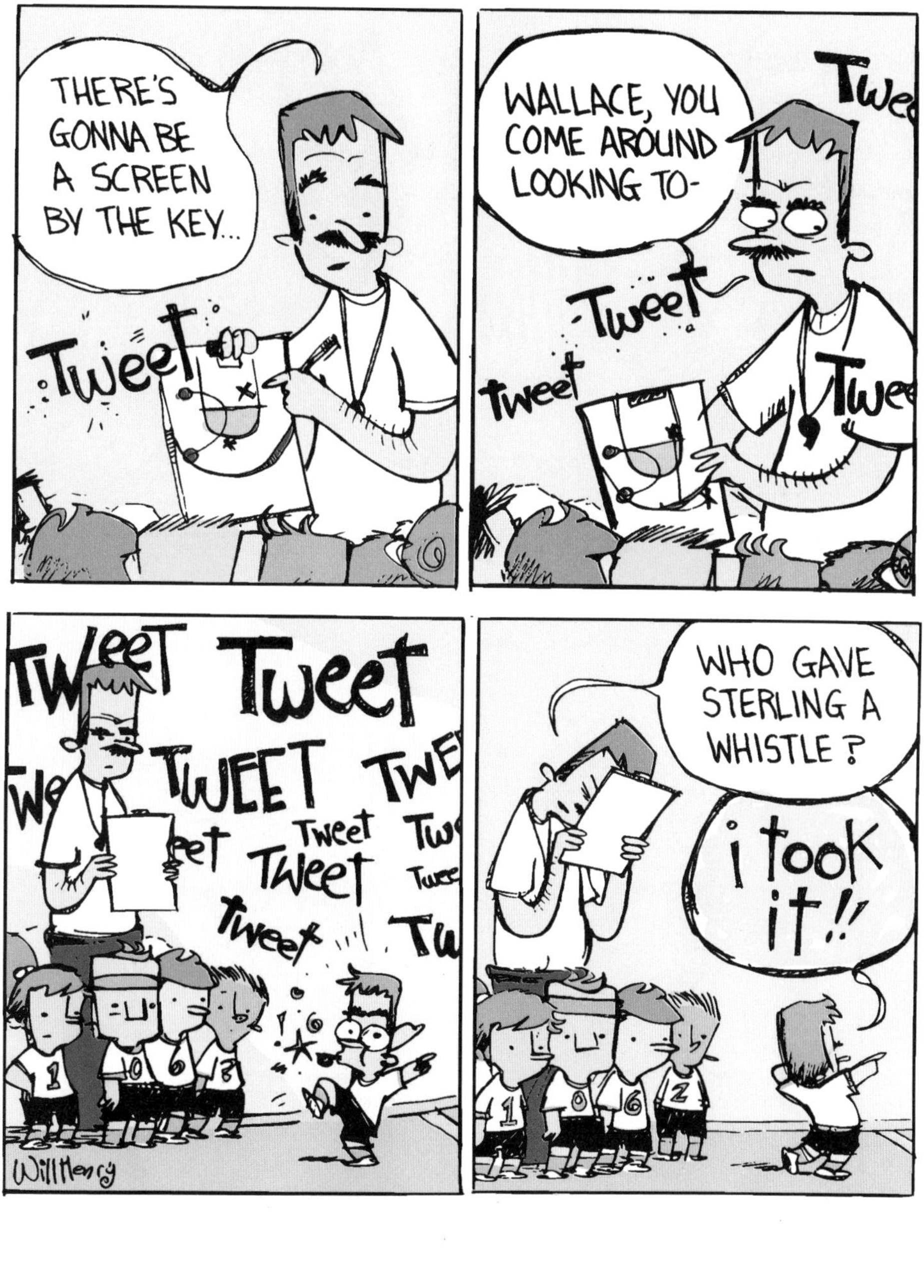
THERE'S GONNA BE A SCREEN BY THE KEY...
Tweet
WALLACE, YOU COME AROUND LOOKING TO-
Twee
Tweet
tweet
Twe
TWEET Tweet
TWEET TWE
Tweet
TWeet
tweet
Will Henry
WHO GAVE STERLING A WHISTLE?
i took it!!

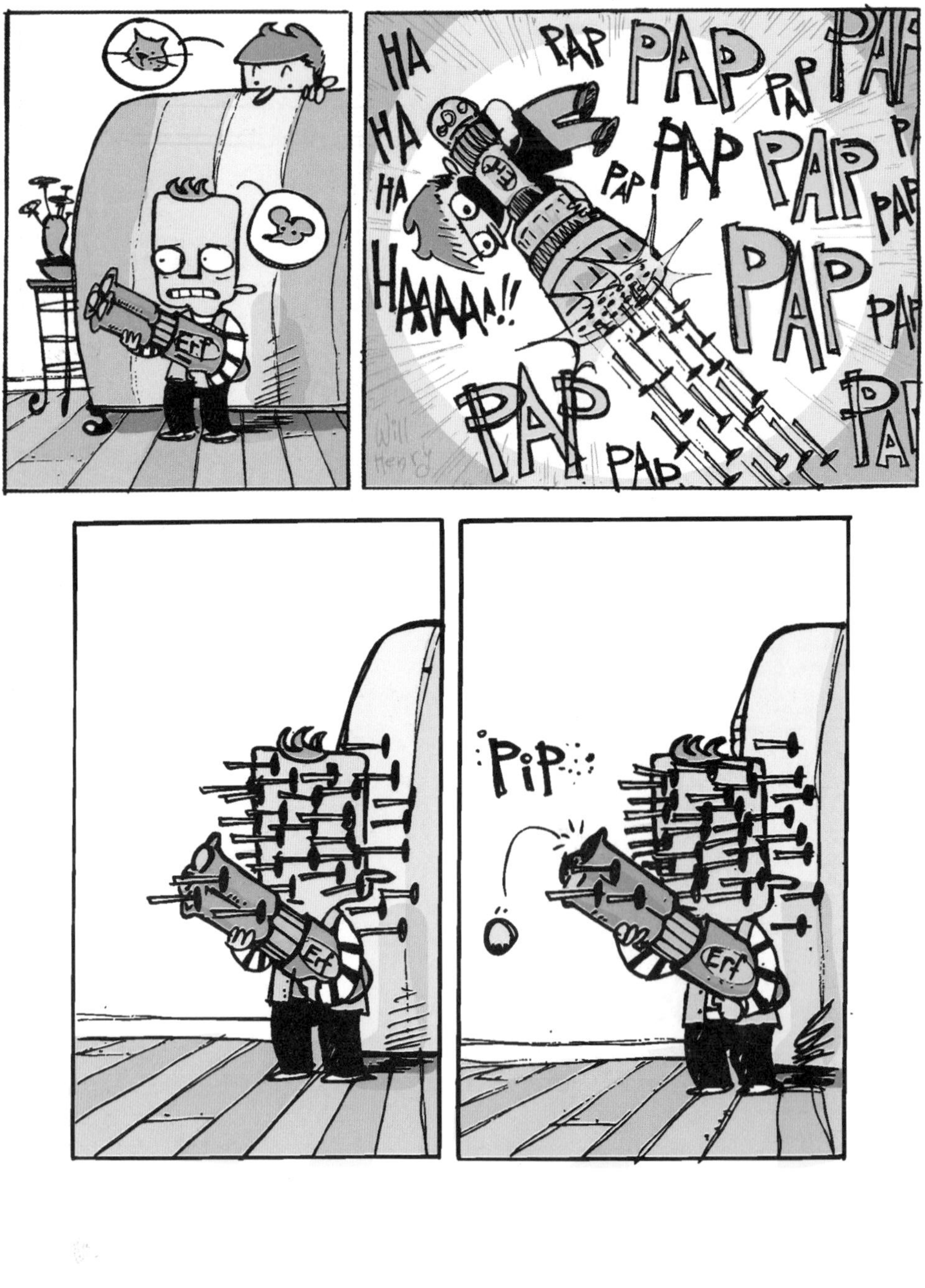
HA
HA
HA
HAAAAAA!!
PAP PAP PAP PAP PAP
PAP PAP PAP PAP PAP PAP
PAP PAP PAP
PIP

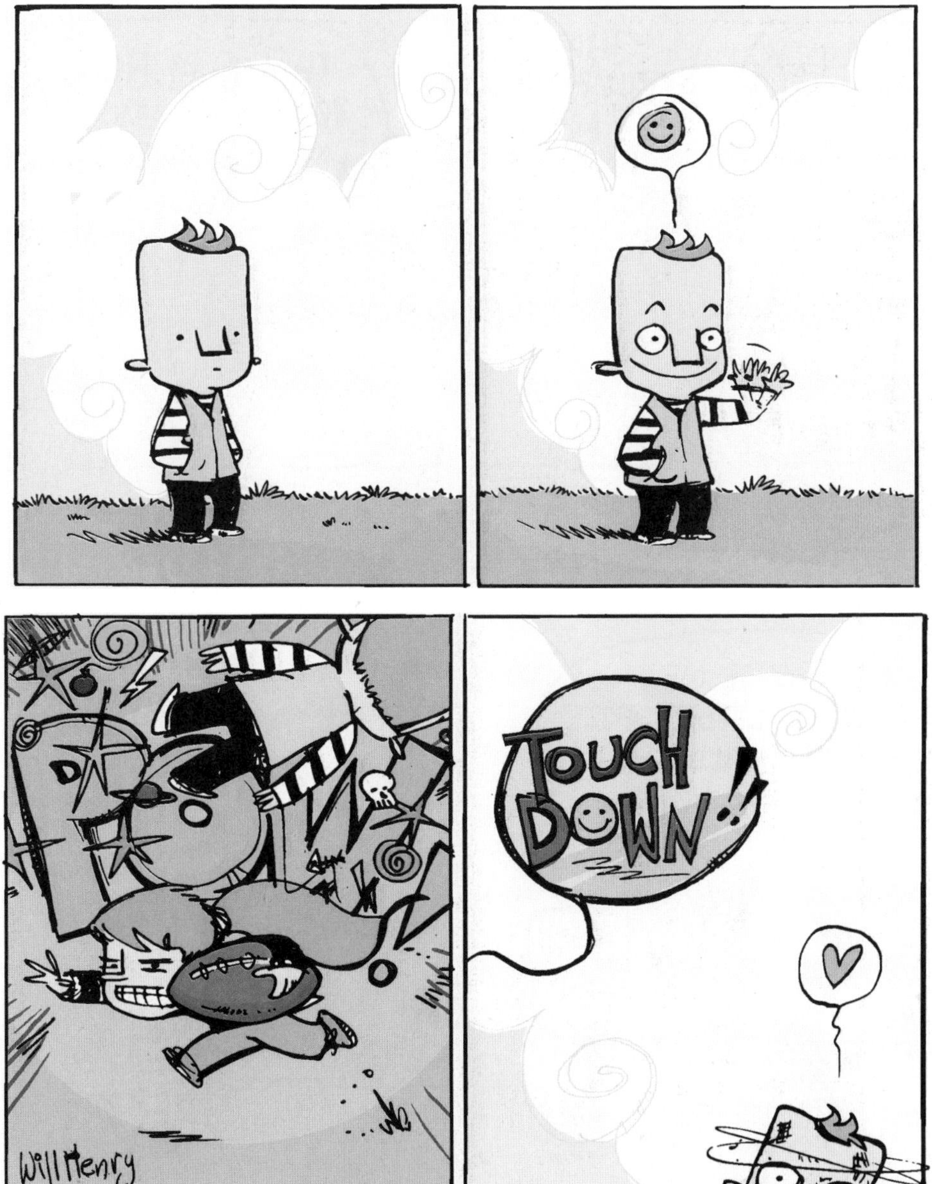
TOUCH DOWN!!
Will Henry

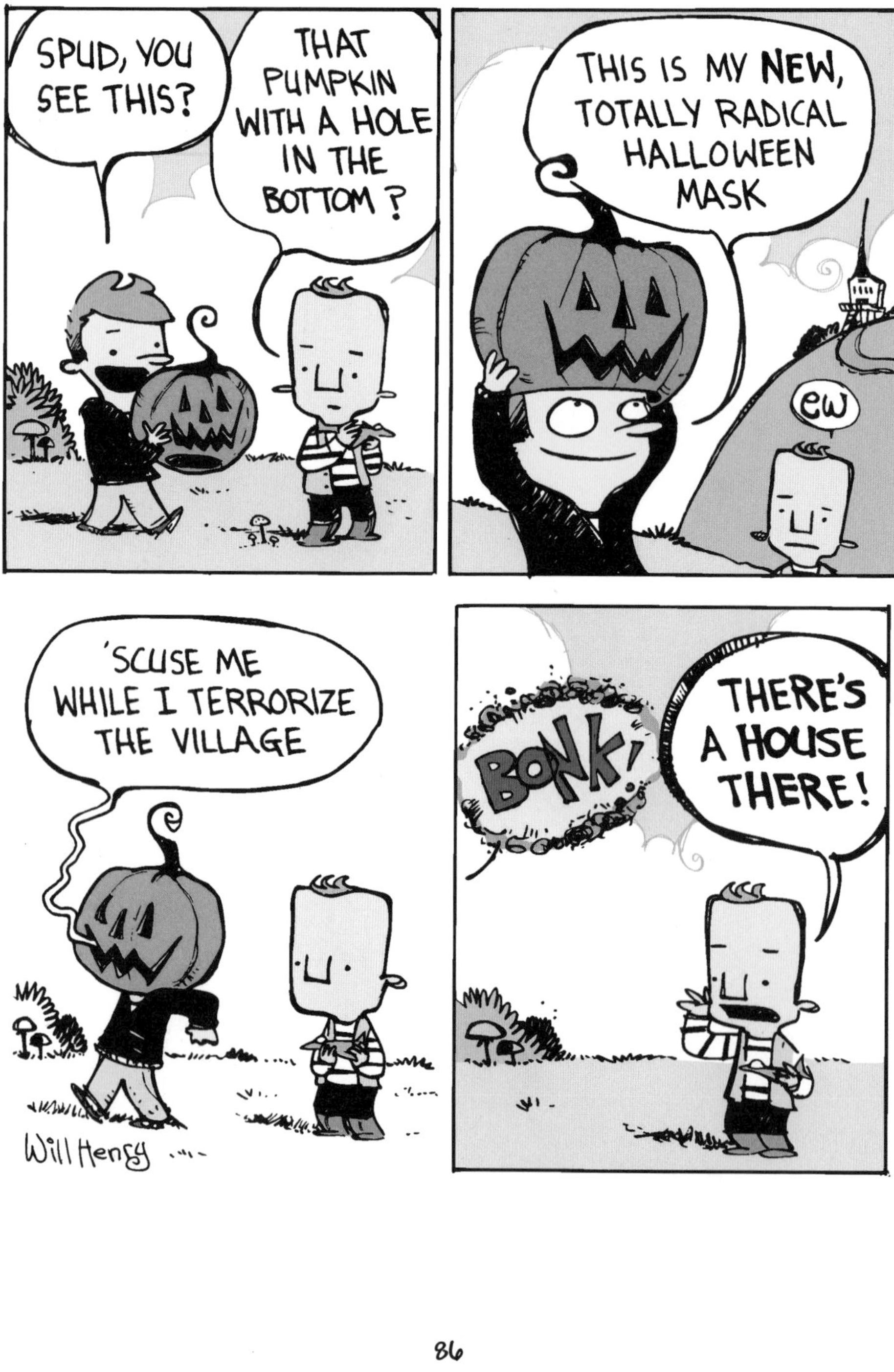
SPUD, YOU SEE THIS?
THAT PUMPKIN WITH A HOLE IN THE BOTTOM?
THIS IS MY NEW, TOTALLY RADICAL HALLOWEEN MASK
EW
'SCUSE ME WHILE I TERRORIZE THE VILLAGE
Will Henry
BONK!
THERE'S A HOUSE THERE!

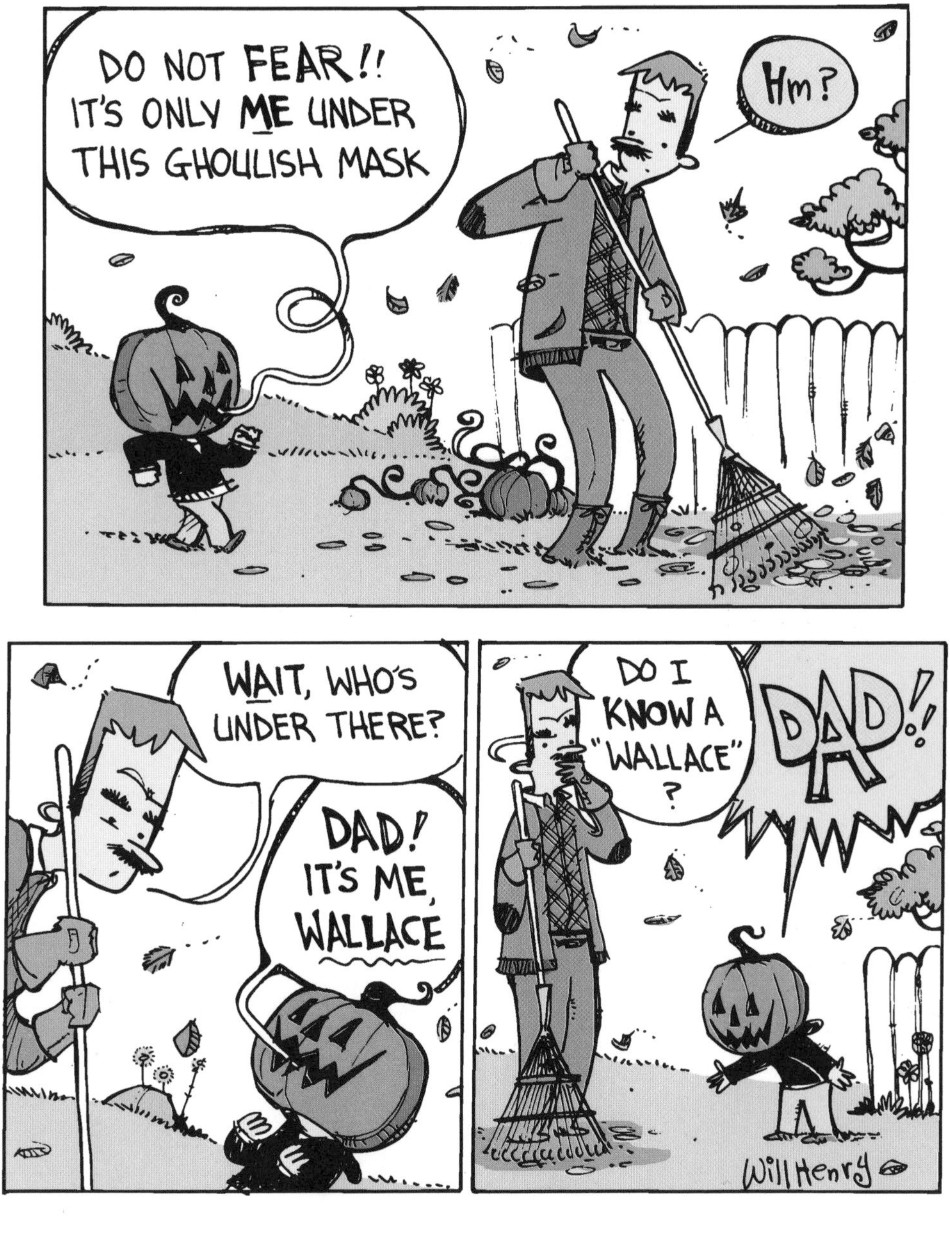
DO NOT FEAR!! IT'S ONLY ME UNDER THIS GHOULISH MASK
Hm?
WAIT, WHO'S UNDER THERE?
DAD! IT'S ME, WALLACE
DO I KNOW A "WALLACE"?
DAD!!
Will Henry

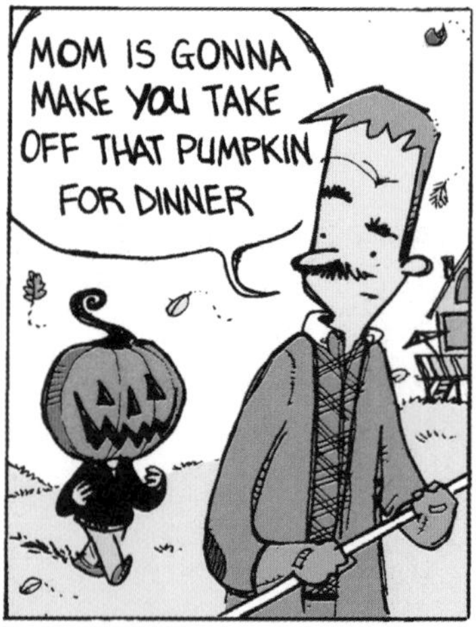
MOM IS GONNA MAKE YOU TAKE OFF THAT PUMPKIN FOR DINNER

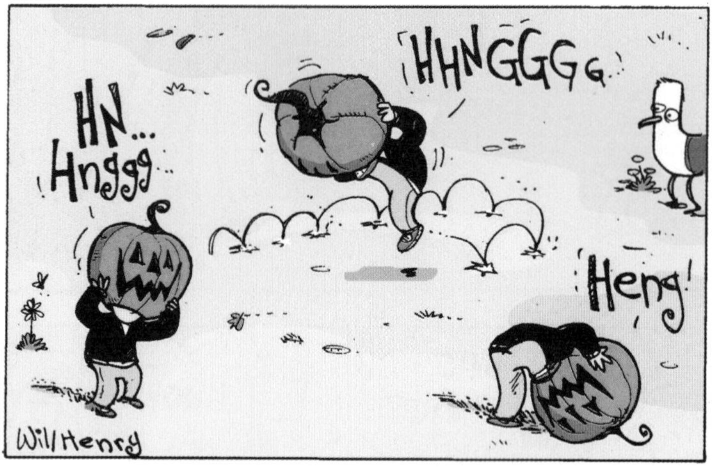
HN... Hnggg
HHNGGGG
Heng!
Will Henry

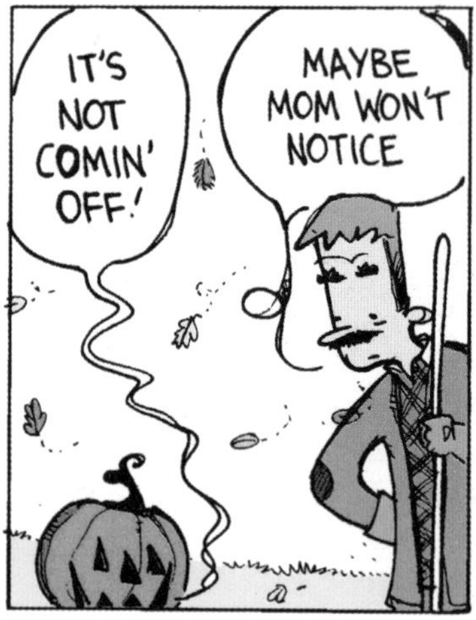
IT'S NOT COMIN' OFF!
MAYBE MOM WON'T NOTICE

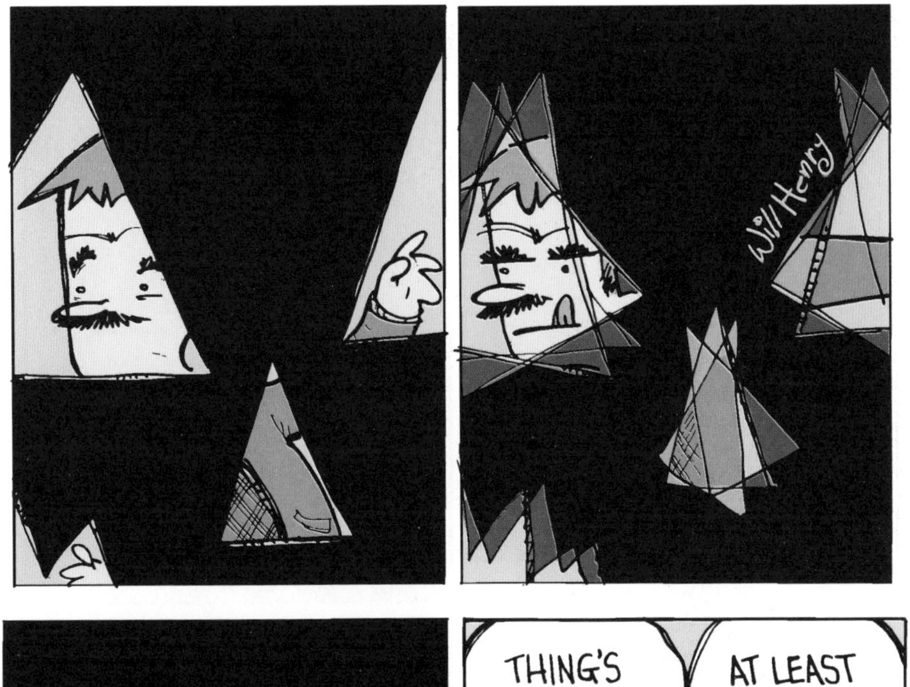
Will Henry
THING'S NOT COMIN' OFF
AT LEAST I'LL HAVE AN **EPIC** SCHOOL PHOTO!

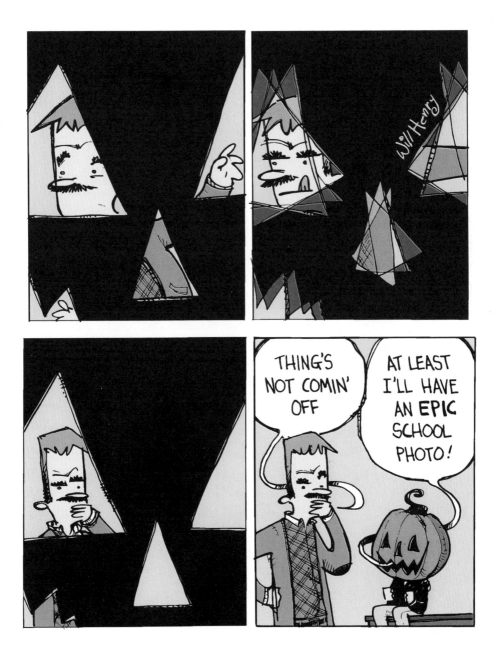

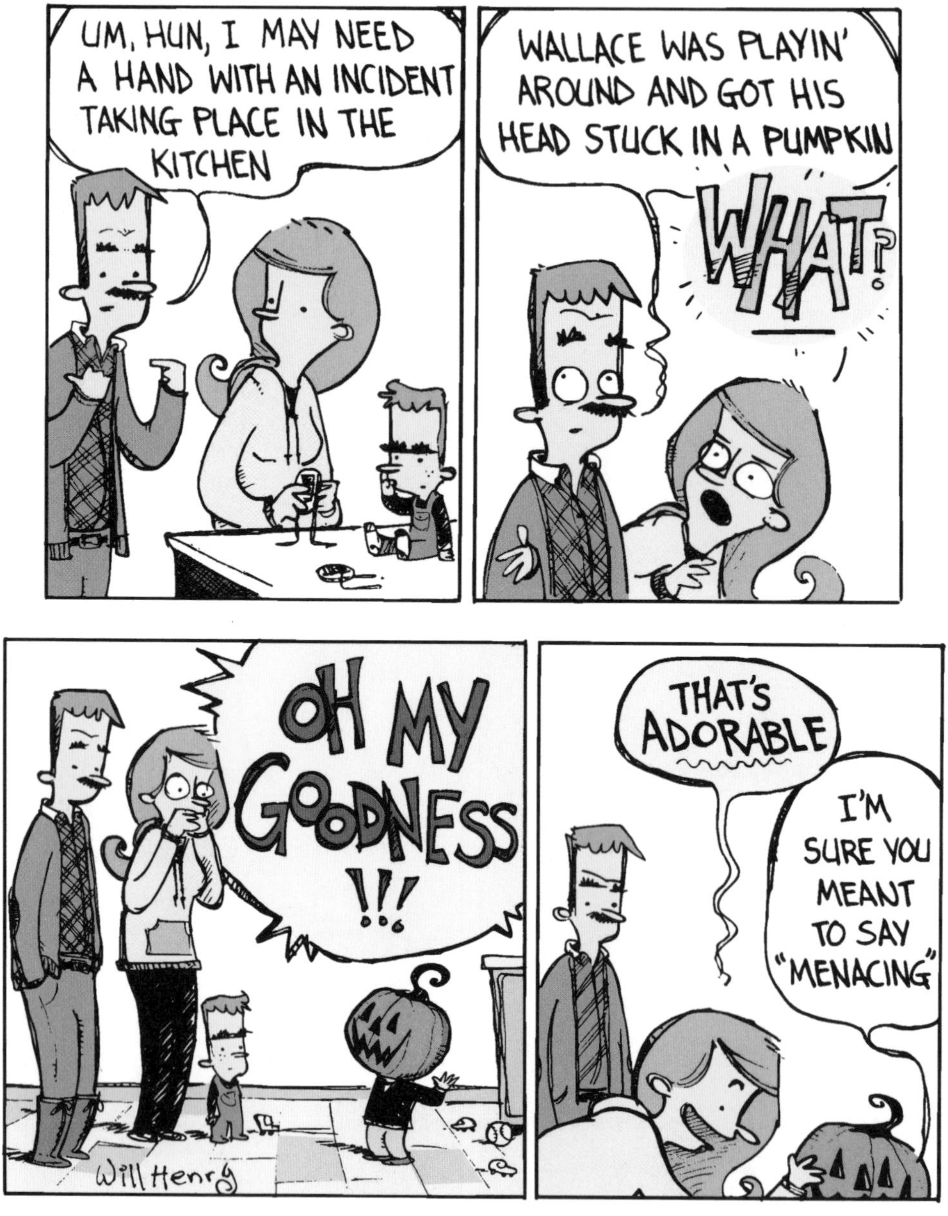
UM, HUN, I MAY NEED A HAND WITH AN INCIDENT TAKING PLACE IN THE KITCHEN
WALLACE WAS PLAYIN' AROUND AND GOT HIS HEAD STUCK IN A PUMPKIN
WHAT?
OH MY GOODNESS !!!
Will Henry
THAT'S ADORABLE
I'M SURE YOU MEANT TO SAY "MENACING"

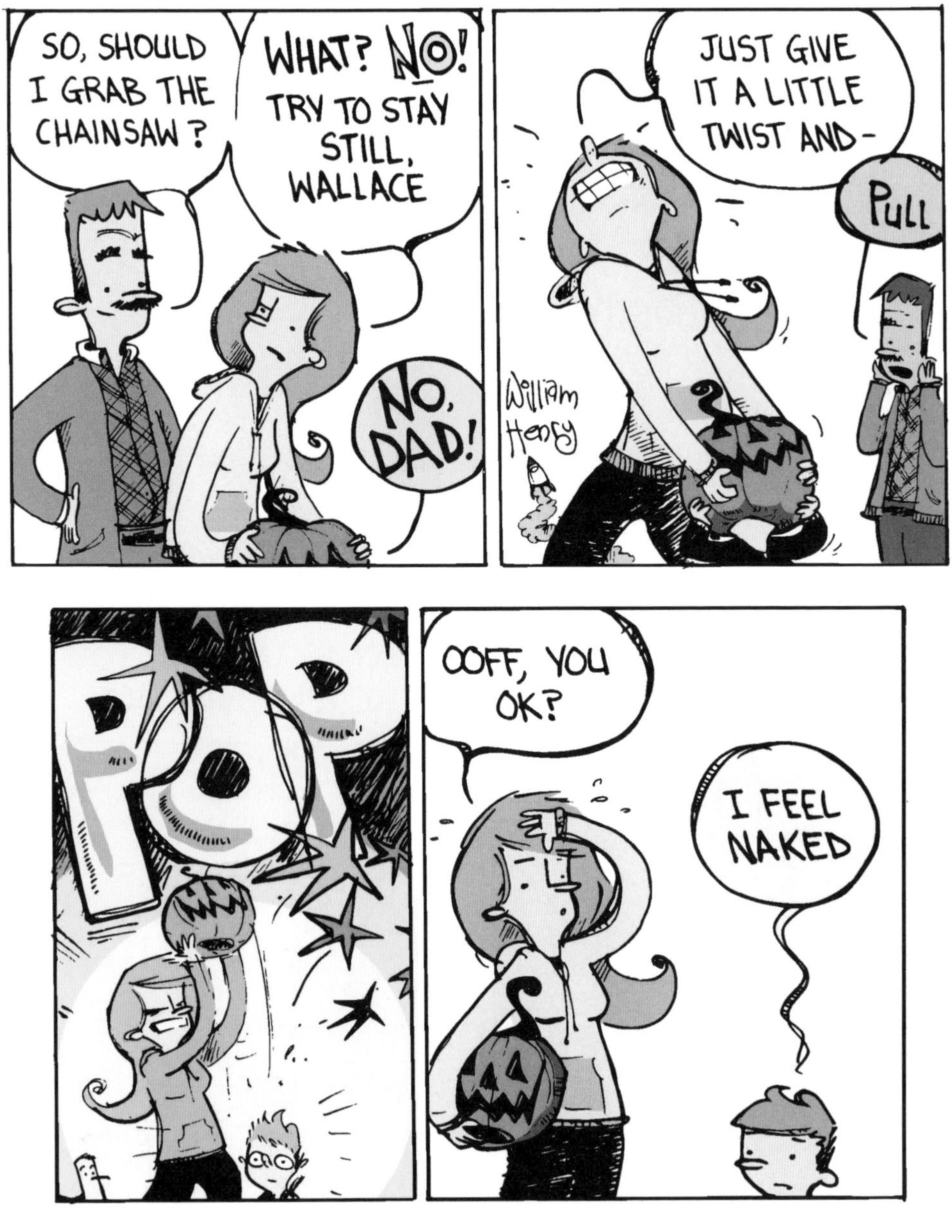
SO, SHOULD I GRAB THE CHAINSAW?
WHAT? NO! TRY TO STAY STILL, WALLACE
NO, DAD!
JUST GIVE IT A LITTLE TWIST AND-
PULL
William Henry
POP
OOFF, YOU OK?
I FEEL NAKED

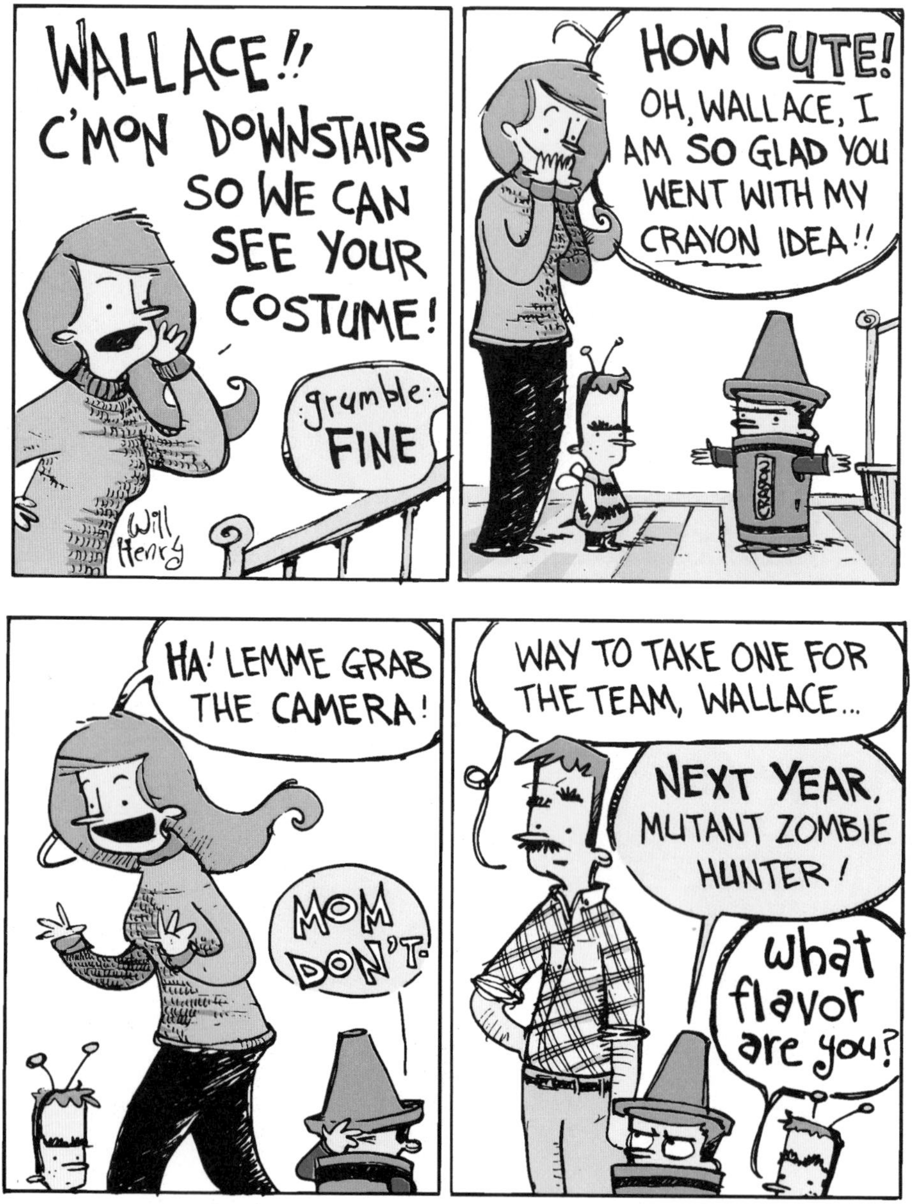
WALLACE!! C'MON DOWNSTAIRS SO WE CAN SEE YOUR COSTUME!
grumble FINE
Will Henry
HOW CUTE! OH, WALLACE, I AM SO GLAD YOU WENT WITH MY CRAYON IDEA!!
CRAYON
HA! LEMME GRAB THE CAMERA!
MOM DON'T.
WAY TO TAKE ONE FOR THE TEAM, WALLACE...
NEXT YEAR, MUTANT ZOMBIE HUNTER!
what flavor are you?

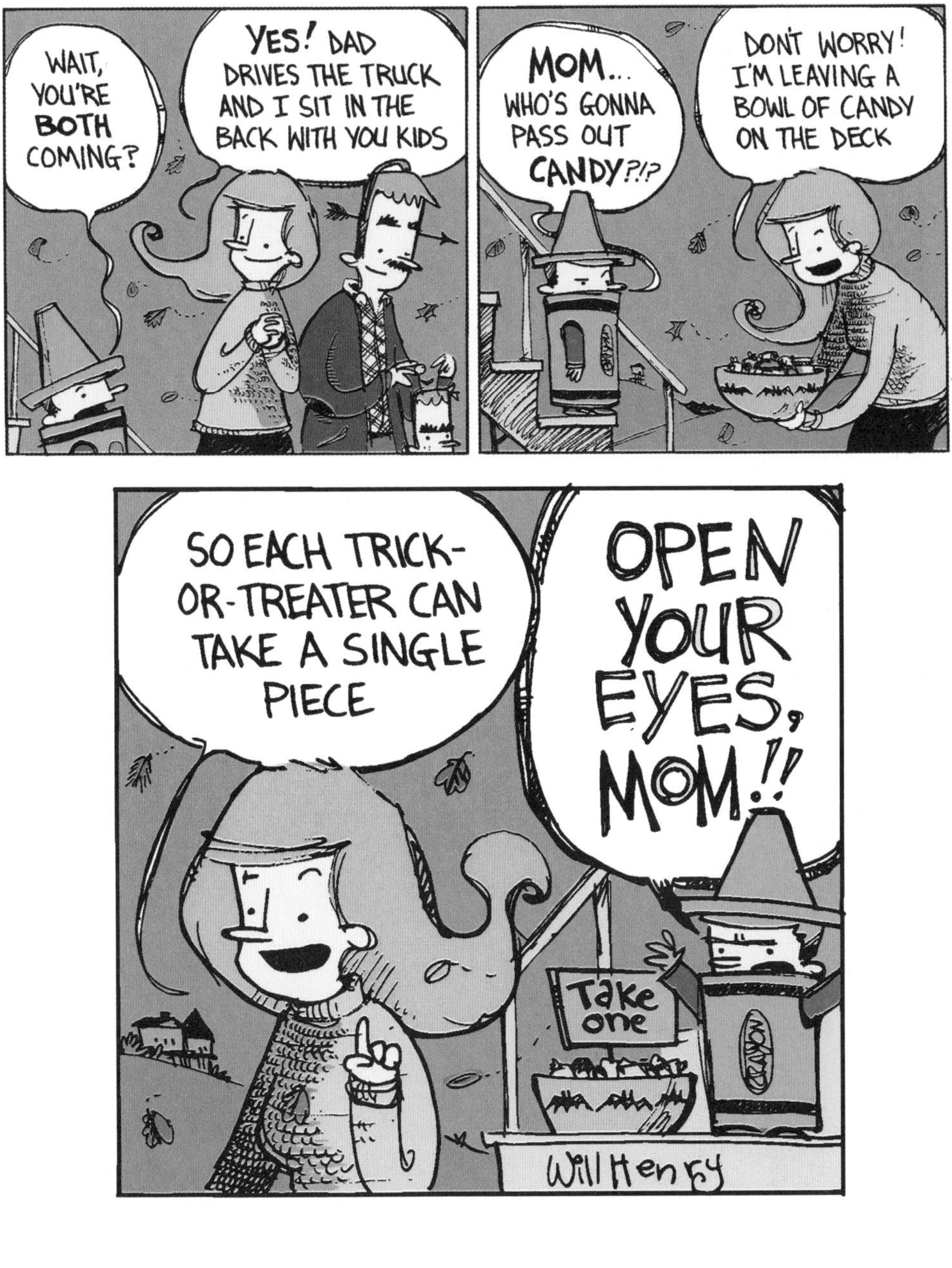
WAIT, YOU'RE **BOTH** COMING?
YES! DAD DRIVES THE TRUCK AND I SIT IN THE BACK WITH YOU KIDS
MOM... WHO'S GONNA PASS OUT **CANDY**?!?
DON'T WORRY! I'M LEAVING A BOWL OF CANDY ON THE DECK
SO EACH TRICK-OR-TREATER CAN TAKE A SINGLE PIECE
OPEN YOUR EYES, MOM!!
Take one
CRAYON
Will Henry

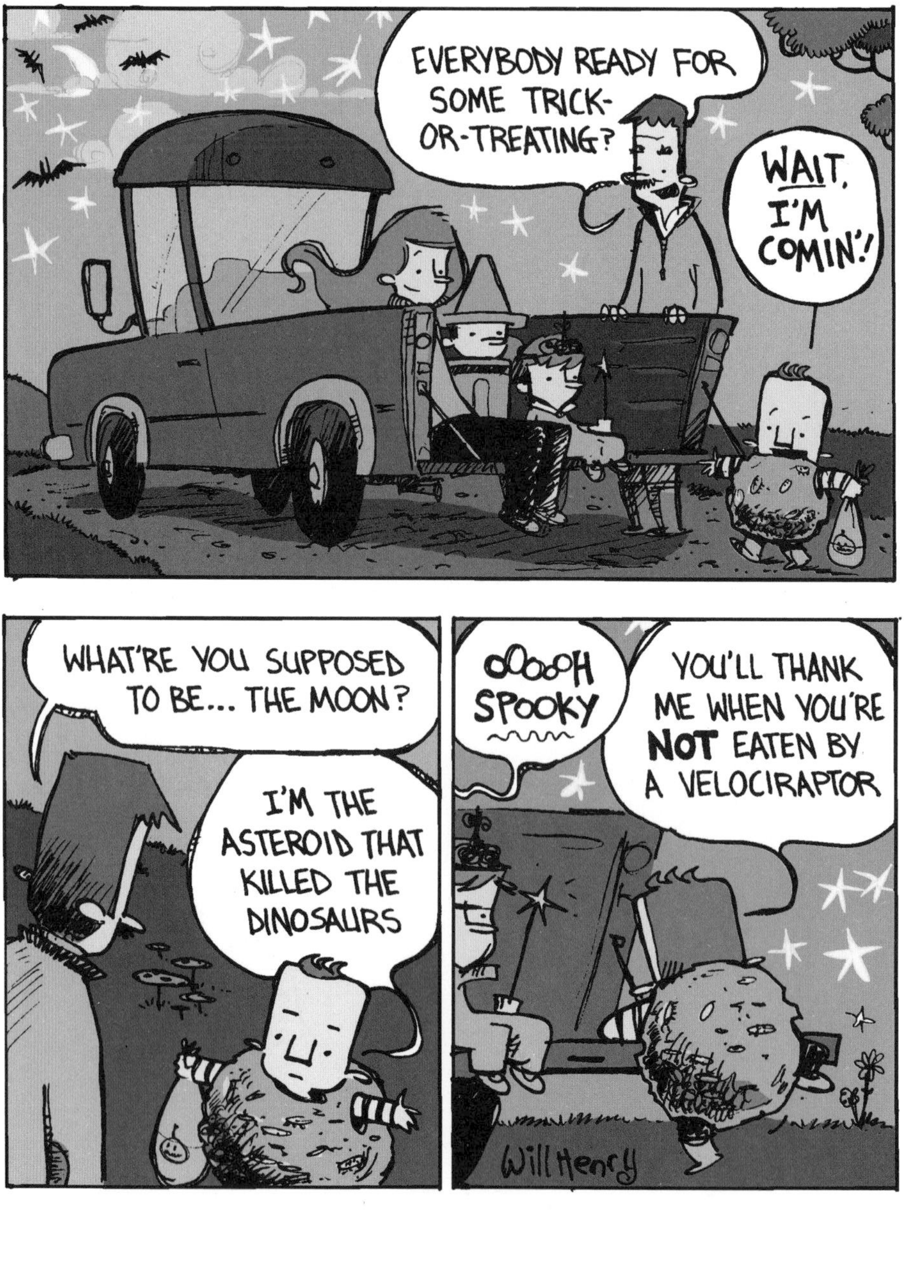
EVERYBODY READY FOR SOME TRICK-OR-TREATING?
WAIT, I'M COMIN'!
WHAT'RE YOU SUPPOSED TO BE... THE MOON?
I'M THE ASTEROID THAT KILLED THE DINOSAURS
OOOOOH SPOOKY
YOU'LL THANK ME WHEN YOU'RE NOT EATEN BY A VELOCIRAPTOR
Will Henry

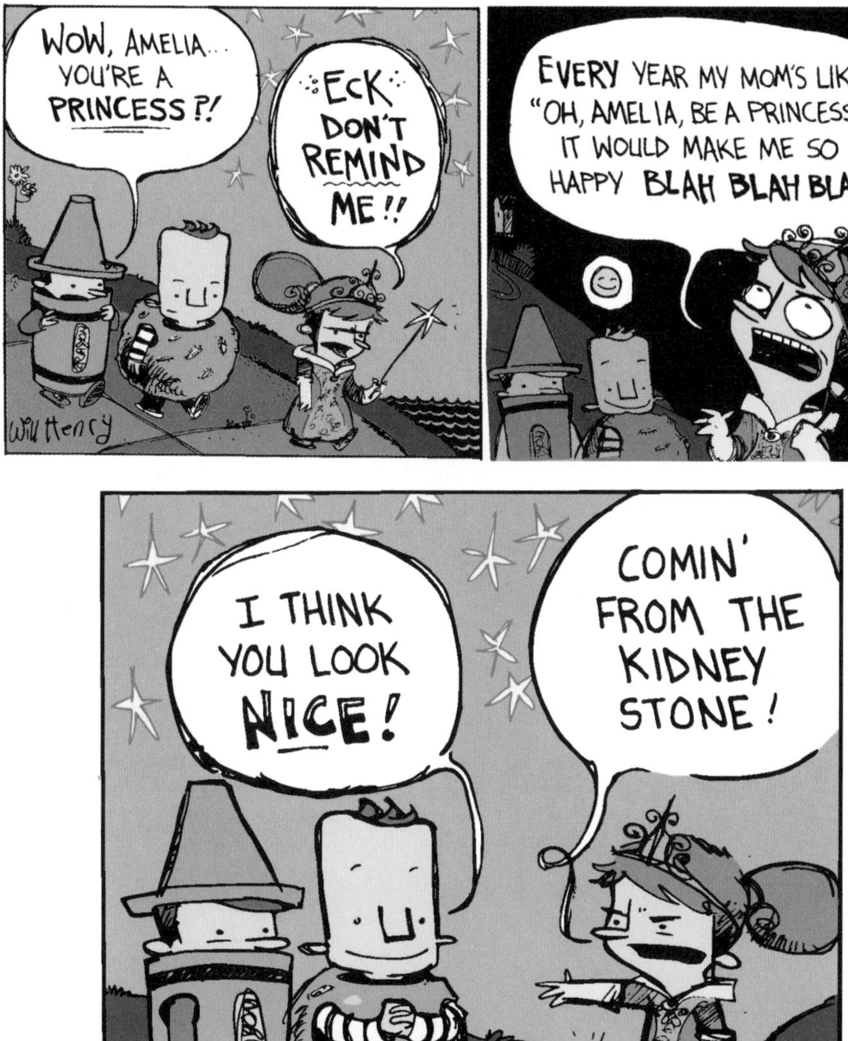
WOW, AMELIA... YOU'RE A PRINCESS?!
ECK DON'T REMIND ME!!
Will Henry
EVERY YEAR MY MOM'S LIKE, "OH, AMELIA, BE A PRINCESS, IT WOULD MAKE ME SO HAPPY BLAH BLAH BLAH"
I THINK YOU LOOK NICE!
COMIN' FROM THE KIDNEY STONE!

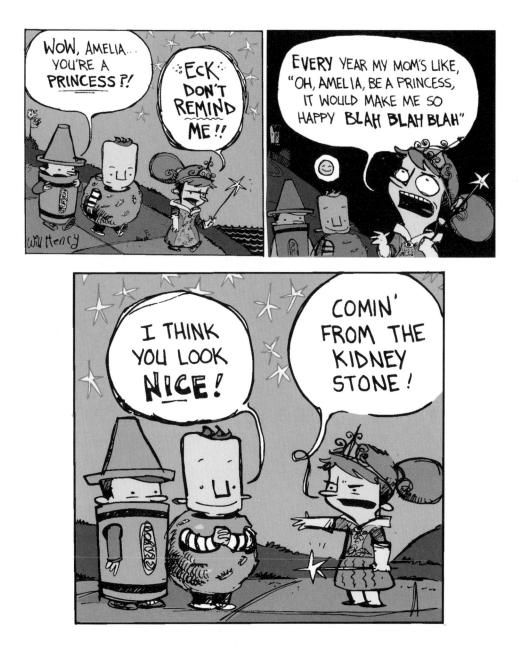

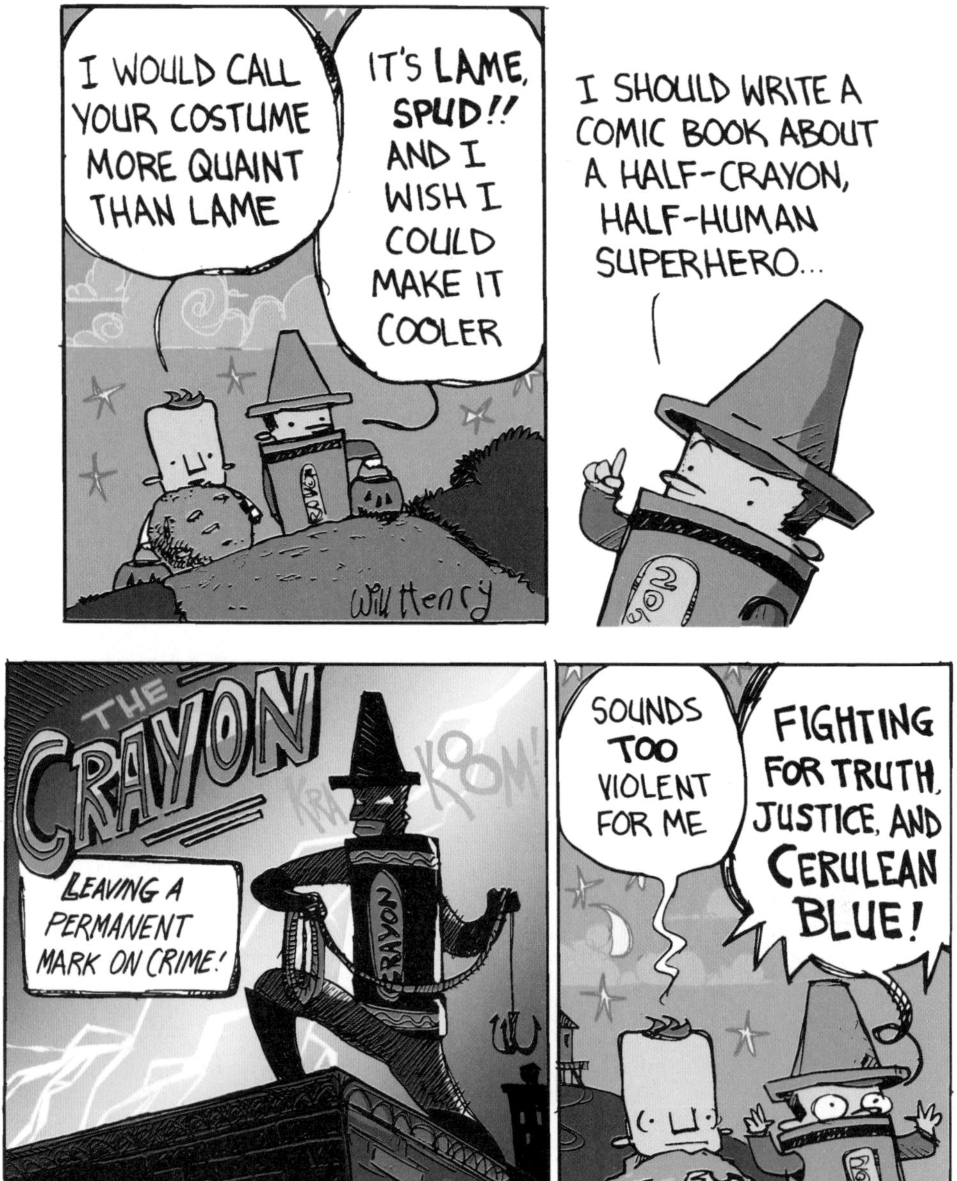
I WOULD CALL YOUR COSTUME MORE QUAINT THAN LAME
IT'S LAME, SPUD!! AND I WISH I COULD MAKE IT COOLER
Will Henry
I SHOULD WRITE A COMIC BOOK ABOUT A HALF-CRAYON, HALF-HUMAN SUPERHERO...
THE CRAYON
KRA-KOOM!
LEAVING A PERMANENT MARK ON CRIME!
CRAYON
FIGHTING FOR TRUTH, JUSTICE, AND CERULEAN BLUE!
SOUNDS TOO VIOLENT FOR ME

97

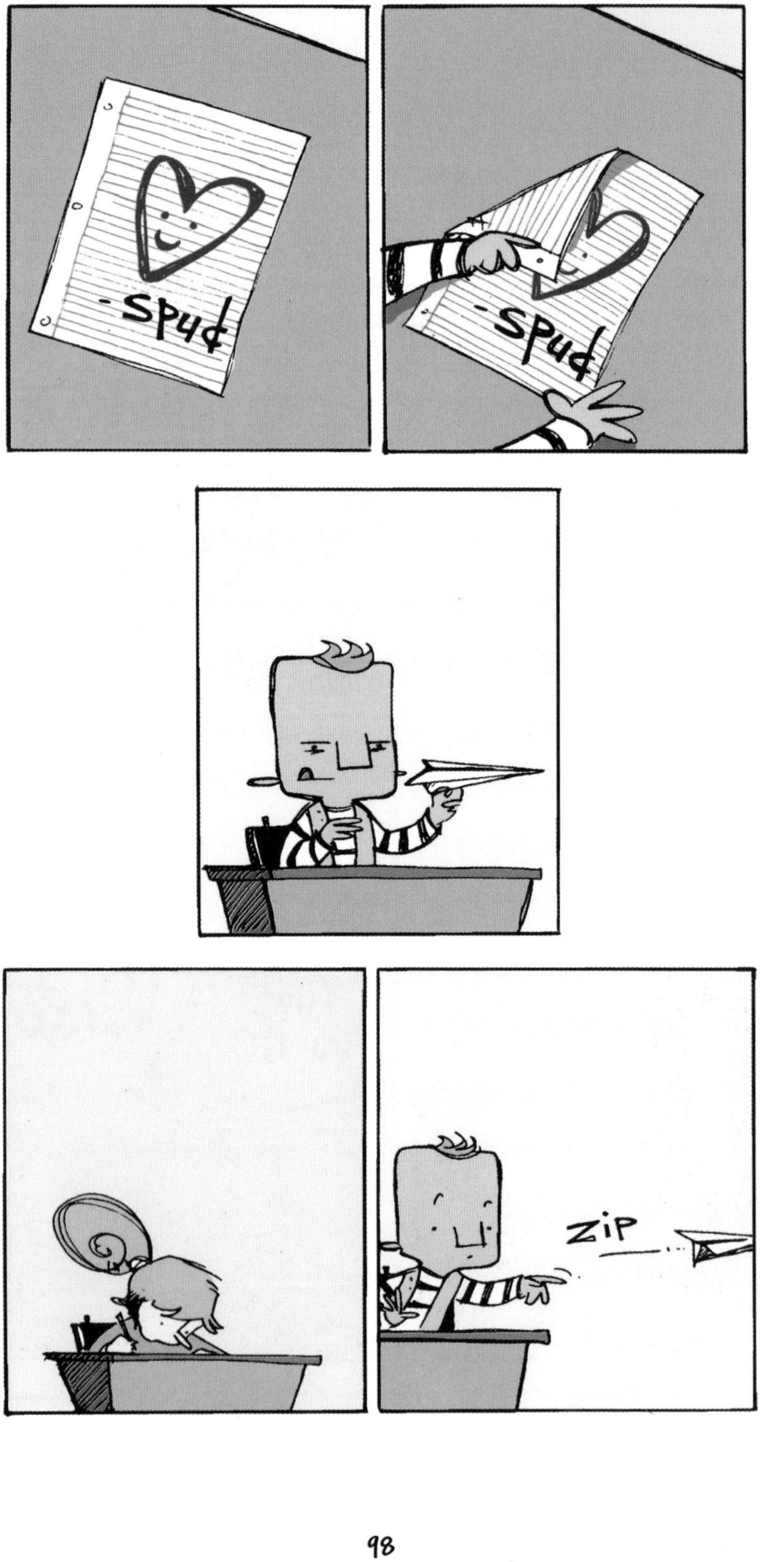
-Spud
-Spud
ZIP

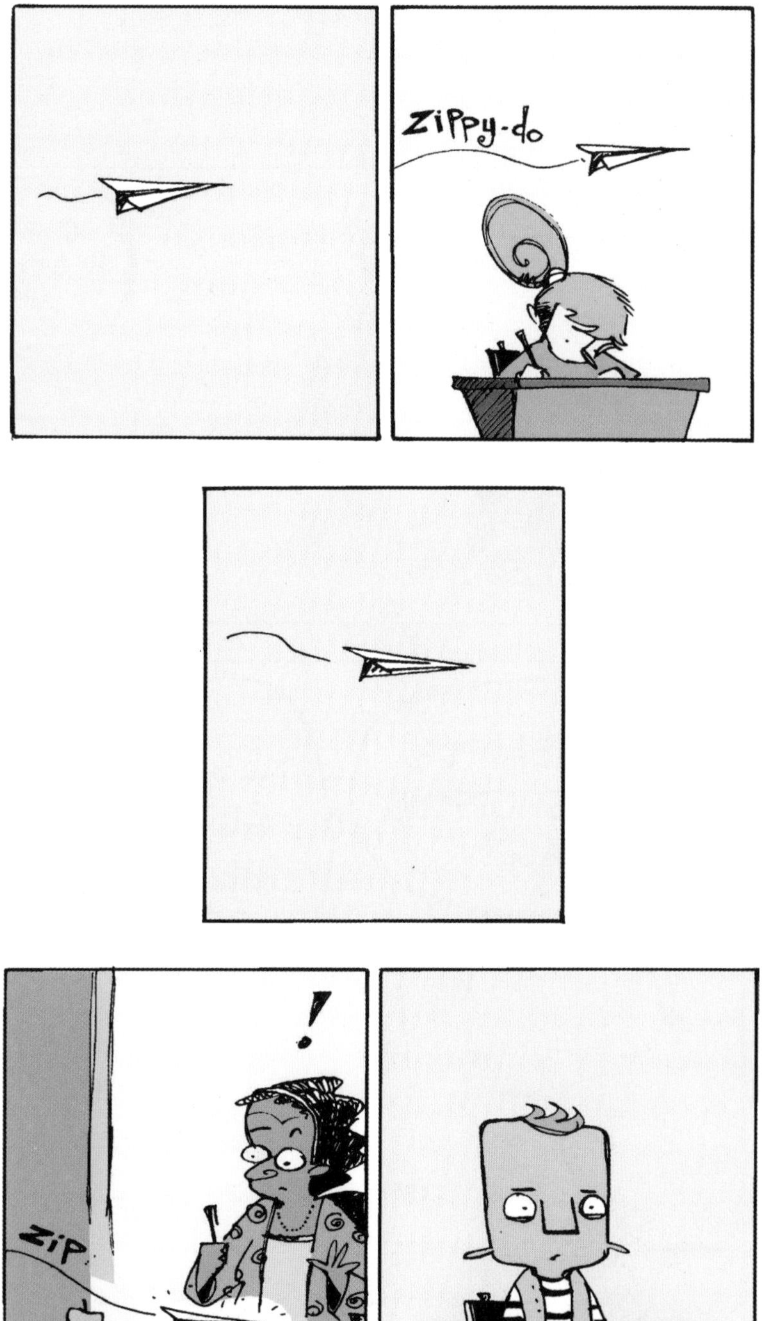
ZIPPY-do
!
ZIP

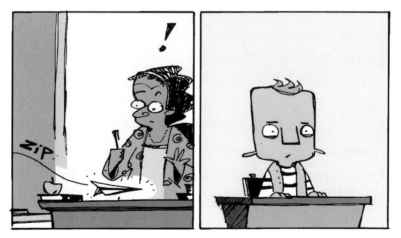

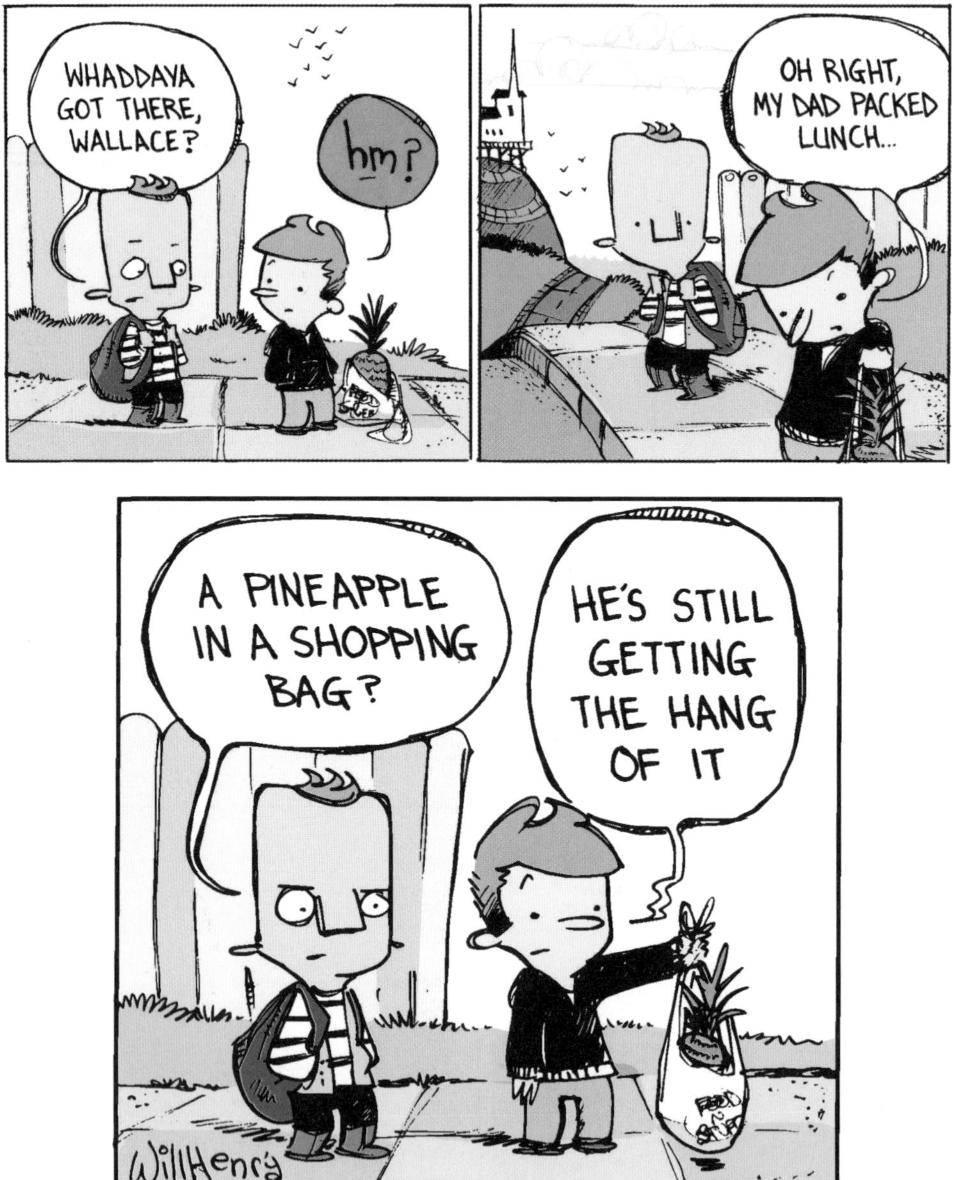
WHADDAYA GOT THERE, WALLACE?
hm?
OH RIGHT, MY DAD PACKED LUNCH...
A PINEAPPLE IN A SHOPPING BAG?
HE'S STILL GETTING THE HANG OF IT
WillHenry

Will Henry

118

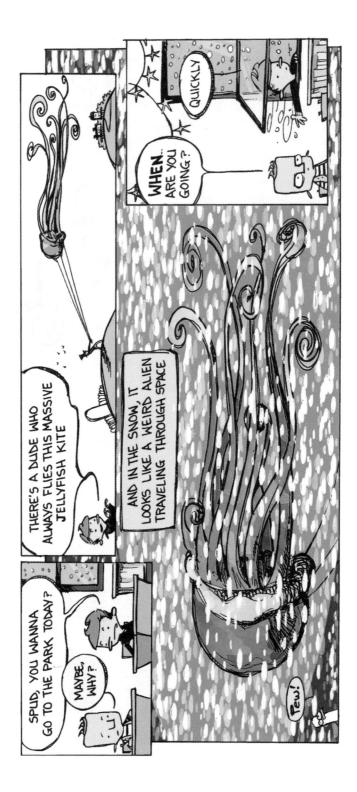

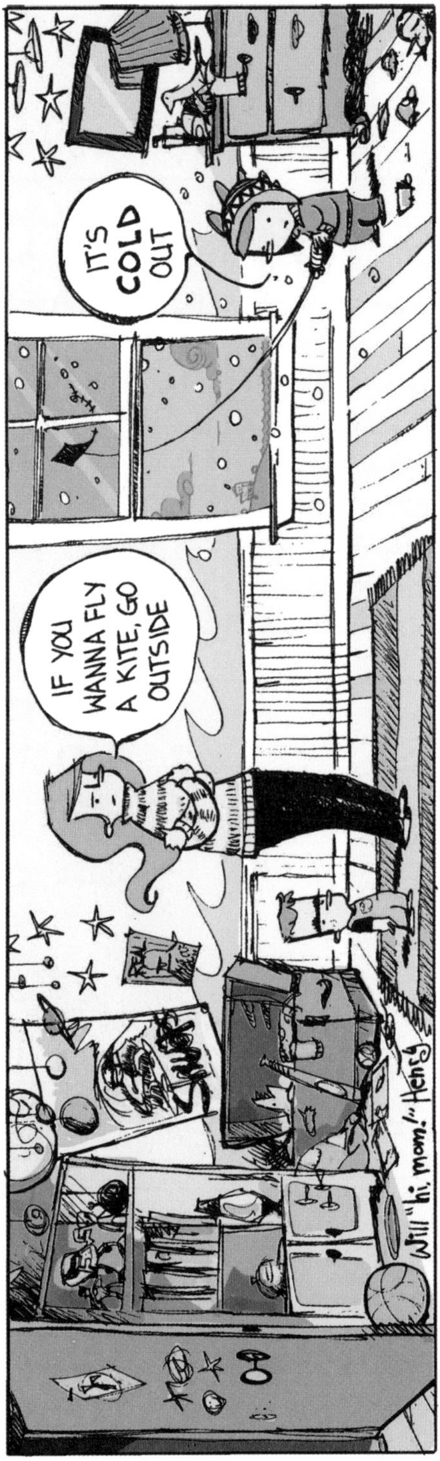
IF YOU WANNA FLY A KITE, GO OUTSIDE
IT'S COLD OUT
Will "hi, mom!" Henry

124

QUICKLY, BEFORE MOM SEES
WillHenry

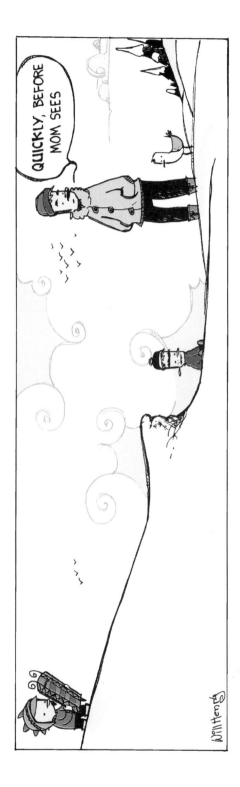

130

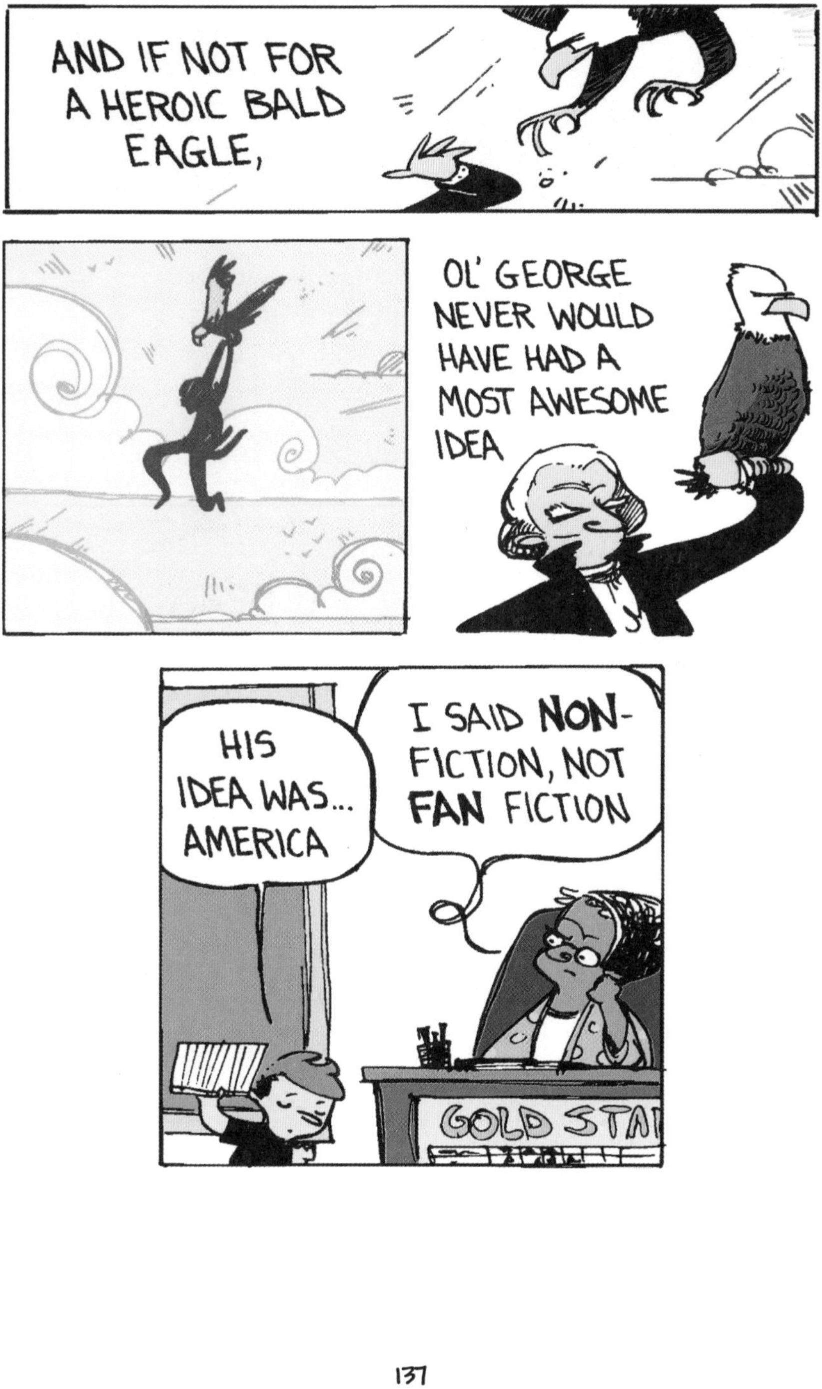
AND IF NOT FOR A HEROIC BALD EAGLE,
OL' GEORGE NEVER WOULD HAVE HAD A MOST AWESOME IDEA
HIS IDEA WAS... AMERICA
I SAID **NON**-FICTION, NOT **FAN** FICTION
GOLD STA

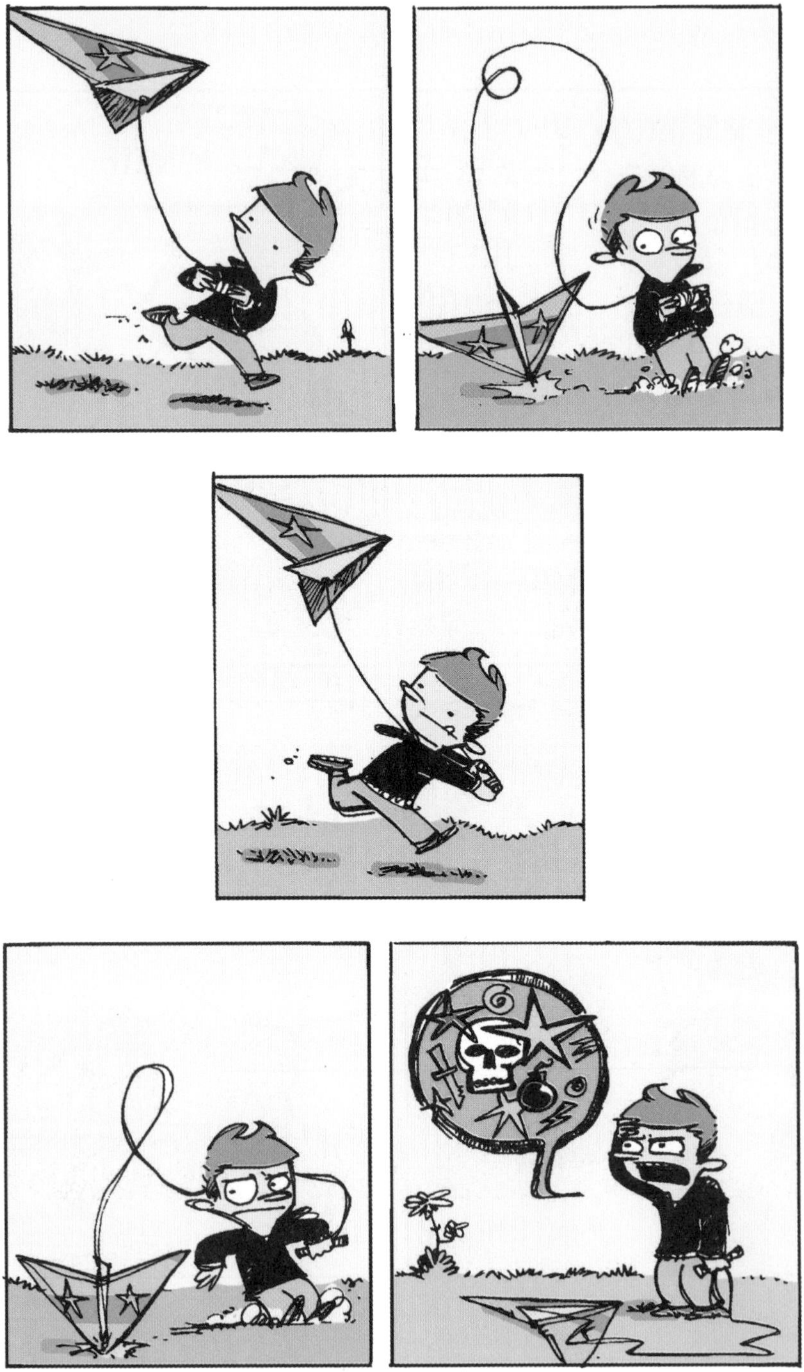

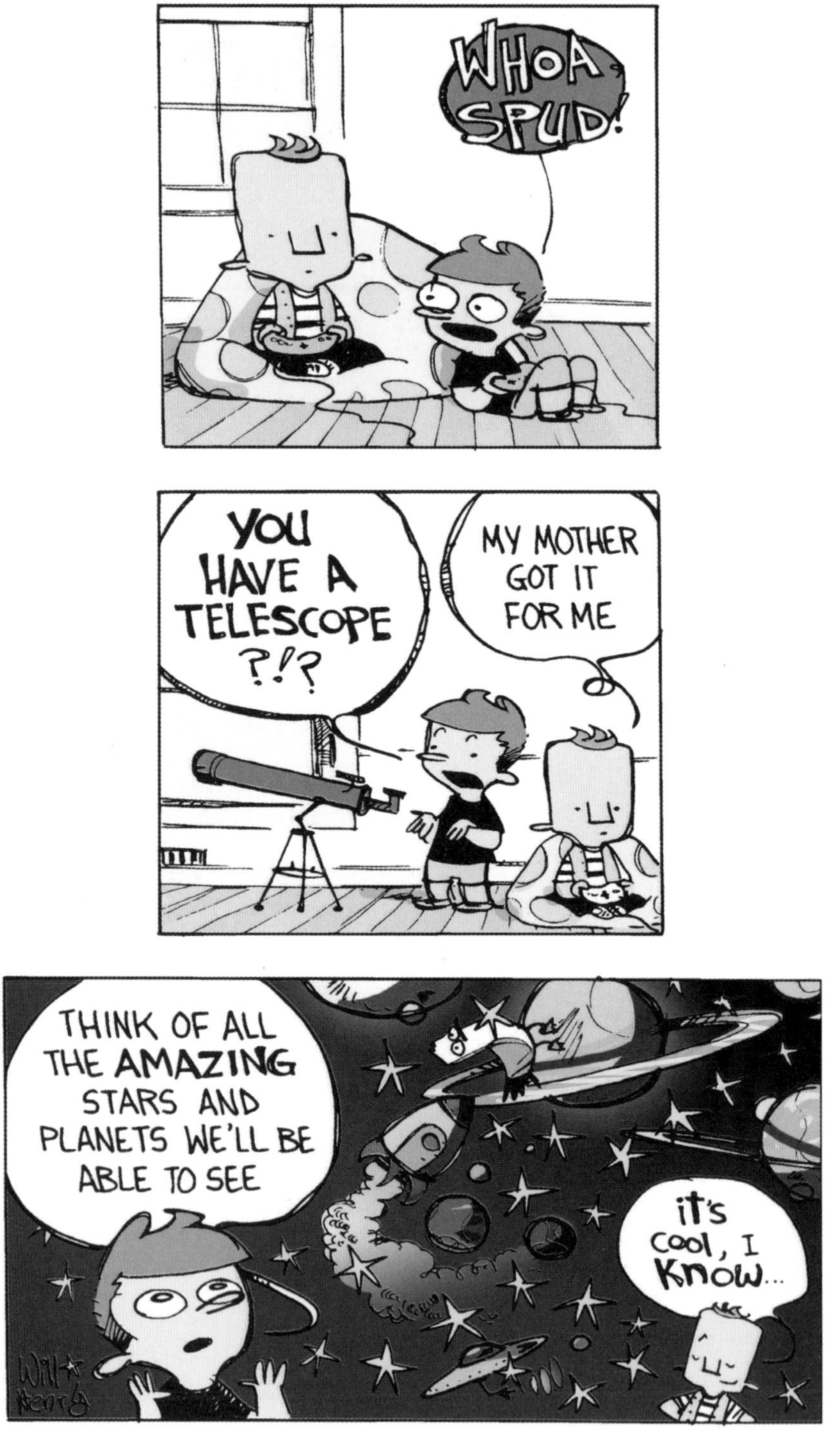
WHOA SPUD!
YOU HAVE A TELESCOPE ?!?
MY MOTHER GOT IT FOR ME
THINK OF ALL THE AMAZING STARS AND PLANETS WE'LL BE ABLE TO SEE
it's cool, I Know...
Will Henry

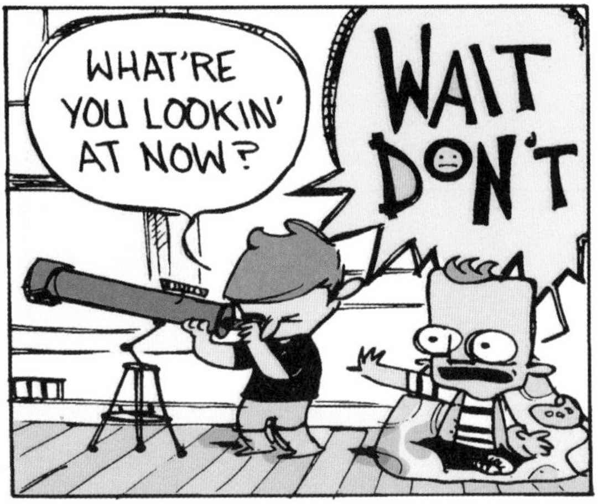
WHAT'RE YOU LOOKIN' AT NOW?
WAIT DON'T

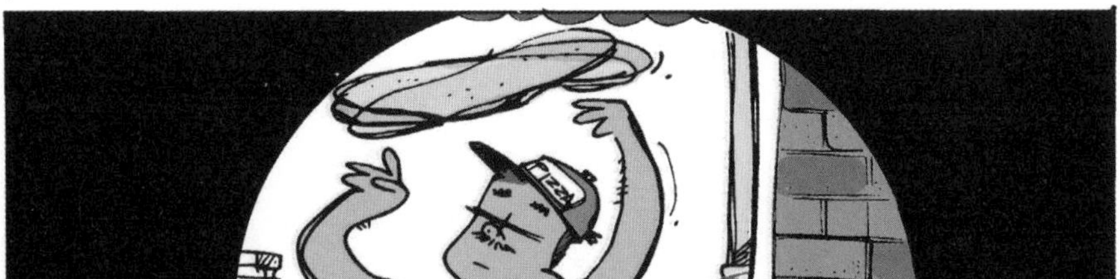
PIZZA
PIZZA
order in
Take out

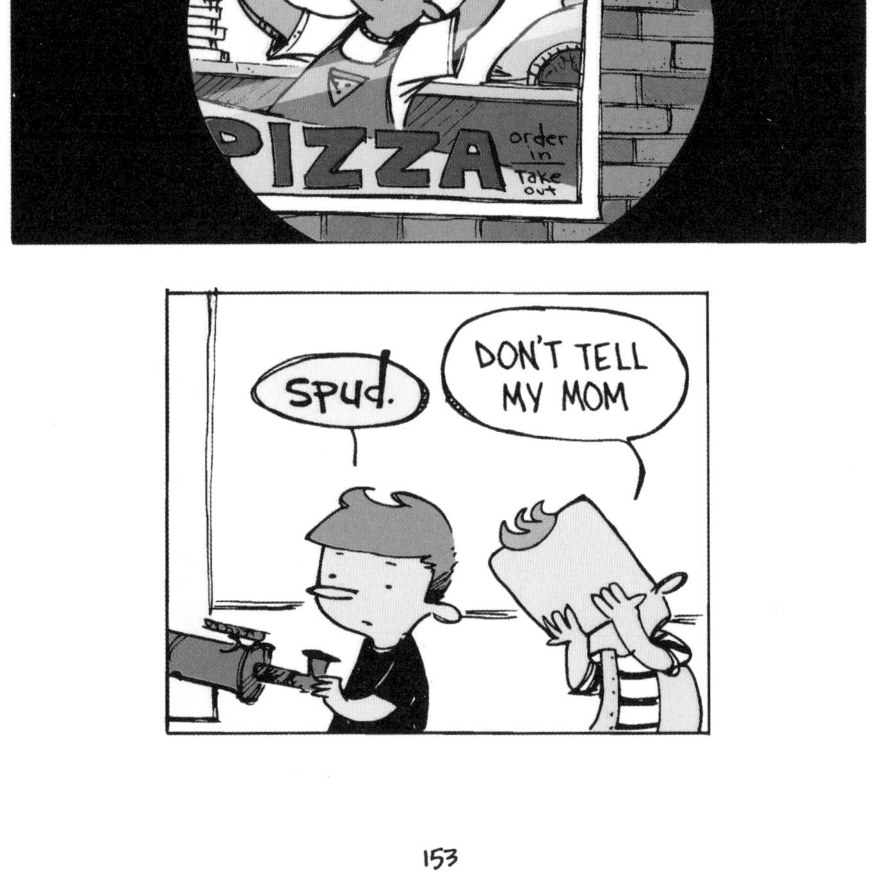
spud.
DON'T TELL MY MOM

157

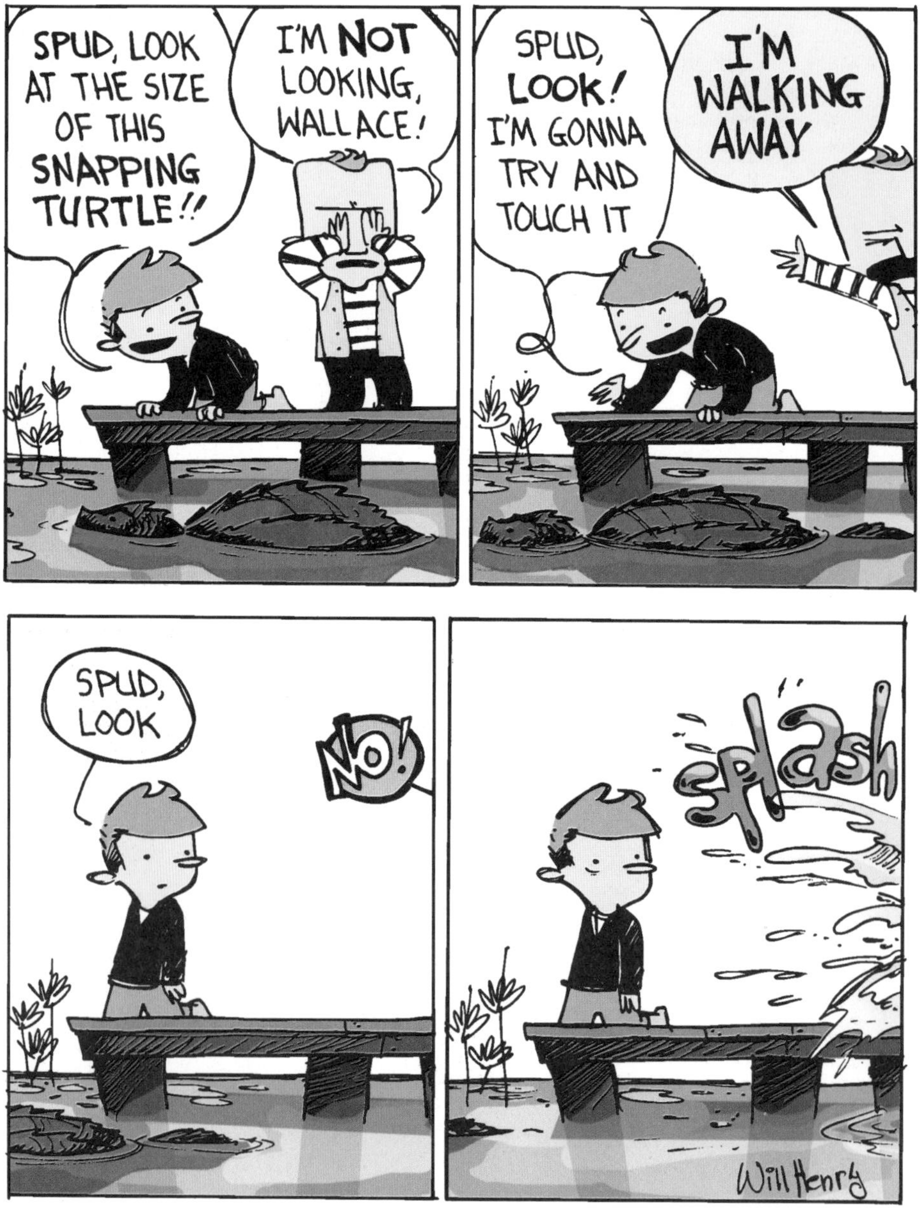
SPUD, LOOK AT THE SIZE OF THIS SNAPPING TURTLE!!
I'M NOT LOOKING, WALLACE!
SPUD, LOOK! I'M GONNA TRY AND TOUCH IT
I'M WALKING AWAY
SPUD, LOOK
NO!
splash
Will Henry

163

WALLACE'S GUIDE TO KEEPING A FIELD BOOK

Trust me, I kinda know what I'm talking about.

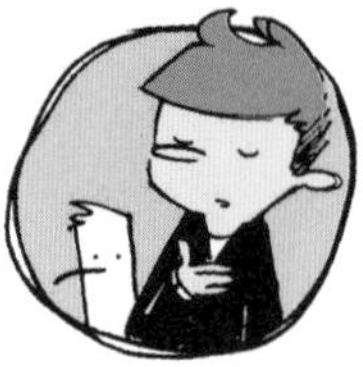

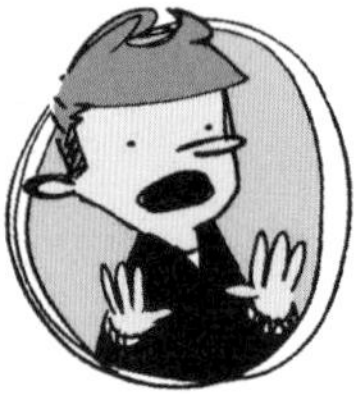

A field guide is a cool way to keep track of all the hikes and parks you visit. I use a regular ol' spiral notebook, but you can use anything you want, from blank sketchbooks to stapled pieces of computer paper. Whenever I get outside with my field book, I always use one page to describe where I am and the opposite page to tape down all the cool things I find, like ferns, feathers, flowers, and sticks.

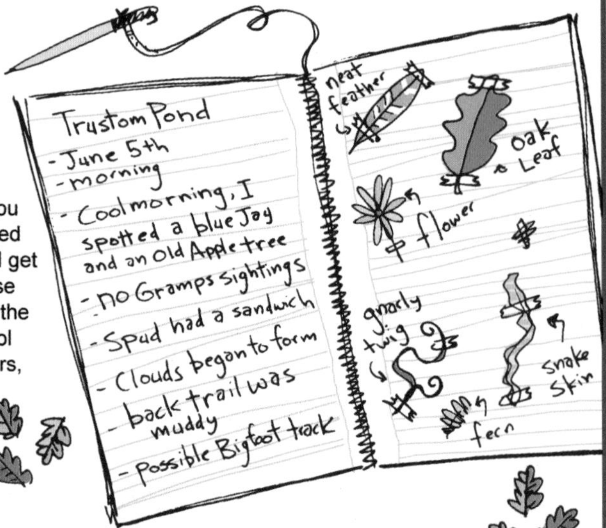

Trustom Pond
- June 5th
- morning
- Cool morning, I spotted a blue Jay and an old Apple tree
- no Gramps sightings
- Spud had a sandwich
- Clouds began to form
- back trail was muddy
- possible Bigfoot track
neat feather
oak Leaf
flower
gnarly twig
snake skin
fern

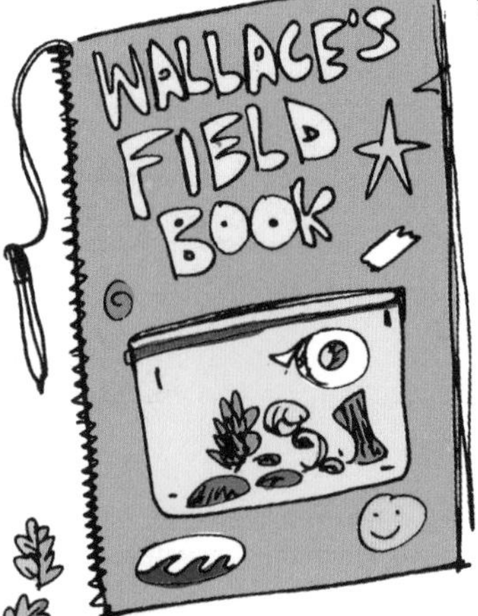

WALLACE'S FIELD BOOK

To keep a good field book, make sure you start each page with the date and time you go on your hikes—it's fun to compare them with the change of seasons. It's also important to have a pen or pencil handy. I tie mine to a string and staple it to the notebook. Staple a resealable plastic bag to the front of your field book to keep bigger objects you find, like neat shells, rocks, and pine cones. It's also where I keep my roll of tape.

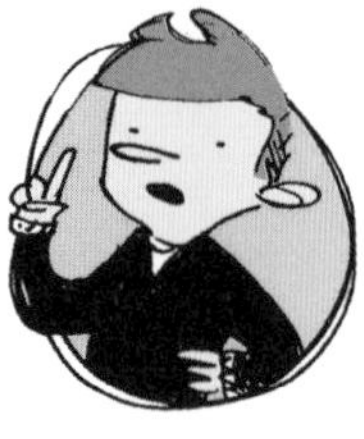

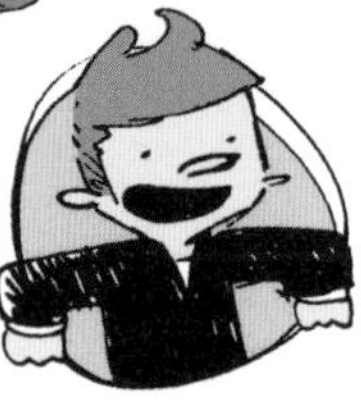

Boom! That's it. Super easy, right?! A good outdoors person keeps track of their adventures! All that's left is to get out there and find some interesting things!

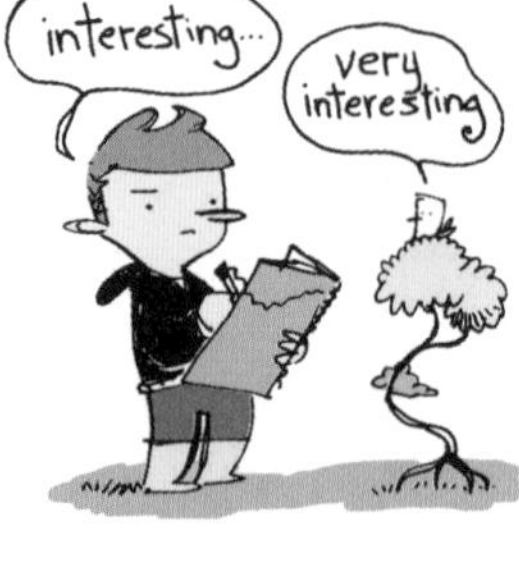

interesting...
very interesting

Winter Mobile

WHAT YOU'LL NEED

Tupperware

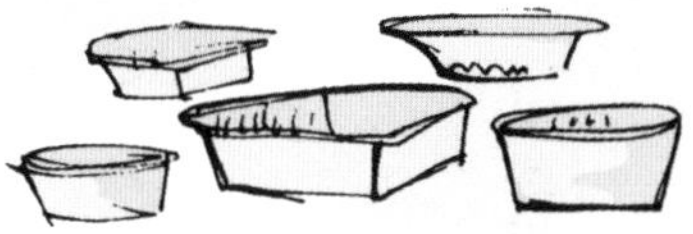

String

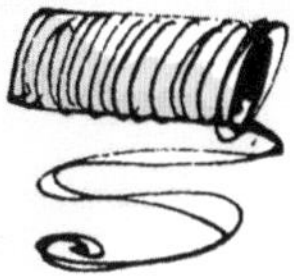

Cool, colorful things you've collected outside, like shells, twigs, leaves, or rocks

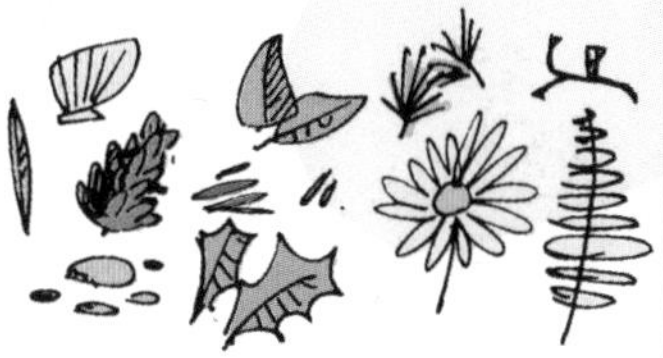

Cut the string 2–3 feet long and lay it on the bottom of your Tupperware.

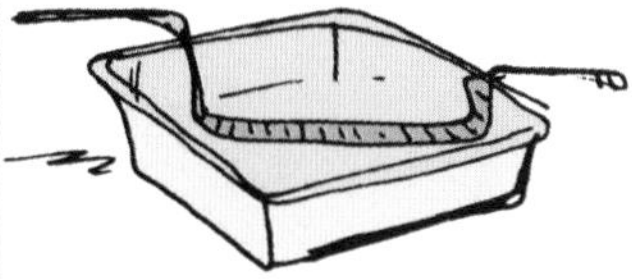

Place your colorful object into the Tupperware on top of the string, and get creative with it!

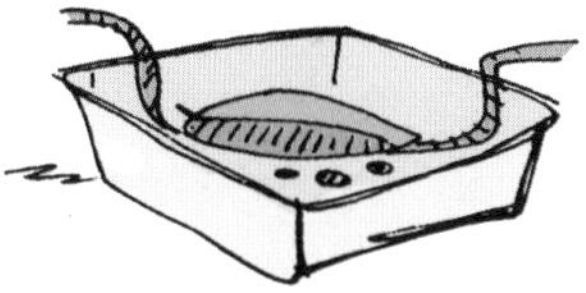

Fill the Tupperware with water just till it covers the objects. It's OK if they float around.

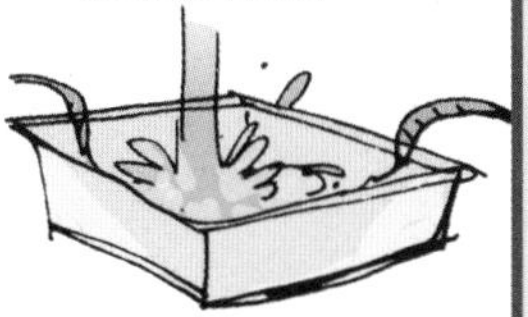

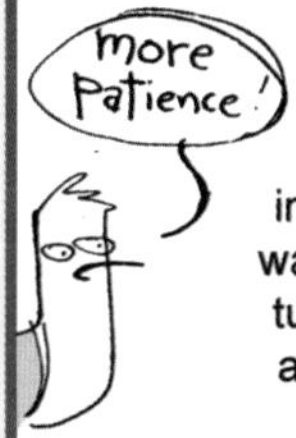
more Patience!

Pop that thing in the freezer, and wait for the water to turn to ice, usually around 2–3 hours depending on the size.

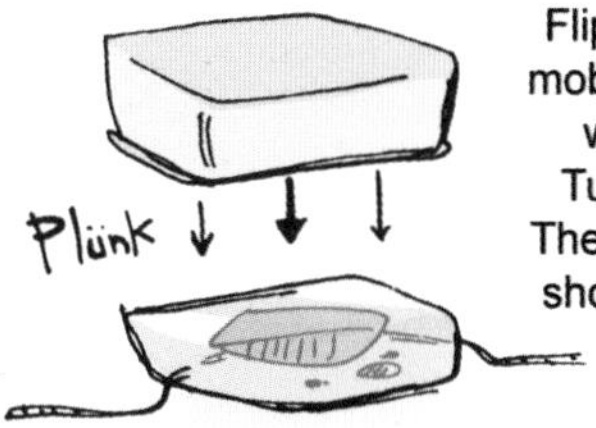
Plünk

Flip the frozen mobile over and wiggle the Tupperware. The block of ice should fall out.

Now you've got your cool winter mobile.

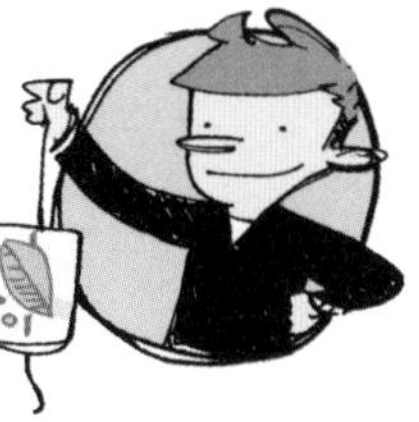

GET CREATIVE!

Try different sizes of Tupperware and connect them with a single string before you freeze them. This will add more parts to your mobile.

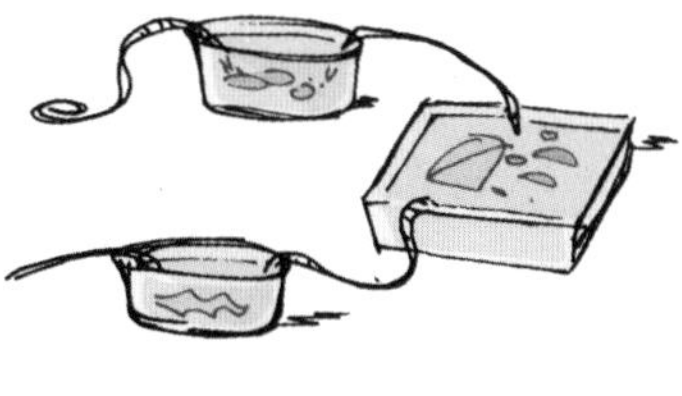

Head outside and hang them in your favorite tree, on your balcony, or in your snow fort.

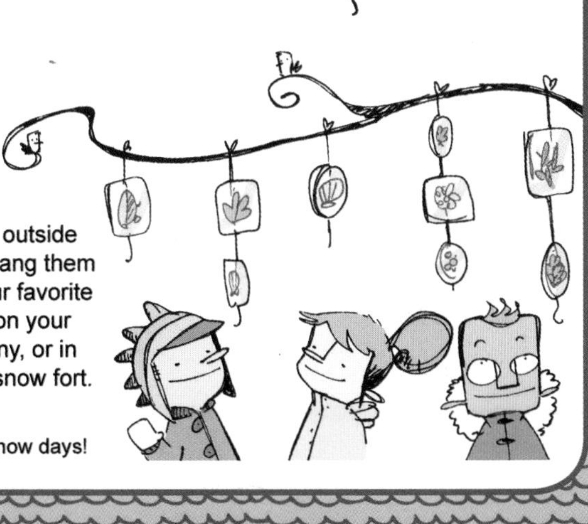

*Note: Winter mobiles work best on colder days or snow days!

Wallace the Brave is distributed internationally by Andrews McMeel Syndication.

Andrews McMeel Publishing
a division of Andrews McMeel Universal
1130 Walnut Street, Kansas City, Missouri 64106

www.andrewsmcmeel.com

19 20 21 22 23 SDB 10 9 8 7 6 5 4 3 2 1

ISBN: 978-1-5248-5177-4

Library of Congress Control Number: 2019932902

Made by:
Shenzhen Donnelley Printing Company Ltd.
Address and location of manufacturer:
No. 47, Wuhe Nan Road, Bantian Ind. Zone,
Shenzhen China, 518129
1st Printing—7/1/19

Look for these books!

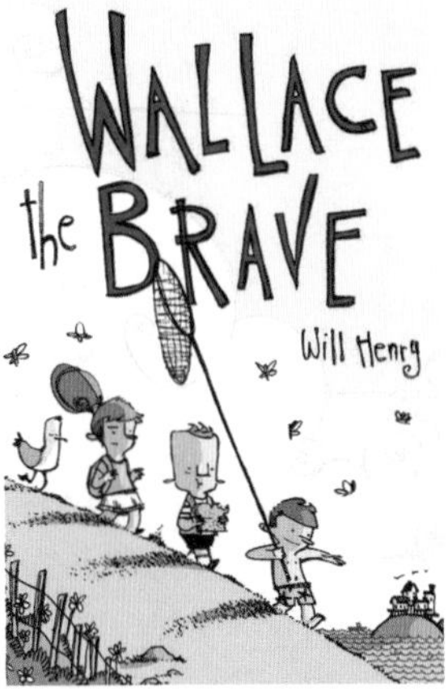

Wallace the Brave
Will Henry

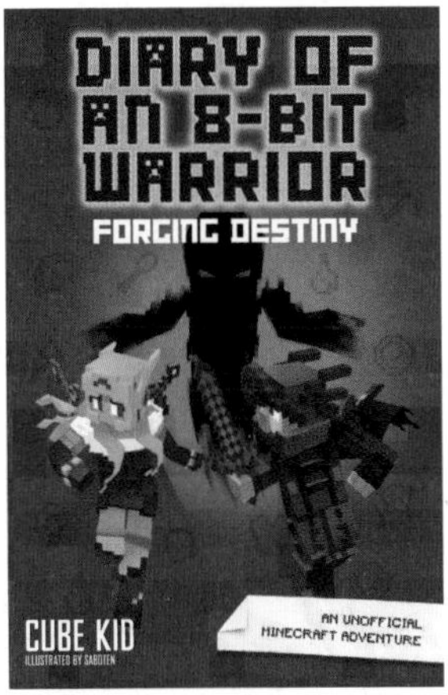

DIARY OF AN 8-BIT WARRIOR
FORGING DESTINY
CUBE KID
ILLUSTRATED BY SABOTEN
AN UNOFFICIAL MINECRAFT ADVENTURE

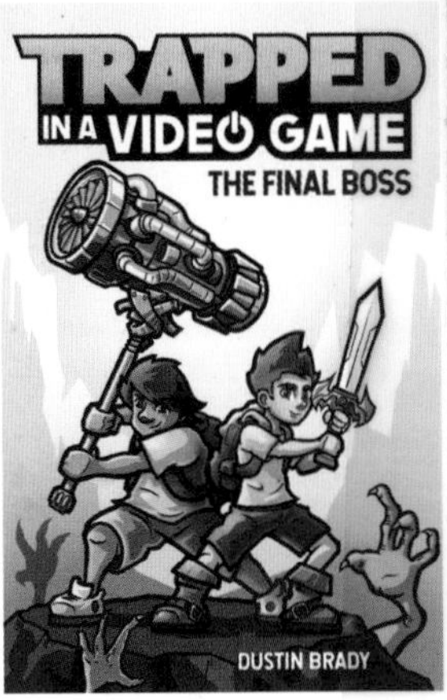

TRAPPED IN A VIDEO GAME
THE FINAL BOSS
DUSTIN BRADY

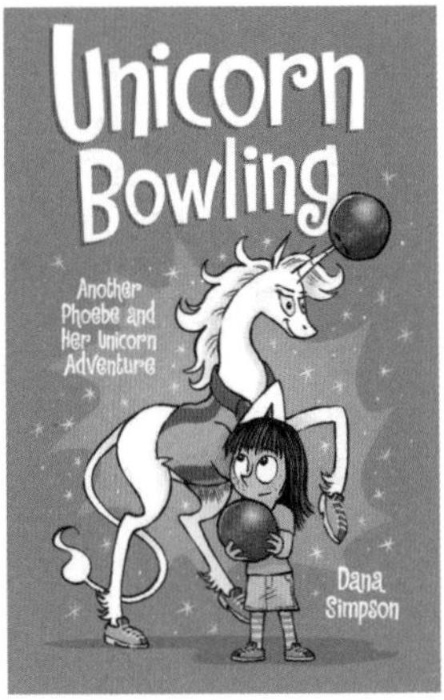

Unicorn Bowling
Another Phoebe and Her Unicorn Adventure
Dana Simpson

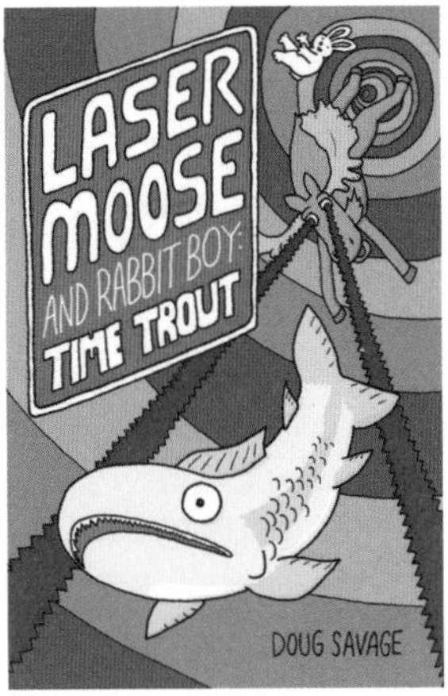

LASER MOOSE AND RABBIT BOY: TIME TROUT
DOUG SAVAGE

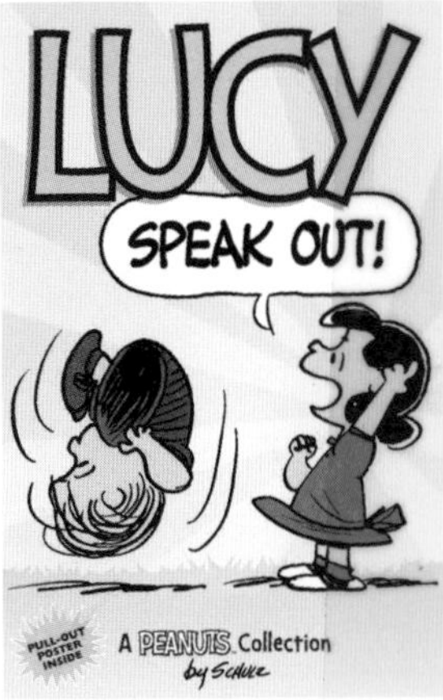

LUCY
SPEAK OUT!
PULL-OUT POSTER INSIDE
A PEANUTS Collection
by Schulz

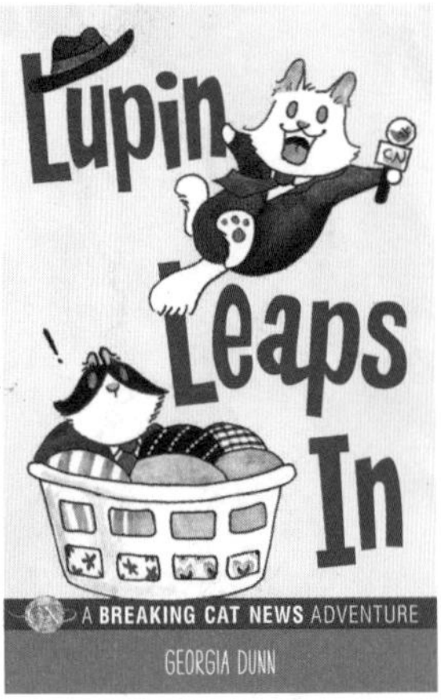

Lupin Leaps In
A BREAKING CAT NEWS ADVENTURE
GEORGIA DUNN

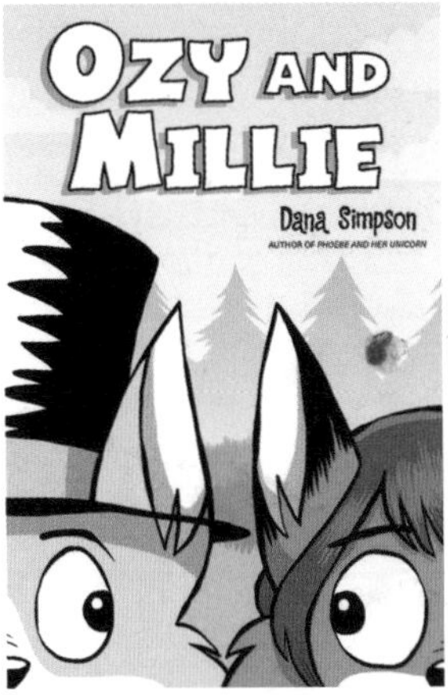

OZY AND MILLIE
Dana Simpson
AUTHOR OF PHOEBE AND HER UNICORN

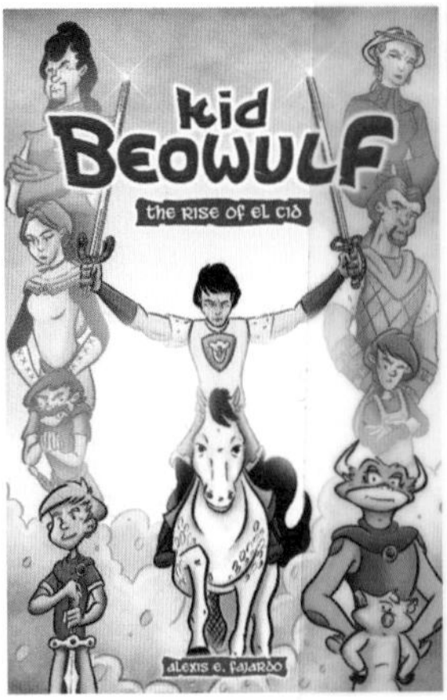

kid BEOWULF
the rise of el cid
alexis e. fajardo